DIRTY LITTLE MIDLIFE DILEMMA

A SMALL TOWN ROMANTIC COMEDY

LILIAN MONROE

Print ISBN: 978-1-922457-77-6

～

WANT THREE BOOKS DELIVERED STRAIGHT TO YOUR INBOX?
HOW ABOUT THREE ROCK STAR ROMANCES THAT WERE WAY TOO
HOT TO SELL?

GET THE COMPLETE ROCK HARD SERIES:
WWW.LILIANMONROE.COM/ROCKHARD

1

NORA

THE SITUATION IS SALVAGEABLE. That's the important thing to remember.

How exactly I'm going to salvage it, I'm not sure. But it will happen. Somehow. Maybe as soon as I get electrocuted and become the newest Marvel superhero, right here in the parking lot of The Cedar Grove Pub.

A line of toppled motorcycles stretches out before me, my hip burning from where it knocked the first one. The bikes fell over like a row of dominos, a horrifying mess of grinding metal and crashing machinery, all because I was startled and accidentally bumped into the first one. I look at the mass of chrome and rubber and steel, blinking, waiting for my superpower-inducing lightning bolt to hit.

Unsurprisingly, nothing happens.

It would have been entertaining to see all those motorcycles fall over one on top of the other if I'd been watching a video while scrolling through social media. It's less fun in real life. Especially when my brain is providing a quick tally of just how much money all this property damage will cost me. I then compare that total to the balance in my checking account, and my brain offers a sad *womp-womp* noise in response.

Lee Blair, the sexiest man I've ever seen, shifts his weight from one foot to the other. He's six-foot-plus of brawny, sexy, motorcycle-riding hotness. Dark hair, bottomless eyes, and enough of a bad-boy edge to make him look dangerous. I can feel the animosity pulsing off him in waves, which is the exact opposite of the teasing, I'm-into-you vibes he was sending me last time we saw each other.

My eyes alight on the first bike in the row, a Harley Davidson with blue smoke painted over its body.

Lee's bike.

"Did you just say 'oopsie daisy?'" His voice is a nice, low growl, and I would totally be thinking about him whispering dirty things in my ear if I hadn't just knocked over his beloved motorcycle.

I clear my throat. "It was an accident. I was startled by the sound of all those bottles breaking in the dumpster."

"Are you blaming *me* for this?" His voice gains a steel-hard edge, and Lord help me, but it makes my insides tingle. And by "insides," of course, I mean my special lady place.

There's something wrong with me. Maybe I'm addicted to danger, and I'm only finding it out at forty-one years of age. I'm secretly an adrenaline junkie who likes bad boys, especially when they want to rip my head off. Up until this very second, I was unaware of that fact, which would explain why my love life has been such a pathetic disappointment thus far.

Focus, Nora.

"No, of course not," I manage to respond, eyes tracing

the long line of bikes before me. I count fourteen. Fourteen motorcycles I just knocked over. Fourteen angry bikers are drinking beer and whiskey just inside this bar, about to find out who just scratched their favorite toys. "I'm not blaming you at all. I'm just explaining what startled me and made me trip."

"You're saying that me taking out the trash made you do this." He sweeps an arm across the junkyard at my feet. "Sounds a lot like you're blaming me."

I could tell him the truth: I saw his motorcycle and was drawn to it like a magnet. I was picturing my front plastered to his back as he took me on a ride on this powerful machine, and I just couldn't help myself from touching the leather seat. I could tell him that I was imagining all kinds of filthy things involving me, Lee, and the bike, lost in the pressure-cooker of my growing lust, and that's why the noise of a hundred breaking bottles startled me so badly.

"I'll pay for everything," I proclaim. "Just tell me how much."

"What the f—" Movement catches my eye from the entrance to the Grove, where a gigantic man looms. When he takes a step, his bulging thigh muscles cause his jeans to strain at the seams. I didn't even know they made jeans that big. His legs look like denim-clad redwood tree trunks. "Buck! Leggy! Get out here! Someone's been messing with our bikes."

I swallow a yelp and force myself to lift an arm. "It was me. I'm sorry! It was an accident." *Please don't murder me.* "I'll pay for everything." *Somehow.*

The giant swings his head to me. His neck is so thick it apparently can't turn on its own, so he has to spin his entire upper body in my direction. Biceps the size of soccer balls

3

flex, and I hear the distinct sound of a seam ripping. Oh, no. No, no, no. He's going to turn into the Hulk right here in the parking lot of the Cedar Grove, when my inaugural Girls' Night with the ladies of Heart's Cove is supposed to happen.

My superhero fantasies are suddenly going very, very wrong.

I look up at the sky, cursing the lack of clouds. This is when I'm supposed to get hit by lightning. Bitten by a spider. Captain America is supposed to land in a circle of crackling pavement to defend me from the bad guys.

I don't even *like* superheroes. My brain is short-circuiting.

"You knocked over my bike," the Hulk growls, spinning his entire body to face me. Goodness. He's even wider than I thought.

Behind him, the door flies open and two men—Buck and Leggy, I presume—tumble out. One of them is squat with a long grey beard that reaches the center of his protruding beer belly. He has an enormous belt buckle and a worn leather vest. The other man is long and lanky, with big bug eyes that cut straight to me.

The Hulk jerks his chin at me. "*She* did this."

Buck and Leggy look at the bikes, then at me. Their jaws clench as they flank the Hulk. There are a lot of balled fists and aggressive male noises happening, which makes my nerves ratchet so tight I think I might snap.

I inhale through my nose and count to eight, just the way Candice says to do it in yoga class. Then I let it out through my mouth and lift my palms. Whatever comes out of my mouth next will make or break this situation. I'll either defuse things, or I'll get my head crushed like a watermelon between the Hulk's meaty paws.

"I—"

"Stand down, Ted," Lee says, taking a sideways step to stand between me and the three angry bikers. "It was an accident."

I blink, staring at Lee's back. He's wearing a short-sleeve tee and low-slung jeans, and my face is in line with his shoulder blades. I can see a damp line down the center of his back, and the thought of Lee Blair sweating through his shirt turns me on so fast I have to take a wobbly step back.

A baseball bat would be really helpful right now. I could use it to beat down my out-of-control libido.

"Look what she did, Lee." Ted—the Hulk—thrusts his arm toward the pile of mangled metal. "My bike! Your father's bike!"

"We'll take care of it," Lee replies, and I frown. *We?* A minute ago he was a card-carrying member of the growly-male-noises club.

Leggy—I assume the lanky man is Leggy, since his legs are about a mile long—points a spindly finger at Lee. "You better take care of it, Blair. Otherwise, we're going to have a word."

The way he says "a word" makes me think he's not actually talking about words at all.

I shuffle around Lee's body to try to smooth things over. "I'll pay for everything. I swear. It was an accident, and I'm really, really sorry."

When I try to take another step, Lee's arm slashes across my body to hold me back. His hard, corded forearm presses up against my breast, which makes my hormones throw a wild party in my veins.

Out of control—my body is utterly out of control. And not in a good way.

Well. A little bit in a good way. But mostly not.

"Let me take care of this," Lee tells me, steely eyes serious. His voice drops to a low, intimate register, his arm still extended across my body. "I need to get these bikes up off the ground so we can assess the damage. Then we'll talk."

He smells like leather, pine, and something musky and male. His arm softens against my body as his hand brushes the hollow of my waist, which sends all kinds of interesting tingles zipping across my stomach. My brain takes the opportunity to put on a pair of sunglasses and go drink margaritas on a beach in Tulum, so all I can do is nod like a good girl.

Lee will take care of it. Then we'll talk. Uh-huh.

Lee jerks his head to the first bike in the line of fallen dominos and uses some kind of wordless man-language to get the other men to help him. They haul the first motorcycle up and set it down on its kickstand, then move to the next. And the next.

They've righted six of the motorcycles when the pub door opens and the sound of cackling laughter floats through. A redheaded woman stumbles out, followed by her dark-haired best friend. Simone and Fiona.

Their laughter abruptly stops when they spot the men at work, glance at the bikes that still need to be picked up, and finally swing their gazes to me. I assume I look as guilty as I feel, because both Simone and Fiona's eyes widen almost comically.

"Nora," Fiona whispers. "What happened?"

"Hold on." Simone lifts a finger, then ducks her head inside the door. "Jen! Candice! Trina! Lily! Get out here," she yells like it's some sort of demented midlife Power Ranger call to action.

I close my eyes. Wonderful. I just officially moved to this town today after months of zipping back and forth between here and Reno, and I was excited to make a good impression on the women who have been so welcoming to me. Heart's Cove is where my brother Fallon has lived for years. It's a cute, artsy town in Northern California, bounded by national parks on one side and a craggy, beautiful coastline on the other.

I like it here. I want to stay. But right now, I also want to jump into a time machine and go back ten minutes so I can stay far, far away from Lee Blair's bike.

The four other women appear and take in the scene. Lee and the scary bikers are on the last two motorcycles, grunting with the effort of tipping them up onto their kickstands.

"Oh my," Trina says, lifting a beautifully manicured hand to cover her lips. "This doesn't look good."

My steps feel jerky and mechanical as I join the ladies in front of the bar. From this angle, I can see the other sides of the motorcycles—the sides that were angled down toward the pavement, where the other half of the damage was wrought.

A vast chasm opens up in the pit of my stomach. This is so much worse than I thought. Every single one of the fourteen bikes is scratched, dented, and dinged within an inch of its life. I know nothing of motorcycles, but I know this is bad.

Lily, who is out for the first time since she had her baby, rubs her hands over her upper arms. She cringes, glancing at me. "How did this happen?"

"I would also like to know the answer to that," Simone cuts in.

"I...tripped," I answer lamely.

"You tripped?" Jen frowns. "And knocked over all these motorcycles?" She scans the destruction, and I just know her logical mind is calculating angles and velocities and probabilities that led to every single bike falling over.

I close my eyes again, as if that will make everything disappear. I nod. "Yeah. Like a bunch of horribly expensive dominos."

There's a silence, then a strange, snorting noise. I crack open an eyelid to see Simone snort again, except her face is so red it looks like she's going to burst a blood vessel. She clenches her jaw and glances at the men, then lets out another snort before clapping her hand over her lips.

"Do. Not. Laugh," I grind out through bared teeth. "Those biker guys almost killed me a minute ago."

"I'm not laughing," Simone says, but it comes out as a squeak. "I swear."

Fiona's lips twitch so violently she has to pinch them bloodless. Candice takes three long yoga breaths, turning her back to the line of dented motorcycles to stare up at the roofline of the building. Trina's hand is still covering her mouth, but I can see the curve of her lips through her fingers. Even Lily, who didn't even want to come to Girls' Night, looks like she's about to lose it.

"I swear," I whisper-yell from the corner of my mouth, "if any of you start laughing right now, I'll come to your house and murder you in your sleep. Or rather my ghost will, because those biker-dudes are about to shoot me where I stand."

"It's just..." Fiona closes her eyes and turns to face the

same way as Candice, her back to the motorcycles. She blows out a controlled breath, shoulders caving inward as she momentarily loses it. "It's just unexpected, is all," she manages to finish. "Girls' Night strikes again."

"This is going to cost me a fortune. It's not freaking funny," I hiss, glancing at the three men inspecting the last bike in the line, deep furrows etched between each set of brows. Despite myself, I feel my lips curl.

Of course this happened to me. Of course. What else would I expect? That my move to Heart's Cove would go smoothly? That I could flirt with Lee Blair and maybe even date him? That things in my life could actually work out, for once?

I'm forty-one years old. I should know better by now. Things don't just *work out* for me.

"Look," Jen says, and we all turn to where she's pointing. "A security camera. I bet it caught everything on tape."

I've never seen a herd of forty-something-year-old women move so fast. They wrestle each other to the door and run through the bar, and all I can do is follow. My steps drag, dread curling in my gut. It was awful enough living through the motorcycle dominos once. I'm not sure I'll survive the embarrassment a second time.

Hamish, the bar owner who also happens to be Lee's father, nearly falls out of his chair when we crash through the door to the back office. We manage to communicate that there's been an Incident (with a capital I) which needs to be reviewed. Once he's finally parsed the scattered information everyone is shouting at him, Hamish nods and pulls up the security feed. The video appears on his computer screen, and all of us crowd around him to watch.

When the first bike-domino falls, all that restrained

laughter finally breaks free from everyone except Hamish and me. The old man grips the arms of his chair with a white-knuckled grip. I cover my face with my hands, unsure if the sounds coming from me are laughs or sobs.

At this point, is there even a difference between the two?

2

LEE

IT'S WORSE than I thought.

Rubbing the back of my neck, I let out a slow breath. Every motorcycle in front of me has been righted, but even in the dimness of the parking lot lights, I can see all kinds of scratches and dents.

The owners of these motorcycles are not going to be happy.

Ted is inspecting his own bike, wheeling it out to a clear patch of pavement to get a three-sixty view. I stalk to my own machine, at the far end of the line, feeling a twinge in my chest at the sight of all that scratched paint. It was a custom job that cost me an arm and a leg, and now it'll have to be redone.

Music and voices get abruptly louder then cut off again as someone steps outside. Glancing up, I see my father with Nora at the entrance to the Cedar Grove.

I don't know what to do with her. Part of me wants to grab her by the arms and shake her for being so careless. The other part of me wants to throw her over my shoulder and take her home, smooth out those worry lines on her brow. And yet another part wants to bend her over my knee and teach her a lesson we'll both enjoy.

My clothes suddenly feel itchy. I tug at my collar and turn back to my bike, seeing nothing.

Buck grunts as he runs a finger over the exhaust pipe on his bike, and Leggy responds with an answering groan.

Nora cringes. She looks at my father, whose lips are pinched in a thin line. He's staring at his bike, which is right in the center of the line. It was crushed under a particularly large machine, so it has significant scratches on both sides.

"I'm sorry," she says so quietly I almost miss it. "It was an accident. I'll pay for everything, Hamish. I promise."

My father doesn't care about very many things. He cares about me and my brother, Mac. He cares about Margaret, the elegant older woman who captured his heart. He cares about his bar, even though it's little better than a dive.

And he cares about his motorcycle.

Tension is written in every line of his body as he takes out his phone flashlight to inspect the damage. Nora hugs her arms around her stomach then drops her chin to her chest. She looks so small in the circle of yellow light from the streetlamp above.

Before I can think, I'm crossing the distance between us to stand next to her. I lift an arm to reach for her, then catch myself. My arm itches to curve around her shoulders, my hands begging to wipe those lines from her brow. But comforting her isn't appropriate. We don't know each other.

I drop my hand. Instead of thinking about all the ways I want to touch Nora, I need to figure out how we're going to break the news to the nine other bike owners inside.

Nora's breath is staggered, but she squares her shoulders as I stand next to her. Then she bends over and picks up a side mirror that got snapped off the nearest bike. She stares at it for a moment, and finally lifts her eyes to me.

She's a beautiful woman. Stunning, really. Olive skin, dark eyes, and inky hair that falls straight down to her mid-back. Tonight, she has something shimmery on her lips that must have been designed specifically to drive men crazy.

To drive *me* crazy.

I've been waiting months for my opportunity to speak to her. We've seen each other around, dancing on opposite outskirts of the same group of friends and family, but never actually speaking to each other. At one point, I was sure she was avoiding me.

This—what happened tonight—is not how I wanted our first real conversation to go.

A gentle breeze dances along the hem of her dress, a knee-length thing with ruffles and polka dots that calls up images of picnics and long summer evenings. She's wearing a light-wash denim jacket to ward off the spring chill, its front open to reveal a dipping neckline. And the way she's looking at me now, with those deep brown eyes open wide, her chin tilted up, the streetlight glinting off her lips and whatever shimmer she applied to her collarbones, cheekbones, and lips—it makes me think of all the curves and hollows hidden under that innocent-looking dress.

Nora's mouth opens, and I don't think I can take another apology. To see her wilt, eyes downcast, shoulders rounded is just...wrong.

"You worked at a magazine, right?" I shift on my feet to face her fully.

Glossy lips snap shut, then part again. I could watch those lips move for an eon and never get bored. "Yeah. I was the art director for a quarterly magazine in Reno. It was called the *Law Review*. I worked with a lot of ex-lawyers."

"Mm," I answer, glancing over her shoulder to meet my father's eyes.

He looks grim, the wrinkled lines in his face carved deep. He lets out a sigh and shuffles toward us, nodding to Nora.

"How bad is it?" she asks him, dark brows drawing together.

"It's...fixable." My father clears his throat and glances at the bar door. "The rest of the guys won't be happy."

"I'll tell them," I cut in. Nora inhales sharply, her gaze cutting to mine. Her eyes are wide, gratitude filling those deep brown pools. My heart gives a hard tug, which makes my brain stumble.

I shouldn't care. Her gratitude shouldn't affect me. Don't I know what happens when I get close to women? How easy it is for them to use a man and then chuck him out?

I really haven't learned anything from my past. All it takes is a pretty woman with glossy lips on to pout in my direction and I'm begging to do her bidding.

Figures.

"Thanks, Lee," Nora says quietly before straightening her spine, "but I need to face this one myself. It was my fault. I'll tell the other owners."

I blink, surprised. Before I can answer, Nora is striding toward the door. My father's brows are arched when he meets my eyes, then we both turn to follow her inside.

My father's bar is well-worn, well-loved, and on nights

like tonight, absolutely packed. The Girls' Night crowd stands around the pool table, cackling like witches around their cauldron. The grizzly, haggard regulars sitting at their usual stools scowl across the space at them. The regulars pretend to hate Girls' Nights, but once they get a couple more drinks in them, they'll be dancing and singing along to Mariah Carey beside Simone and Fiona and the rest of them. A few college students populate the booths on the right side of the room. At tables dotted around the room, various owners of the bikes outside drink and laugh.

Nora's gaze sweeps over all the assembled people, her shoulders back, head held high. She strides to the nearest table, grabs a chair, and stands on it. "Excuse me!" She motions to the bartender, who glances at me and my father, then cuts the music.

Suddenly, the sound of a dozen voices echoes in the space. People frown and glance up, finally seeing Nora standing on the chair. She gulps, clutching her hands at her stomach.

I want to go over there and tug her down, tuck her into my side, and tell everyone to stop staring at her like that. The urge to protect and take care of her sweeps through me like a blaze through dry grass, leaving me reeling. I haven't felt that way in...well, not since Drea. The woman who ruined me.

"There was an accident outside," Nora starts, "and it was my fault."

No one speaks.

Nora drops her hands to her sides and takes a deep breath. "The motorcycles sustained some damage—"

In a rush of movement, every bike owner in the joint jumps up. Chairs go flying. One table flips over, sending a pitcher of beer crashing to the ground. Someone screams. A race to the bar's entrance starts, and before I can stop myself, I'm crossing the distance to Nora and shielding her chair from the onslaught of motorcycle owners streaming to check on their bikes.

She wobbles a bit as someone bumps the chair, putting her hand on my shoulder for a flickering moment. When she takes her hand away, mumbling an apology, I almost snatch her wrist back to bring it back to me, to feel the warmth of her hand against my shirt.

But that would be crazy.

Instead, I give her a curt nod and head back outside to quell the panicked men as they check on their machines.

I'm not a gentleman. I'm not a nice guy. Ask any of my exes, and they'll tell you I'm a selfish piece of shit.

Still, there must be some inkling of gallantry left inside me, because I find myself in the eye of the hurricane for the next hour. I corral all the angry men and guard Nora against them, glaring at anyone who dares raise their voice. It takes me a long while to convince everyone to let me take pictures of the damage and agree to meet at my friend Remy's garage to assess the bikes more closely tomorrow.

When everyone is satisfied that their motorcycles still run despite the dings and dents, my father offers them all a round of drinks on the house, which makes Nora give him the biggest, happiest, puppy-dog eyes I've ever seen.

And for one blazing moment, I'm jealous of my own fucking father.

That's when I know I'm in trouble.

3

NORA

I'M a grown woman and when I do something wrong, I'm not afraid to admit it. Hand up, it was me, tell me the consequences. I'm ready.

Sort of.

The morning after The Incident, I find myself in my apartment, staring in the bathroom mirror. The woman looking back at me has dark circles under her eyes and a haunted expression on her face. Before the disaster in the parking lot, I expected last night to be a celebration. It was supposed to be my first official night as a permanent resident of Heart's Cove, my first Girls' Night. I was expecting to go meet the girls and start laying down more roots in our new friendship.

This morning was supposed to be slightly hungover, but ultimately happy. A fresh start.

Instead, dread squeezes my stomach into a tight ball.

Today, I face the music. And by music, I mean I face Lee Blair and the tally of all the damage my clumsiness caused last night.

It's hard not to beat myself up about what I did. My very first evening as a permanent resident of Heart's Cove, and I go ahead and knock over a row of motorcycles. Who does that?

When I quit my job in Reno, finally admitting that I didn't want to be commuting back and forth every week, it felt like I was stepping up to the big wheel on *The Price Is Right* and giving it a spin. I'd spent the past decade of my life—and more—chasing stability. Safety. After a messy and expensive divorce, quitting my job without having another one lined up was the first time I felt like I was doing something for *me*. Something a little bit reckless. I spun the wheel and watched it *tick-tick-tick* around and around and around, excited to see where it would settle.

I didn't think it would stop on the section that said, "Cause tens of thousands of dollars' worth of property damage before your last suitcase is unpacked, thus wiping out your precious savings account and safety net."

Now it's time to accept the consequences.

Sighing, I force myself to conceal the worst of my dark circles, swipe on some mascara, and make myself look halfway presentable. I'm only putting makeup on because it feels like battle armor and the ritual of it calms me. It has nothing to do with the man I'm meeting this morning. Nothing at all.

And when I slide on the denim shorts that make my butt look incredible, it's simply because they're my last clean pair. I swear.

The push-up bra, I'll admit, is vanity. But what else am I supposed to wear beneath my tight white tank top? This bra is the only one I own that matches my skin tone perfectly. I can't possibly go out in public with the outline of my bra showing, can I? The fact that my cleavage looks particularly good in that bra-and-tank combo is just a happy coincidence.

It's not like I'm dressing up or anything. I'm wearing denim shorts and a tank, for crying out loud.

But when I walk into the Four Cups Café a few minutes later, I start to regret all the happy coincidences that happened when I got ready. I'm greeted with a cacophony of wolf-whistles from my new friends, who see right through my excuses to the real reason I dressed the way I did.

The café is owned by Candice, Jen, Fiona, and Simone. They've created an artsy, eclectic space that serves Jen's incredible pastries and the best coffee in the area. It's been open a couple of years, featured on all kinds of "Best of" lists—especially after Jen's appearance on a baking competition television show. This humble café with local artists' work featured on the walls and mismatched chairs around worn tables has become the soul of the town.

Trina—the middle sister between Candice and Lily—leans a hip against the counter and makes a show of putting her sunglasses on just so she can lower them onto her nose while she checks me out. "Girl," she states, and it's somehow a complete sentence.

"Excuse me, the *body*?" Simone gapes, thrusting her arm toward me. "Unfair. Where's mine? I want a refund. The curves on that woman are insane."

Fiona laughs as she rings up a customer behind the register. "Looking good, Nora. I think we can guess the occasion."

"No occasion." It's supposed to come out cool and casual, but my traitorous voice cracks.

Candice comes in from the back stockroom carrying a huge tub of coffee beans. She stops dead when she sees me and wiggles her eyebrows. "Damn."

Cheeks heated, I wave them all away. "You are all ridiculous. I'm wearing denim shorts and a white tank top. It's hardly a revolutionary outfit."

"We only speak the truth, and the truth is you look incredible," Simone says, tugging me toward the counter. "Now what are you drinking? My treat, as long as you tell me *exactly* how Lee reacts when he sees you."

Letting her lead me to the café's display cabinet, I try to keep my voice casual. "Lee? What are you talking about?"

When the four of them burst out laughing, I wave them away and roll my eyes. Fine. *Fine!* I dressed up because I'm going to meet the hottest man in a hundred-mile radius. Sue me. I may be over forty, but I'm not dead, dammit.

The barista makes my coffee as my shoulders relax ever so slightly. It's been a long time since I felt at home somewhere. I lived in Reno for decades, and by the time I left, I had one friend. One. When she got married and had kids, we drifted apart until we only met up once every six or nine months. While she was living out her happily-ever-after, I was trying to hide the misery of my broken-down marriage.

I'm not too proud to admit I've been lonely.

As Simone calls out a quip that makes Candice laugh, then Fiona responds with a teasing remark of her own, a bit of hope blooms in a secret part of my heart. Maybe in this town, I can have a circle, a community. I can be part of this group of women who laugh together at every opportunity. Maybe that big wheel isn't quite done spinning yet. I have one more tick left, and I'll land on something better.

My coffee slides across the counter as the barista winks,

and it only takes one sip for me to feel a bit calmer about my impending conversation. Calling out goodbyes to my new friends, I brace myself and head out to face the consequences of my actions.

I can do this. I've spent the past few years spinning, stagnant. Even an expensive mistake is better than feeling like my life is passing me by, right?

Remy's garage is on the other side of Heart's Cove, inland and away from the bustling center of town. It's in a more industrial-looking area, between a moving truck rental place and a plant nursery. Across from the garage is a vacant warehouse with a chain around the door handles.

I park on the gravel lot outside the garage, staring at the dark maw leading into the main space. With a deep breath and a sip of extra-sweet coffee, I brace myself. Then I open the car door and walk toward the sounds of whirring machinery and blasting music.

It takes a minute for my eyes to adjust to the relative dimness inside, so I stand in the opening and scan the space until I spot a row of familiar motorcycles. There are only seven of them here, but the sight of all the scratches and dents makes my stomach knot. My coffee churns in my stomach and I bite the inside of my cheek, trying to push down the guilt and embarrassment that threatens to make me turn around and run back to my car.

But, you know. Grown woman. Actions, consequences, etcetera.

"Hello?" I call out as I take a step inside.

From behind the farthest motorcycle, a familiar shape pops up. Lee unfolds his long, strong body and looks in my direction, freezing for a brief moment when he sees me. His eyes burn as they coast down my body and back up again, lingering on my mouth when I swipe my tongue to moisten my lips.

I absolutely do *not* catalogue his reaction to recount to Simone and the girls later. I catalogue it for myself, thank you very much.

Lee is wearing mechanic's overalls that shouldn't be as sexy as they are. They're a dull blue-grey color with grease stains all down the front. He's only zipped them up partway, so I can see the dark tee he has on underneath.

"Nora." He grabs a rag and starts wiping his hands with it. "You're early."

I can't stop watching his hands. The movement of the rag over the long fingers, tendons, bones, broad palm...it makes me wish I had that baseball bat. My libido has not learned her lesson.

"Am I?" I glance at my wrist, which is stupid, because I never wear a watch. Flushing, I try to camouflage the movement by bringing my hand up to tuck a strand of hair behind my ear. "Did you get a chance to talk to everyone whose bike..." I trail off, waving my hand at the row of motorcycles.

"Yeah," he replies. "Come to the office. Remy let me use his computer to do the estimate."

Following Lee to the office, I wave at the other mechanic working on a nearby Volkswagen Beetle. That must be Remy. He nods, then goes back to his work.

The office is a riot of paperwork, random wrenches and socket sets, mismatched chairs, and a computer that belongs in a museum. I take a seat in the chair Lee motions to, preening only a little bit at the way his eyes linger on me.

Rolling forward on the chair behind the desk, Lee

pushes aside a stack of smudged, crinkled papers and taps on the keyboard a few times. "Seven of the guys work on their own bikes, so they'll do the repairs themselves. My bike is here, but I'll do my own repairs too," he adds. "Any paint damage will need to be fixed by a specialist, though. So that leaves the six other bikes we have out here that Remy and his team will work on."

"Okay." I gulp. "Do you have a quote for me?"

Lee lets out a quiet sigh. He flicks his eyes to me, then back to the screen. "Nora, I tried to get the cost down as much as possible. I want you to know that. Remy's only charging us for parts, and the body shop has agreed to a big discount. The guys working on their own bikes appreciated you standing up and taking responsibility, so they're not charging for their time at all. We'll only have to reimburse them for parts and supplies."

As he continues to speak, my nerves crank tighter, and tighter, and tighter. He wouldn't be qualifying this so much if it wasn't going to cost me a fortune. The longer he tells me what a good deal I'm getting, the more I worry I'm about to go bankrupt.

"Most of the damage is cosmetic, but a lot of parts need to be replaced," he continues. "I've checked every bike myself and have photos to document it all, in case you want a second opinion."

"How much?" I croak. "Just tell me how much, Lee."

He's quiet for a beat. Then, "Twenty-seven and a half thousand dollars."

I close my eyes. Shit. *Shit.*

That's a lot of money for a stupid fucking mistake I made. Steeling myself against the pain of parting with that kind of money, I reach into my purse. "Okay," I say. "I can afford that."

I can't, really.

My dreams of buying a home in Heart's Cove flutter out the window like butterflies dancing in the breeze. I've been saving for a down payment for eight years—ever since my divorce. I've scrimped and saved in order to recover from that financial bomb, only to have it all wiped out by my own clumsy actions.

Ignoring the crushing disappointment in my breast, I try to think logically. Hard to do when a sex god of a man is staring at me with all-seeing steely eyes and a sexy mechanic's outfit.

I have the money. I can afford to pay it. I'm responsible, and I've always taken charge of my personal finances. I've been paying my mother's health insurance and part of her rent for eleven years, and even with those expenses—and the cost of my disastrous divorce—I've managed to save up enough to afford a small condo or maybe even a townhouse or a bungalow. Next week I was going to start house hunting.

But now...

I have to start right back at zero, just like I did when I got divorced. Except this time, I don't have a job.

Even worse, this will wipe out almost all of my savings, which means I'll either have to borrow against my retirement funds, get a bank loan, or beg for my old job back just to be able to pay my living expenses. Maybe I can move in with my mother, which would mean I'd only be paying one rent instead of two. I'll delay moving to Heart's Cove for a couple of years. It was irresponsible to move here without a job lined up, anyway.

For someone who's always prided herself on being level-headed, I sure have made some dumb mistakes recently.

Familiar panic starts to mount inside me. This is *exactly* why I always want to be in control. My life, my finances, my schedule—it's usually perfectly planned, with every possible outcome considered. I'm not a risk-taker. I hate making mistakes.

Dating my now ex-husband was supposed to be my last big mistake. Living through the torture of being ground down to nothing, of being used and made to feel small was supposed to be the end of the old me. I escaped that marriage, divorced, and had to carry the debts and alimony payments like a yoke around my neck. *That* was my big life mistake—marrying a leech who sucked me dry, who somehow had money for the best divorce lawyer in the state of Nevada, who made sure I felt the pain of our failed relationship until he remarried.

I wasn't supposed to make another cataclysmic error in this lifetime. I wasn't supposed to have to start over *again*.

"Nora?"

I blink, finding Lee staring at me intently. Swallowing back my panic, I flash him my best smile. "Looks like I'll be moving back in with my mother!" My laugh is tinny and fake. "Good thing the bed in her spare room is comfortable."

Lee's dark brows tug together. Some strange emotion flits across his face. Concern? "I thought you were moving to town. Don't you have an apartment in Lily's old building?"

"Sure do. Thankfully, it's a month-to-month lease. Otherwise I'd *really* be in trouble." My bright smile is fooling no one. Lee's brows draw even closer together and a deep furrow etches itself between them. I curl my fingers into my palm and feel the bite of crescent-shaped nails against my skin. "What account should I send the money to?" I ask, letting my deranged smile widen a little bit more.

Those eyes of blue-grey stare back at me, seeing every little secret I try to keep inside. The shame, the embarrassment, the despair at the thought of starting back at zero all over again.

Seconds tick. My breathing stops. The sexiest man I've ever met watches me like he's cracking my skull open and reading every thought flitting through my brain.

Finally, after an eternity, Lee brings his hands up to the desk and folds them on top of a stack of paperwork. "What if we came to an...arrangement?"

4

NORA

I START AT HIS WORDS, snapping out of my panic. *An arrangement?* What the hell does that mean?

Images of sweaty bodies and rumpled sheets bombard my brain. My body grows taut, shivers coasting over my skin. My nipples are hard little points, and my padded bra does its very best to hide the evidence. Yes, God yes, I want that. I can start paying this off right now on top of this messy desk.

Then my rational brain kicks in, and I reach for my mental baseball bat. *Bad sex drive! Stay down!*

Sleeping with Lee in exchange for a twenty-seven-and-a-half-thousand-dollar debt is not something I want to do. I'm not going to sell my body to pay for my own clumsiness. I believe sex work is work, and more power to the women that can do it, but I'm not one of them. If I sleep with the man on the other side of the desk, it'll be because we both want it and we're coming for it on equal footing.

I learned my lesson when I married Eric—and again

when I divorced him. Relationships need to be equal partnerships.

Why would Lee even *suggest* this? My life is spiraling. I've completely lost control, and I am *not* okay with it.

"I'm not going to sleep with you to pay off this debt," I blurt out.

Lee blinks, then curls his lips in a slow, dangerous smile. "Not that kind of arrangement." *But I like the way you think*, his eyes seem to say.

My cheeks burn. Relief crashes into me, as well as... disappointment? "Oh."

"I was thinking you could work for me."

Eyebrows twitching toward each other, I lean back in my chair. "Work? Doing what? I don't know anything about cars or motorcycles. I guess I could clean this office and do admin, but..."

"I don't work here," Lee says with a shake of his head. "I work for the Heart's Cove Fringe Festival."

I tilt my head. "Oh. Okay."

"The festival has grown a lot over the past five years, and we've started releasing a publication online and in print featuring the artists that travel here to participate. I've been...struggling." He clears his throat. "Our magazine looks amateurish, and it doesn't do the Heart's Cove Fringe Fest any favors."

Despite myself, I sit up straighter. I *love* art. In Reno, I worked for a national magazine targeted to criminal defense attorneys. It was a great job, and I learned a lot, but the subject matter just wasn't what I was interested in. Legal jargon doesn't really get my motor running. I stayed in the job a long time because I needed the money—especially after my divorce—and also, because I found it hard to justify leaving such a stable, solid job.

Working for the *Law Review Magazine* left me in total control of my life...but it also left me stagnant.

Moving to Heart's Cove was the first step I took for myself in a long, long time. A leap into the unknown. Quitting without having another job lined up was scary, but it felt right.

Up until last night, that is.

I try to tamp down the excitement budding inside me. "What would you want me to do?" I shift in my chair. "I'd need to find another job in town to pay the bills, but I'm...interested."

Extremely freaking interested, more accurately. The Heart's Cove Fringe Fest attracts amazing indie bands, potters, painters, sculptors, and all kinds of artisans from in and out of state. It's a week-long ode to art, music, and food. Creating a magazine to celebrate it makes me want to squeal.

"I could pay you a portion of the normal salary. The rest would go toward the debt." Lee's chair squeaks as he leans back, steepling his fingers in front of his chest.

The way he's looking at me makes me want to squirm. All dark-eyed and sexy. Tempting.

I bite my lip, trying to slow down my brain so I can think this dilemma through.

I don't like debt. After the divorce, I was in an awful financial position. I'd been the sole breadwinner in the marriage, which my ex used as a lever to demand alimony from me. He had terrible credit, so a bunch of our joint expenses—like his stupid fifty-thousand-dollar pickup truck—were solely in my name. It took me five whole years to sort all the debt out. He finally got remarried to his next victim three years ago, and I could stop paying alimony to him. Since then, I've been saving every penny to get myself to a position where I *could* quit my soul-sucking job and move here.

Jumping right back into nearly thirty grand's worth of debt is not something I take lightly.

But if I pay for the motorcycle repairs myself, it'll wipe out my savings. I'll have to move in with my mother and delay my relocation to Heart's Cove for another year or two. She relies on me to pay a lot of her housing and health expenses, and I can't just dump all her bills back on her plate when all she gets is Social Security.

Plus, a part of me *wants* to work on the Fringe Fest magazine. How cool would that be? I could work with photographers and artists to feature their best work. I might be able to even interview people myself—I get the feeling the Fringe Fest team is small, which means everyone probably needs to chip in however they can.

And then there's Lee. Do I really want to entangle myself in this crazy scheme? *Owe* him something? It basically eliminates any opportunity for us to come together as equals. If I owe him that much money, I won't want to get involved with him romantically. I'll need to wield my mental baseball bat every day, especially if he keeps looking at me like *that*.

"What are you thinking?" His voice is low, intimate.

That I really, really want to lick your chest.

"Just trying to make a mental pros and cons list," I admit. He doesn't need to know that he falls in both categories. Pro—he's sexy as sin and I'll get to spend a lot of time with him. Con—I won't be able to act on it.

Before Lee can answer, the office door bangs open and Remy the mechanic appears in the doorway. He's a tall man with chestnut-colored hair and dark-brown eyes that have a spark of mischief in them. He lifts a scarred, grease-stained hand to the doorjamb and jerks his head at Lee. "Couple of people here to see you," he announces. "It's about the motorcycles."

Lee's eyes cut to me, then he pushes his long, lean body off the chair. I stand and wait for him to round the desk, catching a bit of that pine-and-leather scent of his beneath the smell of engine grease. We follow Remy out to the main garage, and I try not to stare at the way the coveralls cling to his shoulders, or the way he prowls like he's in complete control of his body.

I don't know what's gotten into me. Ever since I quit my job in Reno, I'm not myself anymore. There's some kind of sex-crazed demon inhabiting my body. I haven't felt like this since I was in my early twenties, before I met my ex-husband.

I was married to Eric for a decade, from the age of twenty-three to thirty-three, and we had a normal, boring sex life. We had sex every second Sunday. A few minutes of grunting in the missionary position, and Eric was able to get what he needed. I didn't always get off, but I never really felt like I was missing anything. It's like the part of my brain that enjoyed sex and intimacy just...faded. I thought that's what happened with age. I figured it was normal.

Then we divorced and I was stressed out about money and housing and court dates and the fact that my life was crumbling around my ears. Sex didn't seem important then, either. After three less-than-stellar dates with men I met on dating apps, including one bout of less-than-stellar sex, I figured I just wasn't a sexual person. The third date was four years ago. Sex was a chore, and what forty-one-year-old woman needs more chores?

Then I decided to quit my job and move. That one action—doing something for me, letting go of the tight fist of control I kept on my life—changed everything. Suddenly, I could see possibilities where there were only problems before. I came to Heart's Cove and imagined a life here with friends and men and sex and good food and *joy*. How long had it been since I even let myself imagine those things?

Now, my body is like a runaway train. I've completely lost control. I've got nearly two decades of repressed sexual urges tumbling through me, and a man like Lee Blair looking at me like he might be thinking the same thing.

The pressure is too much. Like a dam about to break.

But if I agree to this crazy repayment scheme...the dam will have to stay very, very strong unless I want a truly messy disaster on my hands.

As we enter the garage space, I brace myself for angry bikers and hostility. But when I see who's waiting for us on the bare concrete floor, I let out a little breath of air.

"Nora!" Dorothy calls out. The elderly woman beams at me, her long silver hair tied back in a braid that hooks over her shoulder. She's wearing a white shirt with puffy sleeves, a flowing camel-colored skirt, and leopard-print bangles on her wrists. She is the epitome of the Heart's Cove artist. She runs most of the art classes that occur at the Heart's Cove Hotel, which she owns with her twin sister, Margaret.

Dorothy's beau, Eli, is standing beside the nearest motorcycle with his arms clasped behind his back. He's a tall, lanky man with a shiny bald spot on the top of his head. He lifts his gaze to meet mine. "We saw the video."

Of course they did. This town is gorgeous, but the gossip rips through it at light speed.

"We just *had* to come right away," Lottie—Candice, Trina, and Lily's mother—adds. Her pixie cut is styled in funky spikes, which matches the colorful 1960s-style print of her sheath dress. "We heard you were here and decided to come check in on you."

"That's...great," I say, stopping on the other side of the motorcycles from the three of them. Dorothy and Lottie are huge gossips, but they have good hearts. I'm not sure if they're here for moral support or just to see for themselves how much damage I caused last night. "Thank you?"

"Hamish was impressed by you taking responsibility like you did," Dorothy tells me, running a finger along one of the bikes' seats. "He told Margaret that put you in his good books, no matter what happened to his motorcycle."

My heart clenches. "Of course I'm taking responsibility. I'm the one who caused all this."

"Big to-do about a bunch of toys, if you ask me," Lottie cuts in with a huff. "Men and their machines."

"Now, Remy," Dorothy starts, lifting a finger toward the mechanic who wandered over with us. "You better be giving this young lady a good deal. Friends and family discount, all right?"

Remy lifts his working-man's hands. "None of my business. Lee's sorted that out with Nora."

Dorothy and Lottie's heads angle at exactly the same time as their shrewd gazes land on the man beside me.

Lee Blair deploys a smile I've never seen before. It makes his eyes crinkle as they warm, and it turns him from an unapproachable badass hunk into a nice, cozy kind of gentleman. The type of man who would have three devoted dogs that cuddle up to him at every opportunity. The type of man who could cuddle up to *me*.

Everything inside me tightens, especially a place between my legs I really shouldn't be thinking about right now.

"Ladies. Eli." Lee inclines his head. "Nice of you all to come check on Nora."

"We called her mother, but Prisha couldn't make it down in time," Dorothy says, dropping her gaze to inspect the nearest bike.

"You *what*?" My heart takes off, and as if my mother has a psychic line and knows whenever her name is uttered, my phone starts to ring. I fish it out of my purse and gape at the screen.

"Well, don't leave her waiting," Lottie says, nodding to the phone in my hand. "She'll know. I always know when my daughters are avoiding me. Like Lily last year. I knew something was going on."

"You mean you'll tell her you saw me ignore her call?" I ask.

Dorothy just grins. "We wouldn't dare."

Rolling my eyes as my lips twitch, I swipe my thumb across the screen to answer the call. "Hi, Ma." My voice trembles. It's not that I don't want my mother to know about all this, it's just that I'd rather have it all figured out before I tell her. Sometimes I think my mother forgets I'm a grown woman.

Lee shifts on his feet beside me, the back of his fingers brushing my free hand. For some reason that I don't care to investigate right now, the touch calms me. I meet his eyes and that soft smile still lingers in his gaze.

I should refuse his proposal. Definitely. I'm far, far too attracted to him. It'll end in disaster.

"Nora. I saw the video," my mother announces.

I close my eyes. "You and everyone else, huh."

"What made you jump? Are you okay? Who was that man? Why was he looming beside you like that? Was he following you?"

I glance at Lee, whose lips are twitching. Apparently, he can hear every word coming out of my phone's earpiece.

"That's Lee Blair. He works at the bar. Hamish's son. Remember a few months ago when you went to get ice cream with the guys on the motorcycles? He was one of them."

My mother hums. "Well. Dorothy said you had to pay for all that damage. What were you thinking, Nora? Why did you go and touch that bike in the first place?"

I step away from Lee, losing the small contact of his fingers against the back of my palm. My whole body feels colder as I take another step toward the wall. But the thought of him listening to my mother saying all those things...no. That, I can't handle.

"I liked the bike," I answer, unable to stop myself from glancing at the man who owns it. His lips curl ever so slightly, as if he likes hearing me say that. "Going up to touch it was a mistake, obviously." I turn to the wall, staring at the lines of exposed pipes and hydraulic hoses snaking along the concrete.

"Well, I'll say. How are you going to pay for all that? Do you need me to come to town? I told you to find a job before quitting the magazine. Didn't I say that?"

Yes, yes, she did. And I ignored her advice because I was suffocating. I needed out—and look where that got me.

I put my free hand on my hip and straighten up. I saw a TED Talk about power poses. Apparently, they can impart true confidence. As I stand like the superhero I am not, I'm hoping the speaker was right. I try to imbibe as much assurance in my voice as I can. "It's all under control, Ma."

In that moment, Lee's proposition flashes through my mind.

Suddenly, it all becomes clear. If I pay for the damage out of pocket, I'll be taking a step back. I'll be going back to my old, broke, dull, sexless life. I'll be moving in with my mother at the tender young age of forty-one.

That's unacceptable.

If the cost of my mistake is working for Lee—and thus making him utterly romantically off-limits—so be it. I can't go back to the way my life was before. I just can't. My new life may still be sexless, but at least I don't feel like a robot. This way, I can *live*.

So, I turn to look at the motorcycles and make a snap decision. "Don't worry about it. Lee and I came to an understanding." I meet Lee's gaze and see the question in the arch of his eyebrow. "I've found a job."

Is it just me, or did something like relief flash across Lee's gaze? Like he was hoping I'd agree to his proposal?

"Already?"

"Yep. Nothing to worry about. I'll see you next weekend, okay?"

After a few more moments and a hesitant goodbye on

her end, my mother and I hang up. I let out a breath, tucking my phone back into my purse. When I finish fidgeting with my stuff, all eyes are on me.

Dorothy gives me a Cheshire Cat grin. "What kind of understanding did you two kids come to?"

5

SIMONE

AN UNUSUAL WHEEZING noise escapes my old clunker of a laptop. I pause, lifting my fingers from the keys. It wouldn't surprise me if smoke started curling out of this thing. I should buy a new one, I suppose, but I'm still frugal to a fault. Being broke most of your life does that to a person— even when you start two successful businesses, then marry a wealthy man with a gorgeous, wooded property and live happily ever after with him.

Leaning back against my chair, I cast an eye around the Four Cups Café as my computer labors through whatever task it needs to complete to stop sounding like it's about to fall apart.

Sunday morning is busy at Four Cups. There are parents with strollers, hungover-looking young people, and the usual crowd of elderly patrons. A hum fills the air, and I can't quite help the smile that tugs at my lips. When Fiona, Candice, and Jen started talking about this place, I knew I was taking a risk to invest with them. It paid off, though, and now I'm a part-owner of a café that is the beating heart of this beautiful town.

A broad, strong palm slides over my shoulder, and my smile widens. My husband Wes tucks his head into the crook of my neck and places a gentle kiss behind my ear.

"Hey, gorgeous," he says, his fingers tugging at the ends of my red hair. "I didn't want to get up this morning."

My toes curl at the thought of all Wes and I accomplished before the sun came up. "Neither did I."

"How's work going?" He nods to my computer before slipping into the chair beside me, his arm slung across the back of my seat.

"Good. I'll be done as soon as my computer stops thinking so hard. I just need to send off a proposal to a new client, but it's taking forever to save and attach to the email." Along with the café, I have my own business doing social media management for a few local businesses.

"I'm buying you a new laptop tomorrow." Wes's knee nudges mine as he leans back in his chair. His pose looks relaxed, but his voice is unyielding. The man likes to dominate.

I give him a flat stare. "Wes."

"Simone." He meets my gaze with one of his own.

Despite myself, heat sparks in my gut. We've been married a couple of years now, but I still get this feeling every time he's close. I can't believe how lucky I am to have him. My grumpy, growly, solitary man. Our home nestled in the woods on the coast of the Pacific Ocean is my own personal paradise.

Before we can declare a winner in our little staring competition, the bell above the café door opens. A gorgeous woman glides through, immaculately garbed in a designer sundress and a ginormous straw hat. She takes her sunglasses off and tucks them into a hard case that she slips into her purse, then glances at the blackboard above the register before scanning the café.

Her eyes land on me, and she gives me a small nod. She looks familiar, but I can't quite place her.

"Don't think you can use a distraction to call that a win," Wes growls in my ear. "You'll have a new laptop before lunchtime tomorrow."

I roll my eyes. "Stop being a big macho provider, Wes."

His hand moves from the back of the chair to my shoulder. "Why? I like being a macho provider, and I think you like it too." His lips coast over my ear. "You didn't seem to mind what I was providing this morning."

My thighs spasm.

Hmm. What he's saying is true. Still—I can't let him win so easily. Having no suitable retort, I decide to just pinch the delicate skin on the underside of his arm, which makes Wes yelp as I laugh triumphantly. He tucks me against his side and kisses my temple.

The woman in the sundress coasts over to us, coffee in hand. "Simone, right?"

I straighten. "Yes." Recognizing her, I extend a hand. "You're Rudy's friend. I'm sorry, I don't remember your name."

"Georgia." She smiles. "Rudy sold me my house last year."

"That's right." I nod. "You like margaritas."

She smiles, tilting her head from side to side. "Guilty. Although the day you and your friends saw me and Rudy on our way to a margarita date was...odd. I felt a bit of tension from you and your friends. I just wanted to see if we could clear the air."

Straightening, I motion to the chair across from me. I introduce Wes, and the two of them shake hands.

The day she's referring to was a few months ago. Georgia seemed to be flirting with Rudy when he and Lily were dancing around each other. I'll admit that I was a bit defensive, especially since Lily was going through so much. But for Georgia to walk right up to me and ask to clear the air makes me like her. Takes guts to be that direct. A woman like that wouldn't play games.

"Were you and Rudy ever...?" I let the question hang.

Georgia lets out a delicate laugh, the lines around her eyes crinkling. "Gosh, no. Don't get me wrong, he's handsome enough to eat. But not my type. I might have flirted with him a bit," she admits, shifting in her chair, "but that was more...habit than anything else. A bad habit," she adds. "I guess ever since I got divorced, I've been trying to find my feet again." She blinks, as if surprised she shared so much.

"I get that," I answer. I take a sip of my coffee and glance at my laptop screen. My clunker is still thinking. "My default response is snark. It's not always appreciated."

Wes grunts in agreement beside me, and my elbow just slips right into his ribs. An accident, I swear.

Georgia's eyes glimmer. "You two are cute."

"I am not *cute*," Wes says, which makes me laugh so hard I snort.

"Of course not, honey." I let the backs of my fingers coast along his cheek. "You're a big tough manly man who likes to chop firewood and provide for his woman."

"Damn right." His voice is gruff, but I know that gleam of humor in Wes's eyes.

"Well, it was nice chatting." Georgia gathers her purse and her coffee with a nod. "I hope we'll see each other around."

Before she can stand, the door bangs open so hard it rebounds against the wall. Trina runs through, cutting across the café toward me. "You'll never guess what my mother just told me," she says, panting.

Behind Trina, her man, Mac, is shepherding Trina's two kids into the café. Katie, the younger daughter, has her hand in Mac's much larger one and is talking nonstop, as usual. Toby has his eyes on the pastries in the display case.

Trina leans her hands against our table, eyes shining in a way that tells me she has a very, very juicy bit of gossip to share.

"What?" I ask, leaning forward. Trina glances at Wes, then Georgia, and I see her hesitate. I wave my hand. "Trina, Georgia. Georgia, Trina. Now spill."

"Nora and Lee Blair have agreed on an 'arrangement' for her to pay back all the damage to the motorcycles." She arches her brows. "She's going to be working for him to pay it off."

"No." I lean forward. "Really?"

"What happened? What's this about motorcycles?" Georgia asks.

I whip out my phone and pull up the security footage outside the Cedar Grove, which makes Trina gasp. "You saved the security footage to your phone?"

"Obviously," I snort. "You didn't?"

Georgia's eyes grow wide as she watches the video, and

they stay wide as she passes my phone back to me. "That looks bad. How much is that going to cost to repair?"

"Nearly thirty thousand dollars," Trina says, and I gape. Then Trina turns to Georgia and says, "Girl, I love that dress. Where did you get it?"

"I found it at this little second-hand shop in a small town in Washington. Can you believe it? It's a The Row dress. I don't think the shop knew what they had. It was so cheap I felt like I was doing something wrong when I bought it."

"The Olsen Twins' line?"

Georgia nods. "Isn't it gorgeous? And it has pockets!" She demonstrates by sticking her hand in one of them.

Trina hums appreciatively. "You have to tell me the name of the store."

"Never mind the dress," Wes cuts in. "Nora is working for Lee now?"

"My mother said there was something going on. Lots of surreptitious looks to each other when they thought no one was watching." Trina tucks a strand behind her ear. "Which is naive of them, really. They've both met Lottie. She sees everything."

"Why was your mother there?" I laugh. "And where is 'there?' And most importantly, why wasn't I invited?"

"Remy's garage," Trina says, then starts at the beginning and tells us how her mother heard about the motorcycles, and how she, Dorothy, and Eli went to investigate.

By the time she's done speaking, I can't quite help my giggle. I saw the way Nora looked at Lee last night. I saw the way they acted at Candice's housewarming party last year —avoiding each other and gazing longingly across the room.

"Nora's in trouble. It's no good to work for someone you're attracted to," I say, shaking my head. "Take it from someone who knows." I jab a thumb at Wes.

All he does is catch my thumb in his hand and tug me so hard I crash into his chest. "Last I heard, you liked my brand of trouble," he growls in my ear.

Laughing, I let myself melt into Wes's warmth. He tucks me into that place against his side that feels like home until my laptop lets out another wheeze. Finally, I can send my email and shut it down.

Georgia ends up scooting over as Trina, Mac, and her kids join us. I resist the urge to call Nora and demand she come tell us everything.

She's new here. She'll learn that she can't hide from our friendship.

6

NORA

THE FRINGE FESTIVAL offices are next to Town Hall in a small, light-filled office building. The directory in the lobby says the Fringe Fest team is on the third floor, so I call the elevator and make my way up. I walk in to see a sweeping reception desk with a tiny, fierce-looking woman sitting behind it. Her nameplate says Olivia.

"Hello," Olivia says with a smile. Her long, golden hair is braided in two tails and tied at the nape of her neck in an elegant yet quirky bun. "How can I help you?"

"I'm Nora Richter," I say with a tremulous smile. "Lee hired me to work on the magazine?" I'm not sure why it comes out as a question, but it does.

Olivia tilts her head. "Oh. Okay. He's not in yet, but feel free to take a seat—"

The roar of a motorcycle outside makes everything inside me come to attention. I glance out the window to see a man on a big, shiny, badass motorcycle backing into a space in front of our building. Lee takes his helmet off and combs his fingers through the thick, inky strands, then starts stalking toward the front door.

I love the way he walks. His long legs eat up distance in big bites. He's purposeful, confident, in control. Watching him walk makes me feel soft and feminine, and I'm not exactly sure why. Maybe it's the set of his shoulders, or the way his motorcycle jacket hangs on his tall, broad frame.

He disappears from view and I give Olivia a closed-lipped smile. Hiking my purse higher onto my shoulder, I grab the strap with both hands and wait.

The elevator doors sweep open, and there he is. Much bigger than he looked from the window. Much bigger than I remember. His motorcycle helmet hangs from his fist, jacket unzipped. His eyes cut to mine.

"Nora," he says. "You're early."

"Maybe you're late," I shoot back. I tap my wrist, right where my imaginary watch rests.

His lips tilt, then he glances at the receptionist. "Olivia," he says with a nod.

"Hi, Lee. I left the mail on your desk. You have a message from the mayor. He's wondering about the latest permit applications."

Lee's mouth tightens. He doesn't like the mayor?

Olivia smiles at him, sitting up straighter in her chair and arching her back in a way that makes her breasts strain against her bright blue top.

A strange, violent emotion tears through me. Aggression floods my veins, and it takes all my self-control to stop myself from launching across the reception desk and tackling her to the ground.

Deep breaths.

I'm insane. I'm losing my mind. I'm feeling territorial

over a man I spoke to for the first time after scratching up his prized motorcycle. A man who, by all accounts, should hate me. A man who is now officially *my boss*.

"Thanks, Liv," he says, and I hate that he has a nickname for her. Hate it with a fiery passion so strong I'm surprised steam isn't blowing out of my ears.

From the corner of my eye, I take another glance at her. She's tiny. Petite. Is that the kind of woman Lee likes? I'm not petite. Like my brother, I take after my father. I'm five foot eight and a half, but people always think I'm taller. I have hips and boobs and thighs that seem to make it their job to strain the seams of all my clothes.

"This way," Lee says, his hand brushing my elbow. I jolt away from my jealous perusal of the friendly receptionist, mentally smacking myself for my unfounded jealousy. What is wrong with me? She's perfectly friendly and clearly decent at her job. Lee didn't even give her a second glance. And even if he did, who am I to complain? I work for him too. It's not like we're dating.

I blame this out-of-control libido. This shiny new sex drive is melting my brain. I need to leash it somehow. Go back to the old me—if only to survive working in this office.

We walk past a handsome man with salt-and-pepper hair. Lee nods. "Hey, Rick. How was Nate's soccer game?"

"Scored two goals," Rick answers, eyes flicking to me. He smiles warmly. "My son wants to play for the Los Angeles FC when he grows up."

I can't help but smile back. "Sounds like he's on the right track." I'm about to extend my hand to introduce myself when Lee puts his hand on the small of my back and gently yet firmly shoves me toward the corner office.

"We'll introduce you to everyone later."

"Oh. Okay." I give Rick an apologetic smile, which he answers with a wink.

When I sit down in the chair Lee motions to, I notice his jaw is clenched. His movements are jerky as he closes the door and shuffles some papers on his desk.

"Everything okay?" I ask tentatively.

"What?" he barks, then shakes his head. His eyes dart through the wall of glass to Rick then back to me. "Yeah, of course. Sorry."

"You want me to come back in a few minutes when you've had time to settle in?" I make to push myself up, but Lee grunts.

"No."

"Okie dokie," I answer, flopping back down on my seat. Lee places his motorcycle helmet on top of a filing cabinet then strips off his leather jacket. He's wearing jeans and a white T-shirt, which should be the universal uniform for hot men everywhere. He looks delicious.

"I feel overdressed," I say to fill the silence. I'm wearing a silky off-white blouse that has a big floppy bow at the neck. My pencil skirt is brown with a faint cream checkered pattern that comes down just below my knees. My heels are brown patent leather. It was one of my go-to outfits at my old job, where the dress code was business-formal.

Lee glances over at me, eyes skimming my top then coasting down to the fabric of my skirt stretched over my thighs. His gaze moves down to my ankles, which I've crossed. His eyes darken slightly as they move back up my body then shift away. "You look fine."

Heat blazes through me.

Because he told me I looked "fine."

Once again, I need to ask, *What the hell is wrong with me?* That's not even a decent compliment.

Lee hooks his jacket on the back of his chair then drops into his seat with a sigh. His index finger slides along his upper lip as his eyes meet mine. Over and back, his long finger traces his cupid's bow. I'm jealous of his finger. I watch the small movement as everything from my navel to my knees tightens almost painfully.

I reach for my mental baseball bat and beat my libido to a pulp. For some reason, it only seems to excite her.

This was a bad idea. I haven't yet regained control over my body, and now I have to work with the object of Miss Libido's fascination.

"So," I say. "What's the magazine you've been working on?"

Lee blinks as if I've snapped him out of a stupor. He nods, rolling to the filing cabinet on his office chair to pull out an old issue. "It's a quarterly publication. We publish it online as well," he tells me. "I'm hoping we can reach a broader audience of both artists and festival attendees. The growth of the Fringe Fest over the past few years has turned Heart's Cove into a tourist destination. We want to extend that beyond the one-week festival."

I flip through the pages and straighten in my chair. Excitement sparks in my gut. There's so much good content here, but it could be displayed so much more attractively. It's a magazine featuring *art*, for crying out loud. It shouldn't be this ugly.

My lip is soft between my teeth as ideas tumble through my brain. We could do features on different mediums. Interviews with artists. A full photo issue with previous

Fringe Fest attendees. Advertising space to fund it all. A coffee table book to publish during each Fringe Festival. Limited releases to increase the hype. Inspiration goes off like fireworks inside me.

Lee clears his throat. "So?"

When I lift my gaze to meet his, he's frowning. I feel a smile bloom over my face. "I have so many ideas."

He lets out a little puff of breath and leans back on his chair. "Good. Because I don't."

I put the magazine issue down on his desk and point out one of the article headlines, telling him how I would've positioned it with the photos that were chosen. We talk about fonts and spacing and advertising and before I know it, my stomach growls so loudly we both pause.

Lee's brows jump, and I feel a flush sweep over my cheeks. "I didn't eat breakfast," I answer.

"Why not?" His voice is harsh.

"I don't know. Maybe I was nervous about my new job."

A twitch in his lips makes something jump in my chest. Our hands are on his desk on top of the magazine, and he moves his thumb half an inch so it just barely brushes the side of my palm. The touch jolts me, sending heat flooding to all the places hidden beneath my skirt. I don't pull my hand away.

"Don't be nervous, Nora. I don't bite." His thumb sweeps the tiniest bit. "Not unless I'm asked to."

THAT EVENING, when I get home, I feel like I've run a marathon. I ignore calls from Simone and Trina, choosing instead to order takeout and have a long, cold shower.

It still doesn't douse the embers in my veins, and I curse myself for signing up for this particular brand of torture.

If this is how it's going to feel to work with Lee, I'm starting to think I should have moved in with my mother.

7

LEE

IT'S BEEN five days since Nora started working here. I knew I was in trouble as soon as I arrived on Monday morning. She was wearing a tight brown skirt and a silky cream top that made her look like a walking advertisement for workplace fantasies. I wanted her immediately.

I'm such an idiot for offering her this job. Sure, she's perfect for it, and far more experienced than anyone else we'd be able to find at the salary we're able to offer.

Still.

I can't exactly hook up with an employee, can I? Now that we work together, a relationship is off the table. She'll be paying off the cost of the motorcycle damage for somewhere between eighteen months to two years, which might as well be an eternity. It's pure torture to be in the same building as her and not be able to get any closer.

The Fringe Festival team is small, only five people in total. We do all the organizational work, outreach to artists, publicity, and liaison with the Heart's Cove Town Council for permits and approvals. We hire all the volunteers and manage the kiosk rentals. With Nora on board, we'll be able to expand to print and online publications, and hopefully gain more publicity. She knows all kinds of things about media releases and expansion.

And yet all I can think about is dragging her into my office and bending her over my desk.

It's bad. Really, really bad.

Today, she's wearing black, strappy sandals that show off the red polish on her toes. Her hair is a silky black waterfall that slides halfway down her back and sways with every swish of her hips. Her dress matches the polish exactly, hugging every gorgeous curve, stopping just above her knee. When she sits down, I can see a slice of her thigh that has me panting and gritting my teeth to stop my dirty, inappropriate thoughts from showing on my face.

And her lips.

God. Her lips.

I never thought I liked red lipstick until I saw it on Nora Richter. Between the gloss she had on the other night and the lipstick she's wearing today, I'm starting to think I have a new kink. Nora's lips, painted in something shiny and red, wrapped around my—

I tear my eyes away from her as she leans against our administrator's desk. My body is stiff, every muscle clenched to stop myself from looking at the slice of leg that's exposed when she bends over. Legs I want wrapped around my waist. Desperately.

Even with my eyes closed, it takes me long moments to get my breathing under control. My hands are clenched on my desk, my knee jiggling incessantly.

Two years? I signed up for *two years* of this?

I'm an idiot.

But what was the alternative? Let her pay out of pocket and watch her disappear back to Reno? Her reaction said it all. She was laughing, but I could tell she was serious about getting rid of her apartment and moving back in with her mother.

She would have *left*. Heart's Cove would have gone back to the tiny, claustrophobic town it was before she arrived. My life would have constricted back to the dull, meaningless drudgery it was before.

Don't ask me why her arrival changed everything. I'm not thinking about that right now. It's not that I have feelings for her, it's just that she's...she's...

An email hits my inbox.

The sender's name screams at me in bold, black letters. My blood runs cold. Ice crusts over my skin. I'm immediately transported to that horrible day three years ago, the day that cannot be excised from my brain, no matter how much I want to tear the memory out at the root.

My ex-fiancée's name is like a brand on my screen. I read it a dozen times and still, I sit frozen on my chair.

Then I read the subject line. *You're Invited to Roger and Drea's Celebration of Marriage.*

Again. She sent it *again*. It's got to be a hoax...right? Some kind of prank?

The woman wouldn't *actually* invite me to her wedding —she can't keep pestering me with these endless invitations.

It can't be true.

But when I click on the email and open it up, I don't see any evidence of it being a joke. The swooping, cursive font of the invitation laughs at me from the screen. Flowery language about unions and love and happiness.

I remember those words. I remember *our* invitations. She agonized over them for six weeks because she wanted them to be "just right" for the only wedding she'd ever have. She was totally against using Evites, saying it wasn't classy enough. It was one of the thousand decisions we had to make to plan the perfect event that never happened.

What a fucking joke.

I'm unable to look at those two names on the invitation, at the venue right here in Heart's Cove, at the date that falls two Saturdays before the start of the Fringe Festival. I shut the email and roll back from my desk. My ex-fiancée is getting married in six short weeks.

I'm going to puke. My hands are clammy, my heart beats unsteadily, and all I can do is remember that day. The shame, the embarrassment, the heartbreak. It all rushes back to me until all I can do is stare at my screen while a harsh whistling sound pierces my eardrums.

Then, warmth. A hand on my shoulder.

I blink, and Nora's there. She's frowning, searching my face. "Lee? Are you okay?"

"Fine," I croak. "I'm fine. What's up?"

"I was just asking about the sculpture exhibit we're setting up this year. That Texan artist, Sebastian Finch, just confirmed he's commissioning a piece specifically for the Fringe Fest, and I was thinking we could have a walking exhibit throughout the town." She lifts her palm from my shoulder to place the back of her hand against my forehead. Checking my temperature. "You don't look so good. Do you need some water? I can run to the pharmacy if you need medicine."

"I'm not sick," I say, but I still close my eyes as she lets her fingers linger on my brow. She pushes my hair back with a soft, gentle stroke and I nearly groan in contentment.

"You should go home. I can drive you."

"I'm okay, Nora. Really."

Those red-painted lips pinch into a tight little rosebud. I want to run my thumb over them to smooth them out again. Smudge that lipstick onto her cheek. Watch her mouth part...

Blinking, I turn back to my screen. "Sculpture exhibit?" I prompt.

"I was thinking we could set it up in a few parks, maybe even the new community garden. It could be a walking exhibit that coaxes people from Cove Boulevard to the less-traveled parts of town. Spread some foot traffic to other businesses that aren't on the main drag."

"Good idea," I croak. The rusty cogs in my brain are clunking along with great effort. I'm having a hard time keeping up with her words. Half of me is staring at her mouth, and the other half is still stuck on the words *Celebration of Marriage*.

"Olivia said you'd know what kind of permits we'd need. I can draft up a map for the permit application, and we can use it to promote the exhibit online and include it in the next issue of the magazine. What do you think?"

"Yeah." I mentally high-five myself for managing to make a coherent word.

Nora just frowns. Her hand reappears against my forehead, her fingers cool against my heated skin. How is it possible for someone's fingers to feel so good? I close my eyes for a second. I just need the world to stop wobbling.

"I'm driving you home," she announces. "Get your stuff. We're going."

My desk phone rings. I frown at it.

When it rings again, Nora plucks it from its cradle. "Lee Blair's office, how may I help?" She straightens. "Mr. Mayor. Yes. Yes, of course." She covers the receiver and looks at me. "It's the mayor."

I nod, taking the phone from her hands. My grip feels weak, but I force myself to take a long, steadying breath, then I put the phone to my ear. "Roger."

"So you are alive." My former best friend guffaws, the sound arrowing straight through my heart. We used to laugh together, before...before...

"What can I do for you?"

"I'm sitting here looking at a stack of proposals from the Fringe Festival team, but my inbox is still missing your RSVP to my wedding."

Nora's still standing by my desk. I grip her hand, using the contact to steady myself. "I just got the invitation a second ago."

"You mean the third invitation we've sent?" Roger asks. "Is it so hard to tick yes or no on an Evite?"

I clear my throat. "Yeah. Fine. I'll do it. You got our proposals for the road closures?"

I hear shuffling papers on the other end of the line, then the creak of a chair. The pause between us stretches. "I got them," Roger finally confirms.

Silence hangs between us, and I hear what goes unsaid: As long as I keep his wedding invitation unanswered, he'll hold our proposals hostage.

My lids slide shut, and all that keeps me tethered to the ground is the feeling of Nora's fingers in my palm.

"All right," I finally say.

"We understand each other?"

"Loud and clear," I say.

"I want everyone to know there are no hard feelings between us," the mayor says. "There's an election coming up, and I don't want anyone talking about my wedding unless it's to say how beautiful my bride looked in white. No dredging up of old gossip. No talk of you or me or Drea or anything that happened three years ago. Got it?"

Pain lances my chest. I must stiffen because Nora gives my hand a squeeze. I squeeze back, grateful for the contact.

"There are no hard feelings," I tell Roger, and the words taste like a lie on my tongue.

"You were my best friend, Lee," he says, and neither of us corrects his use of the past tense. After what happened between me and Drea—and everything that came after—our friendship never recovered. It was impossible.

"Yeah," I answer noncommittally. "I'll RSVP. I gotta go."

"Good." The phone clicks.

I stare at the receiver in my hand, then gently set it back in its cradle. Nora drops my hand but doesn't move from her spot next to my desk. Her red dress crinkles as she leans against the desk, arms folded as she frowns at me.

"What was that about?"

"The mayor has our proposals. He'll approve them." *As soon as I say I'll go to his wedding and pretend everything is okay.*

"Do you want me to take you home? I'm meeting my mother at the café, and I can drop you off on the way there."

Swallowing tightly, I glance at the clock. Three o'clock. We typically finish early on Fridays, so it wouldn't look weird if I went home right now.

It's all I can do to drag myself to my feet. The office feels stifling. I just need...air. Time. Some space to process what's going on. When I stumble on a wrinkle in the carpet, I know I can't ride my bike back home, even though it's only a short drive.

Nora knows it too. She jerks her head to the door. "Come on," she says. "Let's go."

I watch Nora's hips sway back and forth in that red dress as I follow her out the office door. Squinting against the bright sunlight, I wonder how it is the weather can be so beautiful when my whole world just tilted on its axis.

It's not that I don't want Drea to get married. And it's not that I want her for myself—not after what she did. And I'm not even mad at Roger. I just... I just can't bring myself to pretend that everything's okay. Why do they need me there? Why can't we just ignore each other in peace? Roger'll win the election, easy. He doesn't need me to put on a fake smile and shake his hand to do it.

"Inside," Nora commands when we get to her car, holding the passenger-side door open. She drives a navy Hyundai hatchback, and even when I push the seat all the way back, my knees still hit the glove compartment. I watch her jog around the front of the car, a splash of vibrant red against the black of the asphalt behind her.

Her car smells like her. Fruity and floral. Feminine.

I close my eyes and drag in a long breath, my thoughts slowing down as the scent of her fills my lungs.

She slides in beside me and starts the car. "Where are we going?"

"Take a left at the lights," I answer, angling my head so I can watch her drive. Her hands are clamped on the steering wheel, shoulders tense as they squeeze around her ears. "Thanks, Nora."

"Don't mention it," she says. "What happened? You looked so pale when I walked into your office." She steals a glance my way then turns back to the road. Her neck is a graceful arch that I want to trace with my lips. At some point in the last few minutes, she's tied her hair up in a high ponytail. A few tendrils fall down around her temples and nape. I want to twist them around my fingers to see if they feel as soft as they look.

Gorgeous. She's fucking gorgeous.

And I can't have her. Why would I even want to? I know what happens when I have feelings for a woman. They do what Drea did. They put my heart through a garbage disposal and let it rot with all their vegetable scraps.

"Next right," I tell her as we pass the gas station. "I live in number thirty-four."

She pulls up outside my house and is on my side of the car by the time I have my hand on the handle. She shuts the door behind me and follows me to the entrance to my house.

"I can take it from here, Nora. Thanks for the lift."

"I'm checking your medicine cabinet. You need to drink something, stay hydrated." She motions to the door until I unlock it. "You got any electrolytes? Gatorade?"

It's silly, really. All I did was get an email that sent me reeling, then a phone call that made my stomach churn. I'm not sick. The fog in my head is clearing and as I open the door, I realize Nora is about to walk into my house behind me. I pause at the door, turning to block the entrance. If I let her in, I'm not going to be able to keep my hands off her.

For her sake, she needs to stay outside. I'm not going to be the one who crosses the line when I'm supposed to be her boss.

"I'm fine, Nora. Really. I'll just get some sleep and be fine in an hour."

Her brows are drawn, eyes roving over my face as if she's trying to decide whether or not I'm lying. Whatever she sees must satisfy her because she drops her shoulders. "Fine. But you'll call me if you need something?"

"Sure. I'll even knock a couple hundred bucks off the debt for being so nice and helping me escape the office."

Her lips twitch. "I hadn't realized that was an option. I would've offered to drive you everywhere."

"You still can." I have one hand on the doorjamb, one hand on the door. The top of Nora's head just about reaches my shoulder, and for a brief moment, I wonder how she would fit against my body.

But I already know the answer to that. She'd fit perfectly. That's the problem.

"Okay, well, I'll get going. My mother's probably waiting for me already. And I'm holding you to that couple hundred bucks off my debt," she says with a raised finger. "You can't take it back. I have a spreadsheet."

It's my turn to smile. "Two hundred bucks to drive five blocks." I shake my head. "Most expensive taxi I've ever taken."

"You're the one who set the price," she answers, eyes sparkling. "So don't blame me."

I close the door and watch her through the window as she heads back to her car. She doesn't look back as she drives away.

8

NORA

THROUGH THE WINDOW of the Four Cups Café, I see my mother already seated at a table. Beside her, Margaret is talking animatedly while Dorothy and Lottie argue on the other side of the table. At the end of the table, Agnes, the bookstore owner and Dorothy's supposed mortal enemy, sips a cup of coffee. My mother says something, and they all start cackling.

When I walk in the door, four of the older women cheer. Agnes just scowls. My mother gets up and gives me one of her signature hugs and immediately, my world feels better.

"Hey, Ma."

"Honey." She gives me a smile full of love.

"How was the drive?"

My mother lives in Tahoe, near the border between California and Nevada. It's a couple of hours' drive from here, and I know she gets nervous driving on her own.

"Dan drove," she replies just as a stout, silver-and-white-haired gentleman emerges from the bathroom hallway. I've met my mother's beau a few times, but this is the first time he's made the trip to Heart's Cove. They're staying at the hotel, in one of the honeymoon suites which Dorothy and Margaret reserved for them.

"Hi, Dan," I say, and I get another hug from the man who loves my mother. They met later in life, when they were both in their sixties. My father died when I was young, and for a long time I worried that my mother wouldn't date again. But Dan lost his wife twelve years ago, and he understood that my mom didn't want to replace my dad. He didn't want to push aside the memory of his late wife either, so their relationship grew from that shared understanding into something beautiful and new.

I like him, and I love how he is with my mom.

"You look tired," Dan says, white, bushy brows tugging together. "New job wearing you down?"

"Something like that," I answer. My mother waves me over to the table and pours me a cup of tea from the pot in the middle of the table. Dorothy shifts the plates of pastries around and loads one onto my plate before taking a seat on my other side.

Then, for the next twenty minutes, I listen to the gossip around town. Agnes calls Dorothy an old hag, and Dorothy answers by telling her to take a long walk off a short pier. Everyone nods and smiles like this is normal. I hear about the birds that have visited my mother's bird feeder, and about the new art class Dorothy will be hosting at the hotel. My shoulders relax, and the stress of the day seeps away.

There's no financial pressure here. No sexy man to distract me and drive me out of my mind. Just family and friends and comfort.

As I sip the last of my tea, I realize that there was never

a choice, really. I was always going to stay in this town, no matter what. The dilemma Lee presented me with was woefully unfair, because I would have accepted any arrangement he proposed.

I can't go back to the way my life was before.

"So." My mother puts her palms on the table. "My son is getting married in ten weeks' time."

The elderly ladies at the table lean in. I grin and top everyone's drinks up, lifting the teacup to the barista behind the counter for a refill.

"Fallon says he has everything under control, but I want to know what you've heard," my mother tells her friends, then glances at me. "That boy doesn't tell me anything." Even though her face is stern, I know she's just about bursting with happiness.

Fallon and my mom didn't get along for a long time. When my dad died, Fallon went through a fairly intense rebellious teenage phase. I was the opposite. I became more controlled, more responsible.

A graceful move brings my mother's teacup to her lips. She's always moved like a dancer. Her parents—my grandparents, whom I've only met twice—moved to the States from Kerala, India, and I know from hints my mother's dropped that Fallon gets his rebellious side from her. She rebelled by marrying my white American father, by giving us American names, by splitting from a lot of the customs that were expected of her.

But even as she struck out on her own, my mother never lost her grace, her sense of self. I admire that in her.

Truthfully, my mother's rebellion made me feel disconnected from my heritage, but I can't blame her. I know the split from her parents and her community was incredibly difficult. She didn't like the man they were pushing her to marry, and she wanted a career of her own. I can't even imagine how much strength it must have taken to go out on her own like that, at a time when women were expected to mostly stay at home—not to mention the cultural pressures she was under from her family and community. And after, being all but disowned? I don't know how she survived.

I love her more than anything, and I know that her steel-hardened spine is what got us through the years after my father passed. It's probably her example that got me to leave my steady job and take the leap to move to Heart's Cove.

Now, it warms me to my core to see her proud of Fallon, finally reconnecting with my brother right before he marries the love of his life.

"Jen's planning on making her own wedding cake," I tell her. "Fallon said she's had lots of sleepless nights trying to perfect the recipe."

Ma clicks her tongue. "She should let someone else do that. It's too much pressure." She stands abruptly. "I'll got tell her that."

I grin as I watch her stomp toward the kitchen, knowing she was looking for any excuse to talk wedding plans with Fallon and Jen. Selfishly, I'm happy. Takes the pressure off of me.

When she reemerges, with Fallon gently guiding her back to her chair with his lips tugging at the corners, we finish our last pot of tea and get ready to go. I help bring our dishes to the counter, smile at Fiona, then head out with my mother and Dan.

It doesn't take her long to pepper me with questions about the job, the motorcycles, and the arrangement I've come to with Lee Blair. By the time we arrive at her hotel, she knows the whole story. Trust my mother to move on from the excitement of Fallon's wedding to make sure she knows everything about my life too.

Well, almost the whole story. She doesn't know what Lee's presence does to me.

"I don't like it," my mother finally says, waving Dan on up to the room while she grips my elbow and steers me to a bench in the hotel courtyard.

"It's fine," I answer.

"It's *trouble,* is what it is." She clicks her tongue. "You only just paid off those stupid debts from that man." My ex-husband, Eric, has forever been dubbed *that man* by my mother. Since the day I told her I was getting a divorce, she hasn't spoken his name. She releases a put-upon sigh. "Now you're doing it again."

I shake my head. "It's not the same."

"No?"

"At least these debts are my own." I give her a wry smile. "And I have a funny video to show for it."

My mother rolls her eyes. Her gaze focuses on the middle distance for a moment, then she sets her hand on my knee. "I want you to stop sending me money."

I frown. "Ma, it's fine. I can afford it, and your Social Security isn't enough to pay the rent at the retirement community and your health insurance—"

"Dan was a financial advisor, you know. He helped me make a new budget, and we figured out I'll get by just fine without your help. Tightened up a few areas, but my life won't really change. Your money should go to paying off the motorcycle debt. Get it off the books so you can start over. It's time, Nora."

It might make me a bad daughter or a selfish person, but I feel like a weight has lifted off my shoulders. With the money I sent to my mother freed up to pay the debt, I could potentially clear it within the year. I could *truly* start over—maybe even get that house I've been wanting.

"What about your health insurance? You left enough to pay for that? We were paying yearly, remember? And the date is coming up, so you'll need some money set aside—"

"It's all figured out, honey," my mother says as she pats my knee. "I'm sixty-five and I qualify for Medicare." She arches a brow at me. "There are perks to getting old, apparently."

I start protesting, but my mother interrupts.

"Everything will be fine. You need to start worrying about your own life instead of an old woman's."

"You're my mom," I answer.

My mother turns to me and takes my cheeks in her hands. Her dark-brown eyes are luminous. "I love you, Nora." She smiles. "Let me do this for you. You've helped me so much over the years, and now it's time for me to return the favor."

"If you are ever short on money, you need to tell me," I say sternly. "I won't have you eating cat food and sleeping with a dozen blankets because you can't afford the heating bill. You hear me?"

"Loud and clear." My mother smiles. She lets out a sigh and shakes her head. "I'm sorry, Nora."

I frown. "For what?"

"For making you feel like security was the most important thing. I drilled it into you about getting a good job and to save, save, save. And where did that get you?" She pauses. When she speaks again, her voice is quiet. "I failed you. I should have taught you how to live properly, but..."

I curl my fingers into my mother's hand and lean my head against hers. "Things were hard after Dad died," I say quietly. "And then everything happened with Fallon's troubles...I think we both needed to feel secure."

"I'm glad you're taking a few risks now," my mother tells me. "I'm glad we both are." Her eyes drift to the edge of the courtyard, where Dan appears. His face lights up at the sight of my mother. She straightens, a smile blooming on her lips.

I leave her in the care of a man who treats her like a queen and wander home, heart feeling heavy and light all at once.

THERE'S a package waiting for me when I get to my apartment. I stare at it for a beat, thoughts of my mother drifting away as I come back to the present. The sight of the box—and the knowledge of what's inside—makes me think of my new boss. Was it really only a couple of hours since I drove Lee home? I have to wait an entire weekend to see him again, and I know it's going to drag on, each grain of sand taking an eternity to fall through the hourglass.

I've already gotten used to seeing him in the office, his dark head bent over his desk. Sometimes he wears glasses to look at his screen, and he turns from a badass motorcycle-riding hunk to a sexy librarian fantasy. Whenever I catch myself looking at him, I slap myself and open up the spreadsheet detailing my debt payoff.

Shaking my head, I grab the box by my front door and duck inside. Knowing what's inside the package, I set it down on the kitchen table like I'm holding a bomb and back away. I keep an eye on it as I toe off my shoes. As I potter around the kitchen, the box sits on the table. Waiting.

Inside the box is a solution to my Lee Blair problem. Not only am I grown woman who owns up to her mistakes, but I'm also solution-oriented. When I have a problem, it doesn't take me long to fix it.

I thought working in the office would be like exposure therapy. I was supposed to get over this odd infatuation, because I'd be close enough to see all his warts and imperfections. My body would normalize, and I'd recover from this runaway libido.

It's been a week, though, and I don't seem to be recovering at all. If anything, it seems to be getting worse. As far as I can tell, through careful observation, he has no warts. No imperfections. His nose is very slightly crooked, which could be classed as a flaw, but it only makes him look more handsome.

Yesterday, he leaned against my desk to point at something on my screen and my head spun at the heat of his bicep so close to my cheek. Today, when he was sitting in my car, I had to breathe through my mouth to avoid inhaling his pine-and-leather scent until it was imprinted in my lungs. Every minute I spend in his presence, I wind myself tighter and tighter and tighter.

That is a problem I haven't been able to solve —until now.

My mental baseball bat isn't doing the trick. Putting my hands on my hips, I stare at the discreet brown box on my kitchen table. My stomach tightens, but I don't have the guts to open it. I need some food first. Then I can shower off my day, and *then* I'll open my package.

I'm halfway through putting a salad together when I huff, set my knife down, and wash my hands. Screw it.

It only takes a moment to slice off the packing tape and flip open the box. It's about the size of a large, rectangular Tupperware container, and it's filled with brown packing paper along the edges. I pull out a sleek black box from the packaging and stare at the glossy lettering on the top.

My heart pounds against my ribs, which is silly. This shouldn't make me so nervous. I'm alone in my kitchen with an item I purchased myself with my own money. Nothing to be embarrassed or apprehensive about.

Tearing off the plastic from the item, I let out a shaky breath. Then I take the top of the black box off and stare at what rests inside.

Smooth white silicone stares back at me, gleaming in the light of my kitchen.

My first ever vibrator.

Tearing my gaze away from the device, I jog to my front door to make sure I locked it. The last thing I want is for my mother and her pack of cackling cronies to burst in while I'm...otherwise occupied. Satisfied that the lock is indeed engaged, I put the chain on for good measure and return to the kitchen table. Approaching on soft feet, as if the vibrator were a wild animal about to attack, I peer at my new purchase.

It's the shape of a large microphone, with a smooth round head attached to a wand with three buttons. I did a *lot* of research on Monday, putting in a late-night order after my first day of work. This vibrator was highly recommended. It made multiple "best-of" lists, which were thoroughly tested by multiple women.

Now that it's in front of me, I'm intimidated. My palms are clammy and my heart beats unsteadily. I've seen pictures of the Hitachi Magic Wand, of course, and this particular vibrator is like a sleeker, updated model by a different brand. It's wireless, which many reviewers said was useful. Why they need a gigantic portable vibrator is beyond me, but I trust their experience and judgment. I'm a novice, after all.

Slowly, I take the wand out of its box and run the pads of my fingers over the silicone head. It's buttery-soft, and it makes my heart beat just a little bit faster.

This is ridiculous, really. Most people buy vibrators when they're in their twenties. They complete most of their sexual exploration in college and figure out what they want. Maybe after a decade of marriage, they get more adventurous and enter a new stage. I...didn't do that. I studied design and threw myself into my internships. I was busy chasing my passion. I met Eric and got married, and our sex life didn't really include experimentation.

So yeah. I'm late to the party.

Tentatively, I run my thumb over the hard plastic buttons on the wand and press the up arrow. I yelp when the thing starts buzzing, then stare. My mouth grows dry. This thing is vibrating *hard*. It seems like a lot. Like that would be far, far too intense if I were to put it...down there.

But the thousands of five-star reviews wouldn't lie, right? This vibrator gave women faster, more intense orgasms than any other vibrator on the market. Why would I be any different?

I square my shoulders. I'm no chicken. I'm a woman. An adult.

This is a good solution. It was a great idea. I'm finally going to see what all the fuss about vibrators is about. If I can't get the real thing and I can't ignore my sex drive, I'll take care of the problem myself.

See? Solution-oriented. A doer.

Nora Richter, creative problem solver. I should put that on my resume.

Grabbing the toy cleaner that came with the wand, I give it a quick spritz and wash off the head, then leave my half-made dinner on the kitchen counter and head to the bedroom. With shaking hands, I pull off my pants and panties in one quick movement then lie back on my bed.

It's dark in the bedroom, with the light of the setting sun streaming through the cracks in my closed blinds. Everything feels heightened as I grab my new vibrator and lie back on my pillows. The blanket is scratchy against my bare behind. My breathing is too loud in the quiet room. My heart beats far, far too fast.

But if I'm going to survive working on the Fringe Fest team, watching my boss slide those sexy glasses on and off his face every day, holding my breath as he prowls to the office kitchen and back, I'm going to have to take the edge off. He presented me with a dilemma, and I made a choice to work for him. I will not muddy the waters by pursuing a relationship with my new boss; I'll take care of the problem on my own.

Right here. Right now.

I turn on the vibrator. The buzzing is deafening in the stillness of the room, but a dollop of excitement spreads over my stomach. With a trembling breath, I bring my new toy to my inner thigh, and slide up.

Oh. *Oh.* I...*whoa.*

Yes I *am* solving problems. Look at me go.

Closing my eyes, I sink into the unfamiliar sensations. It's a lot, but it's not bad. Quite the opposite, actually. As I inhale through the vibrations and try to find the right spot and pressure, Miss Libido takes over.

That's where it all goes wrong.

With intense, pleasurable buzzing between my legs and a winding tension in the pit of my stomach, my brain provides images to help me along.

Images of a certain man in a certain leather jacket. Of his weight pressing me into the pillows. So heavy and so, so nice. His harsh breaths panting my name.

He'd dominate me. He'd pin my hands by my sides and spread me as wide as he wanted. He'd fit me perfectly; I already know. His broad, rough hands sweeping over my skin. His teeth sliding along the dusky brown of my nipples. His cock pistoning in and out of me with punishing thrusts.

I can almost feel it. The sweat-slicked skin against mine, the hands pulling my knees apart, and the harsh breaths ghosting over my skin. Flipping me over, pushing me down, tangling those hands into my hair to pull—

An explosion detonates inside me. I arch clean off the bed, back bowing, breath whistling. I buck my hips against my new toy, imagining my new boss pinning me down and fucking me so hard I see stars.

And then suddenly, it's too much. I pull the wand away and fumble to turn it off, accidentally turning the vibrations up instead. It slips from my grip and bounces to the floor, hitting the nightstand and buzzing so hard the whole room vibrates. With trembling hands and harsh breaths, I fall off the bed and lunge for it, legs up in the air, hips against the mattress, face mashed against the carpet. Finally, I manage to power the wand off and slither to the floor, unable to move.

That was...

I mean.

Wow.

The ladies reviewing this thing were not lying.

Closing my eyes, I enjoy the final few thrills zipping between my thighs as my heartbeat returns to a normal pace. Slow as molasses, my thoughts start filtering back through my mind.

And I realize that I'm a massive, monumental idiot.

My eyes fly open as I stare at the ceiling, then at my new vibrator. My cheeks heat at the thought of what I just did. What I just *imagined*. How hard I came. The fact that I'm lying on the floor after it all, boneless and sated.

Monday morning, bright and early, I need to go into the office, look Lee Blair in the eye, and pretend I didn't just propel myself to another galaxy with a fantasy featuring him in the starring role.

Shit.

9

LEE

Nora's acting weird.

I bought coffees for everyone in the office and she didn't even look at my face when she mumbled, "Thank you," and set the coffee aside. Her cheeks were pinker than usual. I asked her how her mother's visit was, and she just said, "Good," before turning back to her screen. An hour later, she emailed her proposal for the sculpture exhibit, but she didn't come into my office to discuss it face-to-face.

Is it because of Friday? She feels awkward about driving me home?

Even her clothes seem different. She's not wearing one of those sexy business outfits today, just jeans and a loose blue top. Her hair is thrown up in a messy bun. It's like she's trying to sink into the background, stay unnoticed.

Because I'm a huge, inappropriate asshole, I still think she's hot as hell. The top slips to reveal a slice of her shoulder, and my cock throbs behind my zipper. Her outfit makes me wonder how she'd look first thing in the morning with her hair splayed across my pillow.

Tearing my eyes away from the top of her head poking above her computer screen, I turn back to my own work. I've got phone calls to make and artists to confirm for the live shows we're doing at the Fringe Fest. The youngest member of our team, Hailey, wants to start posting promotional information on the Fringe Fest's social media pages. We need content for her.

But as I blink at my computer, I see nothing. My gaze drifts back to the messy bun jutting out above Nora's screen.

I need to talk to her. I'll clear the air and tell her that I appreciate her driving me home on Friday, but there's no need to feel awkward. We're colleagues. That's all.

Except...

I fist my hands on my desk. Friday, after Nora left, I went on a five-mile run then punished myself in my home gym. I sweated out the stress and shock of Drea's wedding invitation until I felt normal again, then I took a shower. That's where things got interesting. And by interesting, I mean inappropriate.

Every time I inhaled on my run or in the gym or in my house, I could smell the fruity, floral scent from Nora's car. Despite my workouts I still had excess energy, so I took a cold shower...and my hand ended up wrapped around my cock. Nothing like a quick tug to blow off some steam, right?

Except the woman who popped into my head was Nora. Splayed out on my sheets for me to enjoy. I thought of tasting her, burying my face between her legs, tasting her orgasm on my tongue.

It's only a fantasy, right? No harm. I've fantasized about plenty of women I'll never sleep with.

But if Nora feels uncomfortable in the office, or if I did something in the car on Friday to make her feel uneasy, I'd rather deal with it right away. I don't want her to email proposals across the office and avoid eye contact. It's bad enough to have the debt hanging between us. If she keeps me at arm's length, I'll go crazy.

"Nora," I say from my office doorway. "Can you come here for a minute?"

Her wide brown eyes meet mine for the first time all day. Those lush lips drop open, and she rolls back from her desk. "Sure."

"Close the door," I say when she's inside. She does as I ask, then stands behind the chair across from my desk.

God, this woman is irresistible. Her jeans look painted on, hugging her curves to perfection. Her lipstick is dark pink and only slightly glossy. I wonder how it tastes.

"Yes?" she prompts.

"I wanted to make sure you weren't uncomfortable about what happened Friday."

Her cheeks flush as her gaze slides away from mine. "Friday?" Her voice squeaks on the word.

I frown. "Driving me home? I appreciate it, and I want you to know I won't ask that of you again. I should have just taken a taxi."

Her throat works as she swallows. "It's fine, Lee. Really." She meets my eye and gives me a tight smile. "No problem. Is there anything else?"

I shake my head. "No. Thanks again."

I watch her walk back to her desk, wondering what the hell happened between us.

· · ·

SHE KEEPS me at arm's length for a whole week. On Tuesday, she comes to my office to tell me she'll be making larger payments for the debt, which means she should have it paid off in nine months instead of eighteen. We agree on a new number, put it in writing, then move on.

On Wednesday, I get a reminder email for Roger and Drea's wedding, which I ignore, because I'm a responsible adult in total control of his feelings.

On Friday, she sends the team her proposal for the walking exhibit and produces a couple of layouts for pages in the magazine. Her work is incredibly good. We're lucky to have her.

It's all very professional.

How it's supposed to be.

But it's killing me.

By the time Monday rolls around again, I'm coming out of my skin. I don't want her to linger at my doorway anymore or give me curt nods when she says good morning. I want her to act how she did her first week. Warm and blushing.

That probably makes me an asshole. Not to mention the fact that my cock gets hard every time she's near, and how I can't stop fantasizing about her whenever I need release. I've had so many dirty, depraved thoughts about the woman that I wonder if they're written on my face every time I look at her. She's gotten under my skin in a big way.

Lunchtime rolls around, and I glance through the glass to Nora's cubicle. All I have to do is head over there and ask her how she's doing, maybe tell her to come grab lunch with me so we can check in after her first two weeks of work. I could take her to Taqueria, the taco place just around the corner. If we leave now, we'll beat the lunch rush.

Just two coworkers grabbing food together. Nice and professional.

Rolling my chair back, I brace my hands on the arms and get ready to stand—

When Rick saunters over to her desk.

He smiles at her, leaning on her desk to say something. I hear Nora laugh, and Rick ducks his head closer. He points at something on her screen, and they both smile.

My body is burning up. My skin is too tight.

And when Nora nods, grabs her purse, and stands with Rick, I nearly grab the edge of my desk and flip it over. Then I sit back down, close my eyes, and take a deep breath.

A second later, I jump out of my chair and stalk across the office, catching the elevator door right before it closes.

Nora's deep brown eyes are wide. "Lee."

"Nora." I nod. "Rick."

"Hey, boss." He smiles at me, but it looks slightly forced.

As I stare at the scant space between his shoulders and Nora's, my fists tighten. Forcing my face into a natural, casual expression, I jerk my chin at the two of them. "Going out for lunch?"

"Tacos," Nora says with a quick flick of her eyes toward me. Her cheeks flush pink again.

I hate that Rick wanted to take her to the same restaurant as me. Even though it's the closest one to the office and they have a killer lunch deal, I still hate the idea of him inviting her out.

"Mind if I join?" I ask, my voice coming out as a low growl.

"Oh." Rick clears his throat. "Not at all. The more the merrier."

We ride the rest of the way down in tense silence, the three of us watching the numbers descending above the door. When the elevator slides open, I extend a hand to let Nora exit in front of me. She doesn't make eye contact.

Why? What's going on? Is it me? I can't deal with another week of this, let alone a month. Six months. A year. I'll go insane.

The sun is shining, and soon the last chill in the air will melt into summer. The Fringe Fest happens every year during the first week of June, which means we have seven weeks to finish planning. And five weeks until the mayor's wedding.

The town will explode with tourists, exhibits, musicians, and stalls selling food and artisanal goods.

For now, though, Heart's Cove is the same quiet town where I've lived my entire life. The three of us turn onto Cove Boulevard and head toward Taqueria, walking in silence until Nora clears her throat.

"Lee, your brother is a potter, right? Do you think he'd be willing to sit for an interview for our next edition of the magazine?" She turns her head to meet my gaze, the sun shimmering on her inky hair.

"I can ask him," I say.

A strand of hair falls out of Nora's bun, and she lifts a hand to twist it back into the hair tie. She turns to Rick. "We could feature his work on the cover."

"Love it," Rick answers, flashing a smile. His face is full of crinkles and laugh lines, eyes lingering a bit too long on Nora's body.

I want to punch him. I've known the man for years, and

he's an important part of the team, but right now, I'd fire him just to make sure he never looks at Nora with that kind of hunger in his eyes. What kind of man does that make me?

We get to the taco restaurant, place our orders, and sit at a small table outside to eat. Nora tilts her head toward the sun, closing her eyes and letting out a soft breath. "This is such a great town," she says.

Before either of us can answer, Rick's phone starts ringing. He leans over to pull it out of his back pocket, brows drawing together when he sees the name on the screen.

"Everything okay?" Nora asks.

"It's my son's school. Excuse me." He stands up and walks a few paces away, putting the phone to his ear.

Nora watches him for a beat, then turns to find me staring at her. That wash of redness returns to her cheeks, and she takes a big bite of her lunch. I shift my gaze to my own food, unable to think of something to say.

Smooth. Real smooth.

We munch in silence for a while until Nora clears her throat. "How are the motorcycle repairs coming along?"

"Waiting on the body shop guys to get back to me with an appointment, but otherwise fine. I was able to find the parts I needed to replace, so I'll probably be nearly done fixing it up by the end of the weekend. Works fine, just a bit scratched up. Hasn't stopped me riding."

Her shoulders drop, and she nods. "Good. I'm really sorry, by the way."

"Stop apologizing, Nora. It's fine. Really. Leggy called to say he finished the repairs on his bike. My dad's machine is at the body shop getting a fresh coat of paint. No one's mad at you."

She nods and lets out a breath, her lips curling at the corners. "Good. That's a relief."

"Is that why you've been avoiding talking to me?" The words fall out before I can stop them.

Nora's eyes widen, and oddly, her blush deepens. Even the tips of her ears are red. "I... No. I'm not—"

The hum of a small engine gets louder, cutting Nora's words off. We both turn toward the sound as a woman on a red scooter zooms past. Her gauzy dress flaps in her wake, a gigantic smile plastered on her lips.

Nora lets out a laugh. "She looks like she's having fun. I've always wanted to get one of those."

I know she's changing the subject, and it's fine. Her blush was answer enough. She hasn't been avoiding me because she's mad or uncomfortable. Is it possible she's feeling the same way I am? Trying to keep her distance to stay professional?

I jerk my head toward the woman's retreating shape. "You ever ridden a scooter before?"

She shakes her head, taking another bite.

"What about a motorcycle?"

Nora meets my gaze as she wipes her hands on a paper napkin. "Nope."

The glimmer in her eyes makes me hard. Obviously. I should be used to my body's reaction by now. I open my mouth to ask her to come ride with me, but Rick reappears at my elbow.

"I have to go pick Nate up from school. He just threw up at his desk. I'll come in early tomorrow, all right, Lee?"

"Oh no! Is he okay?" Nora asks, brows arching.

Because I'm a Neanderthal, it bothers me that she's concerned about another man's child. I need to get a grip.

"He'll be fine. It's my week with the kids, though, and I'm not going to be able to find a babysitter on such short notice."

"Go. We'll be fine," I tell him.

Rick wraps up his food then hurries away, and I'm left alone with Nora. The savage monster inside me relaxes, which I know is insane. I know I have no right to Nora's attention or affection. But still. I prefer being here without another man staring at her like...like...

The same way I am.

Crap.

Wanting to get on solid ground, I turn our conversation to work, and we discuss her sculpture exhibit and ideas for interactive classes during the Fringe Fest. It's easy to talk to Nora. I hired her for the magazine, but her mind is intricate, interesting. She'll present ideas by talking about how we can announce them in print, how the design will look on the page, while also giving us fresh inspiration for the content.

"We'd have to run it by Town Hall, of course," she says, wiping a few crumbs up with her napkin. "Do you think the mayor would approve a large exhibit like that?"

My throat tightens. "Maybe." *If I go to his wedding.*

"I'll put a proposal together with Rick and Hailey," she says.

On the way back to the office, my shoulder brushes hers as we walk and talk. The lady on the red scooter passes us twice more, each time looking more exhilarated than the last.

When we get to our building, we hear the scooter approaching once more. Pausing to watch the woman go by, Nora and I follow her progress until she's out of sight.

Nora's gaze turns to my bike, her fingers running along the chrome handlebars. I feel that touch as if it's on my skin. Between my legs.

Giving me a squinty look, she tilts her head. "What's it like to ride one of these things?"

My lips curl, heart leaping. "How about after work, we go for a spin and you can find out?"

10

GEORGIA

MY HEART THUMPS SO HARD, I might as well be riding a roller coaster. I gun the throttle on my brand-new, cherry red Vespa scooter, doing a fourth loop of the town before turning onto Cove Boulevard once more.

I. Am. In. Love.

I laugh to myself, wanting to howl like a wolf.

Slowing down in front of my new favorite café, I park the scooter on a little patch of unused pavement, pull off my helmet, and let out a breathless laugh.

"New wheels?" Simone asks from the café doorway, her arms crossed as she leans against the frame. Her lips are pulled in a bright smile. "We've been watching you zoom up and down the street for the past half hour."

As I slide off the scooter, my legs feel like jelly. I grin at Simone. "It's so much fun. I've always wanted one of them, but my ex-husband used to make fun of me for it. He insisted I only drive SUVs because they were safer." Sometimes I wonder if it had more to do with his image than my safety.

"Nothing wrong with a little danger," Simone answers, grinning. She pushes herself off the frame and saunters over, whistling as she takes in my new vehicle. "It's kind of hot."

"It's the most fun I've had in ten years." I glance at my new scooter, patting the handlebars fondly. I felt like such a rebel buying this thing. I went to the dealership, pointed to the red model, and without even saying hello, told the salesman I was buying it.

Today, I finally got my M2 motorcycle license and can legally drive my scooter on the roads. So I did. And I'll do it again, because *hell yes*.

Being a little bit reckless isn't something I'm used to. But ever since the divorce, something inside me snapped. I was so worried about being responsible and acting like the good little wife my ex wanted me to be—and look where that got me! Divorced, heartbroken, and alone. Fighting through a bitter separation for the better part of a year when my ex-husband did his best to drain me dry of everything I earned and inherited.

Why not get the scooter I want and do half a dozen laps around town?

"Mind taking me for a ride?" Simone asks.

I bunch my lips to the side. "I've never ridden with a passenger before." The street is free of traffic when I glance up and down. "If I crash, promise you won't blame me."

Simone giggles. "Cross my heart."

I put my helmet back on and wheel the scooter out onto the road. Turning it on, I take a deep breath and glance over my shoulder at Simone. "Hop on."

The scooter wobbles. Simone's feet can't touch the ground, and we both fumble with the footrests. When they're lowered and Simone's flip-flop-clad feet are resting on them, I take a deep breath.

"This is so unsafe," I say. "You have no helmet, no shoes, and you're wearing shorts and a tee. If we crash, you'll be hamburger meat."

"I know. Isn't it great?" Simone puts one hand on her shoulder, the other hand on the handle at the back of the scooter.

I huff a laugh. "Ready?"

"Gun it, Georgia."

So I do.

It's, uh, *very* different riding with a passenger. The center of gravity of the scooter is shifted way back, and the extra weight makes it slower to accelerate. We wobble like crazy for the first minute. I scream, gripping the handlebars with all my might as I try to stay upright. I weave all the way onto the wrong side of the road until I get the hang of it, both of us screeching like a couple of middle-aged banshees.

When I finally get on the right side of the road and drive mostly in a straight line, Simone lets out a whoop and a laugh. "I need to get one of these!"

I take the same roads I've been riding all morning, doing a long loop through Heart's Cove and back onto the main drag. When we stop outside the café, Simone's face is flushed and she's laughing like crazy.

"Fun?" I ask as we dismount.

"I'm getting one. I'm serious."

I pull my helmet off and grin. "I can give you my driving instructor's information."

"Judging by the first couple minutes of that ride, I'm not sure I want the same teacher."

"Oh, shut up," I say, then laugh. "I *was* pretty wobbly, though."

"My life flashed before my eyes."

"You asked for it."

Simone just giggles, then waves me inside. Candice is standing behind the register, and she gives us both a Mom Look. "Did you just ride on the back of a scooter without a helmet, Simone?"

"You going to call the police?" Simone quips, leaning her hip against the counter.

"Worse. I'll call Wes." Candice looks at me. "But before I call him, I want a turn."

"Coffee first, please," I ask. "My arm muscles feel like jelly. I was clinging on way too hard to keep us on the road."

The three of us giggle like schoolgirls, and an unfamiliar feeling settles over my skin like fresh spring rain. It's been a long time since I had girlfriends who weren't my ex-husband's coworkers' wives. Friends that were mine first.

I'm not sure I can call these women friends yet—they only just opened up to me —but it feels like a possibility. For the first time in years, I could actually have a community.

"Oh my word," Simone says quietly as I thank the barista for my coffee. I follow her gaze to the big plate-glass windows that look out on Cove Boulevard.

And my jaw drops to the floor.

A pickup truck is parked in one of the spaces out front, and its driver is sliding out in full cowboy regalia. Tight Levi's jeans, tucked-in shirt, enormous shiny belt buckle, and a cream-colored cowboy hat. He pauses to check one of the straps holding down the bulky, tarp-covered object in the back of his truck, leaning over to give it a tug and in the process, giving all of us ladies a direct look at the way his butt looks in those faded jeans.

"Holy moly," Simone whispers.

"Is there another movie shooting in town or is that guy an actual cowboy?" Candice says quietly, her hands frozen in midair, paused while making a latte.

The man turns, and my eyes drop down to his crotch. I'm not a pervert, I swear, but...there's a bulge. A very big bulge. And his pants are tight enough to show off every bit of it. His hat is tilted low, obscuring his face.

I'm from just outside of Dallas, Texas, originally. Left when I was eighteen, but the sight of a man dressed like that...

Let's just say it gets me a little more hot and bothered than I like to admit.

"Do you think he stuffs his underwear with tube socks?" Simone asks.

I try to answer, but my tongue is glued to the top of my mouth. Because the rest of this man is a walking wet dream. Broad shoulders, working man's hands tanned to a color that betrays long hours spent under hot sun.

For the first time in a long, long time, I'm turned on.

Here's a little-known fact about me: I haven't been attracted to a man in nearly a decade. Maybe longer. I flirt a lot, because it distracts me from the garbage fire that my life has become. I'm an expert flirt. I do it for fun, for shits and giggles, for a bit of entertainment. I flirt to keep people at arm's length, because you can't be vulnerable and sincere when you're putting on that kind of mask.

But I rarely feel any kind of connection. It's all a game. A bit of razzle dazzle I started employing years ago to hide the fact that my personal life was falling apart. When my ex-husband stopped touching me—stopped loving me—it was the only bit of connection to other humans I had. Men and women both respond to it. Flirting is the armor that keeps me safe—but I don't ever feel attracted to the person I'm flirting with.

But I feel a visceral, physical attraction to this man. This *cowboy*.

Maybe it's the way he stalks along the sidewalk and glances up at the Four Cups Café sign. Maybe it's the way he takes a long, sun-burnished index finger and rubs it over his stubble-lined jaw. Maybe it's the fact that he's dressed like an honest-to-goodness cowboy and he doesn't look ridiculous. Far from it.

The bells above the door tinkle gently as he pushes his way into the café. He pauses in the doorway, his strong frame silhouetted against the daylight beyond. Hooking a thumb into his belt loop, the man starts walking toward the register. His worn brown cowboy boots make a *clop, clop, clop* sound on the wooden floors.

Then he finally takes his hat off and I get a good look at his face.

And my lungs seize right there in my chest—because I know this man.

His face is lined and craggy and sun-burnished, but it's the same face I remember from twenty-five years ago. The same icy blue eyes, strong jaw, and long, straight nose. The same teasing arrogance in the arch of his eyebrow.

This is Sebastian Finch. My first love. My first boyfriend. The man who took my virginity...then turned around and shattered my heart.

Simone and I are still standing frozen beside the counter. Sebastian glances up at the blackboard on the wall, his Adam's apple bobbing as he swallows. Without looking at what he's doing, he starts rolling up his shirt sleeves, revealing corded forearms inch, by inch, by inch.

Heat gushes in my thighs.

I wish it wouldn't. Really, truly wish I were in control of myself right now. Because I *hate* this man. I want to stomp over to him, slap him across the face, then throttle him, and ask him to strip down and show me the kind of body he's been building for the past twenty-five years.

My own body seems to be having a *lot* of reactions to this man without my permission, and it's starting to make me feel unbalanced. Maybe it's the scooter's fault. My nerves are frayed. I wasn't expecting this.

Sebastian's gaze lowers and meet mine. Recognition flares, and then that teasing, familiar smirk curls his lips.

Fuck. Him.

How dare he look at me like that? Like all is forgiven just because time has passed? Like he has a right to flash that arrogant smile at me?

His eyes are pale and piercing in the midst of his golden-brown face. He glances at Simone, then at Candice, saying nothing for a long moment.

Then, he puts his hat back on his head, brings long, calloused fingers to the front, and tips his hat.

Tips. His. Hat.

Like a cowboy from a movie.

I've entered an alternate dimension where men like this exist.

"Afternoon." In his deep, deep voice, I hear a twang of a southern accent that makes me remember what it was like to grow up in Texas. What it was like to slide into Seb's pickup after sneaking out of my parents' house and make out with him until our lips were bruised. My thighs clench involuntarily, and I mean, *really*? This is the man who makes me remember I used to be a sexual creature? This twangy cowboy with a sizable bulge? This...this...this complete and utter overbearing *asshole*?

His gaze comes to rest on mine. "Sweet Peach," he drawls. "Didn't expect to see you here."

"Do *not* call me that," I grit out.

I can feel Simone's frown on me, and I ignore it.

Sebastian's brow arches. He's grown into a beast of a man. I hate that my body is reacting to his. I hate that heat is twisting in my belly, that my breasts feel heavy and puckered.

He comes closer, towering over me. His eyes are shuttered, that teasing smirk still playing on his hard lips. "Small world, ain't it?"

"What the hell are you doing here?"

His hard gaze slides down to my body, lingering on my breasts, my thighs. I should slap him. When my hands ball into fists, he meets my eyes again. "Time has been very kind to you. Guess California was a better fit." There's an edge of bitterness to his words.

He's still mad that I left. After twenty-five freaking years. After everything he did.

Then again, I seem to be mad at him too. Or maybe I'm just turned on.

Cold, blue eyes slide over my face, down to my lips. Goosebumps prickle over every inch of my body.

Then he glances at Simone. "Any of you lovely ladies able to tell me where I can find Lee Blair? I'm supposed to talk to him about the Fringe Festival this year. Name's Sebastian Finch. I would have called him but my phone ran out of juice, and I figured someone in here might be able to help."

"Uh..." Simone looks at Sebastian, then at me, then back at him. "Sure." She grabs the café phone from its cradle and hands it over.

"Thank you," he replies, pulling a scrap of paper out of his back pocket.

When I meet Simone's gaze, I know she wants me to explain. But I just say goodbye and leave as quickly as possible. When I'm straddling my scooter, I make the mistake of looking up.

Sebastian has the phone to his ear and he's speaking, but his eyes are trained on me. Even at a distance, through the café window, his gaze feels like a physical touch.

It takes me two tries to start the scooter. I wobble onto the road and my hands don't stop shaking until I'm safely at home and away from the ghost of lovers past.

11

NORA

"You're *here*?" Lee pauses by my desk, frowning as he speaks into his phone.

I jiggle my mouse to turn on my screen, but stop before actually signing in. I look up to meet Lee's gaze.

"Wow. Okay. Actually, my colleague Nora was just putting together the plan for the sculpture exhibit. We could take a look at what you've got. Uh-huh. Okay. Yeah, we'll be over in a few minutes." He hangs up and lets out a huff. "That was Sebastian Finch, that artist from Texas."

I let out an inelegant grunt in surprise.

"He's here. Said he came up early and was hoping to do an installation in town ahead of the Fringe Fest."

I blow out a breath. "Wow. Already? The festival isn't for seven weeks." I frown, then spread my palms flat against my desk. "Okay. That's fine. What kind of approvals do we need for that?"

"Let's meet him and see what he has in mind. He's well-known enough that the town council might consider it a coup to have him design something specifically for Heart's Cove." Lee's frown deepens. "If the mayor approves it."

"If all else fails, we could feature him in the next issue of the magazine."

Lee grins. "I like the way you think. Come on. Let's go meet him."

A short walk later, we're entering the Four Cups Café and it's immediately obvious which patron is Mr. Finch. After all, there's only one man in here with a cowboy hat. He's sitting on a bright-red chair, with one cowboy-boot-clad foot leaning against the opposite knee. He sips an espresso in a tiny cup, his hat clasped in his other hand, tapping against his thigh to the beat of the Spanish-style music playing in the café.

"Mr. Finch?" Lee asks as we approach.

"Sebastian is fine." He gives us a broad, disarming smile, and I feel a funny kind of twist in my lower belly. This man is attractive. Viscerally so.

Or, perhaps more accurately, my body has gone off the rails, and I have no hope of ever regaining control. I mean, did I really think buying a vibrator would *help*? That was my genius solution? It took me all week to work up the courage to look Lee in the eyes again after what I did. What I *imagined*.

More than once.

Now some Texan sculptor with a nice smile is getting me all hot and bothered? This is a problem.

When I moved to Heart's Cove, I wanted to loosen the reins a bit, but I didn't want to put a pack of wild horses in charge of my life.

"Nora is the newest member of our team. She has extensive experience as an art director and has been heading up the creation of our magazine. She's also got some interesting ideas about a sculptural exhibit around town." Lee puts his hand on my lower back as he introduces me, and the touch feels...not quite professional.

I like it more than I should.

I extend a hand toward the artist. "Sebastian. So nice to meet you. I'm a big fan of your work."

"You're too kind." His voice is deep, with a musical kind of cadence that makes heat flush up my neck. It's not that I want this man—he doesn't make me hot like Lee does—it's just that he's...he's...

He's so *masculine*. Unapologetically so.

And he's dressed like a cowboy.

I didn't know that was hot until right this minute.

"This town has more than its fair share of gorgeous women." Sebastian nods to the table where Simone, Candice, and Fiona are blatantly eavesdropping. Even Jen is hovering near the opening in the wall between the kitchen and the front of house. The Texan turns back to me. "Y'all are making me think I should move here for good."

Lee clears his throat, sliding his hand from my lower back to my waist before gently, yet forcefully, shoving me back. As if he doesn't want Sebastian to get a good look at me. I glare at Lee, hip-checking him back out of the way. He stumbles, then smirks at me, which has the unfortunate effect of turning me on even more.

I reach for my mental baseball bat, but all I find is the wand-shaped vibrator. Damn it.

"It's a great town," I answer with a slightly strangled voice. "And it'll be made better by a few Finch installations, don't you think?"

Sebastian's smile widens. "I do, indeed."

"Here's what I've been working on," I say, pulling out the map of the town where I've noted the location of various art exhibits. "I'm thinking we can install sculptures that people can interact with throughout the town. Your pieces, due to their large scale and sense of drama, could be placed here or here." I point to two central locations in town.

"I'd be honored," he says, his voice almost somber. "Why don't I show you what I had in mind? I've got part of my newest sculpture in the back of the truck. Looking for some workshop space to put it together. If you were interested in more than one piece, I would need to start working on it right away."

He stands, and I'm slightly shocked at how tall he is. I feel like a shrimp between him and Lee. The surprise must show on my face because Sebastian just grins and winks. Lee's hand appears at my waist, and a zip of heat flows through my belly.

There are too many hot men here. Far, far too many. Heck, *one* was too many, and I was the idiot who decided to work for him for the foreseeable future. That was a problem *before* I decided to masturbate to the thought of him.

I've now reached Situation Critical. I need to get my body back under control ASAP. I either need to pick up the reins of my own libido, or I need to have sex with someone to let off some of this pressure.

Lee's hand tightens on my waist, as if he can read my thoughts and is volunteering for the job.

We head outside and the men loosen the straps holding down the tarpaulin in place in the back of Sebastian's pickup truck. When the blue fabric comes off, I see bits of rusted iron, what looks like an old wagon wheel, and a bunch of metal brackets.

"It don't look like much right now, but she's going to be beautiful," Sebastian says, patting the old wooden wagon wheel that has gone grey with age.

"What's it going to be?"

"An ode to my ex-wife," Sebastian replies. "This hunk of junk is damn near all she left me in the divorce, so I figured I could make it into something she'd hate."

"Oh," I answer. "Well. That sounds...poignant."

Sebastian lets out a belly laugh. "Poignant. That's exactly what I'm going for."

I open my mouth to answer, but catch a strange, panicked look on Lee's face. I only have a moment to frown before a graceful, gorgeous woman glides into my field of view.

"Lee!" she cries, spreading her arms like she wants a hug.

Lee stands stiff as a board, clinging onto one of the straps that held the tarp down. "Drea."

"Roger and I haven't gotten your RSVP yet," she says with a pout. "Did you get the invitation? I re-sent it over a week ago. Roger said he spoke to you about it."

Lee clears his throat, his eyes darting back and forth. Sweat beads on his forehead, and I get the sense that he's a second away from a panic attack.

The realization hits me like a ton of bricks. Roger is the mayor. I was there when Lee got the call, after which he was so ill I had to drive him home. So...there's something about a wedding, and Lee isn't happy about it. This woman must be marrying the mayor, and there's something going on between the three of them. Some history I'm not aware of.

And right now, it looks like Lee's about to keel over and gasp for air like a dying fish.

I stick my hand out at the woman. "Hi. I'm Nora."

She blinks at me, glancing down at my hand then back at my face, as if she only just realized I was standing here. "Hello." She gives me a limp handshake with the tips of her fingers. Her gaze turns back to Lee. "So, I—"

"That's a great purse," I say a little too loudly. "Nice and big. I always need a bigger purse for all my junk. Sometimes I clear this thing out"—I slap my shoulder bag for emphasis—"and half of the contents are garbage. Literal garbage. How crazy is that?" I give a deranged laugh, sidestepping until I'm directly in front of Lee. Out of the corner of my eye, I see his hands still white-knuckled around the strap he's holding. "Old receipts, expired lip gloss, food wrappers. I mean, maybe I should just go for smaller purses, but then where I would I put my trash?" I nod to her purse. "Don't you think?"

"Oh, I, um..." She frowns. "I guess?"

"You should try pockets," Sebastian cuts in, spinning to give me a view of his tush, where the outline of a wallet stands out, its imprint faded into the pocket of his light-wash jeans. He pats his butt, and I swear, I feel those pats on my own behind. The man has no right to be this hot. But maybe I'm feeling hot and bothered because the heat of Lee's body blazes all along my back. The strap he's holding taut brushes against the curve of my ass.

The sensations are too much. I'm going to spontaneously combust.

"Pockets? In women's clothing?" I scoff, clinging onto

the lifeline Sebastian throws me. "Please. You'd have an easier time finding a unicorn. Back me up here, Drea."

She clears her throat, putting a hand on her slim hip. "Yeah, I mean, pockets aren't actually *useful*, unless you want to hold a bobby pin or two."

"Plus, if I didn't have a purse, where would I keep my expired lip gloss?"

No one laughs at my stupid joke, and I realize I'm glancing around for Simone or Fiona or any one of the friends I know would be in my corner.

"Did you know"—I gesture at Sebastian and unfortunately point in the general direction of his crotch—"that the small pocket on Levi's Jeans was originally designed to hold a watch? How cool! Fun fact." I give the woman another deranged smile, gently nudging my butt back to get Lee to say something. I'm not sure how much longer I can stall.

But then my butt makes contact with his crotch, and my brain fizzles and sparks. Whoops.

"Yeah." The woman squares her shoulders. "Look, I really just wanted to talk to Lee about his RSVP to my wedding. We've sent it four times, Lee, and we really need an answer."

Behind me, tension seems to buzz in the space surrounding Lee. He clears his throat, ghosting his fingers over my waist to tug me to the side. To my surprise, once I've moved over, he doesn't remove his hand.

Drea's eyes flick to the fingers gripping my waist, and her lips pinch ever so slightly.

"I was surprised to get the invitation," Lee says in a scratchy voice. "Considering."

"What? All that old history?" A delicate, tinkling laugh.

"Come on, Lee. Water under the bridge. You're not still upset, are you?"

Lee's body is stiff as a board next to mine.

The woman cocks a hip, tilting her head so that a hank of golden hair slides off her shoulder. "Everyone is coming. If you don't, they'll all think you're holding a grudge. It's been years, Lee. Everyone else moved on. Don't you think you should too? Roger would *so* appreciate you being there. He's been so busy with the election, you know. A friendly face would be welcome."

A grudge? About what? And what does the election have to do with anything?

I glance at Lee, frowning.

He seems to sense my stare because he gulps and gives the woman a jerky nod. "Fine. I'll come."

"Marvelous," she says, her lips curling into a smile that looks half-predatory. "And are you bringing a plus-one?" She sniffs slightly, eyes flicking to me and away again. She hikes her gigantic purse higher on a slim shoulder, then rearranges her perfect hair just a touch more perfectly around her face. Every movement is prim and feminine and affected. This woman is not someone I'd want to be friends with—not on first impression, anyway. I doubt *she'd* laugh uncontrollably at motorcycle dominos.

She lifts her chin. "We need to know. For the caterers."

"Yeah." Lee's hand tightens around my waist. "I'm bringing Nora."

12

NORA

I'm GOING TO EXPLODE. My body is a pressure cooker with a faulty valve, and I'm about to blow right here in the middle of the street. They'll find pieces of grey matter splattered on the front of the Four Cups Café for weeks.

It takes long, long seconds for Drea to strut her way down the street, by which time I'm clinging onto my sanity with the very tips of my fingernails.

"Excuse us," I say to Sebastian, then grip Lee with said fingernails and tug him toward the red door next to the Four Cups Café. It leads up to the library above the café, where the girls like to hang out. Wes built it for Simone a couple of years ago, and now it's packed full of comfy chairs and romance novels.

The bottom door is unlocked, thankfully. I stomp up a couple of steps and spin around. "Shut the door."

Lee shuts the door. He makes to start up the stairs but I hold up a hand. I need the height difference now. I can't be craning my neck up at him when I eviscerate him with well-chosen words.

"Nora—"

"No." I cross my arms. "Absolutely not."

"Let me explain."

"Explain what? That you hate that woman? That you have some sort of history, a grudge, whatever? I don't want to know." I stick out my index finger and point it at his face. I don't care if it's rude. Foisting this wedding on me is rude. He can deal with a damn finger. "This is the type of thing my ex-husband used to do all the time. He'd use social pressure to make me act a certain way, do certain things. For *him*. Because I cared what people thought, I went along with whatever he said. From the outside, we had a picture-perfect relationship, because that was the only thing I could control. I cared so, *so* much, and he *broke* me. I became a person I didn't like, and he used his power over me to suck me dry. I moved to this town to start fresh. I will *not* be pushed around by some macho-man who thinks he can bully me into doing his bidding."

Lee deflates in an instant. He scrubs his face with both palms, then combs his fingers through his hair. When his eyes meet mine again, he looks tortured. "You're right. I'm sorry."

I huff. "Thank you."

"I shouldn't have sprung that on you."

"No, you shouldn't have." I lift my chin and cross my arms. *Hmph.*

Don't think about how hot he looks with his hair sticking up in all directions. Don't think about how badly you want to kiss him right now. Definitely *don't think about the vibrator waiting for you in your nightstand.*

"What if... What if I knocked off part of the debt for the motorcycle repairs?" Lee asks, desperation skating at the edges of his words. "I get that you don't want to go to some random wedding, but we could scratch off, say...two grand?"

It's an effort to keep my face steady. He wants to knock off nearly ten percent of the total I owe him to be his date to a wedding? Two thousand dollars off the debt is a massive chunk. If I combine that with the money I'll save with my mom's new financial plan, I can almost *see* myself walking through the front door of my dream home. I could call a real estate agent and start looking *today*.

Hmm.

"Come on, Nora." Lee takes a step closer, rising onto the bottom stair. Now he's taller than me.

I resist the urge to back up again. "Don't 'come on, Nora' me."

My bulldog face has no effect on him. His lips twitch. "Please?"

"What's the deal with the two of you, anyway? Why do you need me to go with you?"

Lee's eyes slide away. He's quiet for a long while. "If I don't go, I'll look bitter. We know a lot of the same people and going to her wedding will make me the bigger person. I...need to be the bigger person."

My eyes narrow. "Did you used to date?"

He dips his chin once.

"So you want me to be your plus-one to your ex-girl-friend's wedding, just because some friends—who don't seem like really great friends if they think you need to go to this wedding in order to prove anything—will judge you if you don't?"

A sigh, and Lee is rubbing his thumb and forefinger over his brow. "She's marrying Roger. The mayor. When he called last week, he made it clear that the Fringe Fest approvals we're waiting on were conditional on me attending the wedding."

My eyes widen. "That's not right."

Lee shrugs with a bitter huff. "It's a small town. Local politics are full of that kind of thing."

"He'd really reject some of our proposals because you don't want to go to your ex-girlfriend's wedding?"

"Ex-fiancée, actually."

I gape. "Wow."

"When we broke up, it was the talk of the town. Roger thinks if I show up, it'll smooth everything over and prove there are no hard feelings. It'll look good for him right before the election."

"Are there any hard feelings?" The words slip out, and I don't realize how badly I want to know the answer until I say it out loud. Drea was graceful and gorgeous and tall and I'm... God, I'm none of those things. I'm a control freak who can't even handle moving to a new town.

Lee's lips twist. He's quiet for a few long moments, then finally releases a breath. "I don't even fucking know anymore."

I chew my bottom lip, thinking. This is going to complicate an already complicated situation. I don't like that the mayor is holding this above Lee's head. I don't like the fact that Lee felt he could blindside me with this.

But the faster I pay off this debt, the better.

"So?" he asks.

"So what?"

"Will you go with me?"

"I'm considering all angles."

"Maybe you could consider the fact that I'll effectively pay you two grand for a couple hours of your time."

I roll my eyes. "I'm flattered. But based on your reaction, I'm thinking I should charge you more."

A low growl rides out through his clenched teeth as he lifts his gaze to mine. "Don't push it."

"Listen, buddy. *I'm* doing *you* a favor. Don't growl at me like some sort of wild animal." I huff, relieved to see the tension in his jaw dissipate.

His lips twitch. "So it's a yes?" His voice is quiet, hopeful.

My heart gives a mighty lurch. I'd say yes to anything to see this man smile. I am an utter fool. I've learned nothing.

I stick out my finger again, because it makes me feel like I'm in control of this quickly spiraling situation. "I want it in writing that this is worth two grand off my debt. Plus the two hundred bucks for driving you home the other day." Why not? He's the one who offered.

Lee's smile widens, and before I can react, he has an arm hooked around my back and he's slamming me into his chest. We spin on the stairway as I yelp, then Lee puts me down on the same stair tread he's standing on. He hugs me close. "Thank you."

God, he smells good.

"I'm only doing it for the money," I lie, my face mashed against his chest. The truth is, I'm also doing it because I hated seeing his face freeze when he saw that woman. I hated feeling the tension in his body. I want to help him.

A small part of me also points out the fact that the sooner I pay off my debt, the sooner we'll have one less thing standing between us. I still won't let myself act on this attraction when we work together, and when I owe him such an astronomical amount of money. If I enter a relationship—even a purely physical one—it'll be as equals. I've learned my lesson from my ex.

Ignoring Lee didn't lessen my attraction to him. Dealing with it in more creative ways—with my new toy—only made things worse. The only solution I can think of is to pay this off as quickly as possible, and then see if there's anything real between us.

His arms are still around me, his broad hand spread across my lower back. His fingers span from the waistband of my jeans all the way up to my bra strap. I feel small and delicate and all I want to do is melt into his embrace. Without asking my permission, my fingers seem to have curled into his shirt.

I glance up at him, shadows playing over the hollows of his face in the darkened stairwell. Suddenly, I realize how alone we are. Hidden.

My body comes alive and all I can think about is my chest pressed against his much larger and harder one, my legs tangled in his. I tighten my hold on his shirt, tilting my face up toward Lee's.

Would it really be so bad to give in to temptation? Maybe there is some kind of power in my position. We could still come together as equals—keep my debt separate and indulge this attraction once and for all.

Beneath my bra, my nipples turn to hard pebbles. Heat tightens in the pit of my stomach as his hand presses against the small of my back just a little bit harder. I can feel him everywhere, plastered against my front. My eyes drop to his lips, and I know I'm going to kiss him. Let him kiss me. Whatever. We're going to kiss.

"Nora," he says in a low, rumbling voice that sends

tremors rushing through my veins. His eyes are dark. Dangerous. His gaze traces my lips and I can't help licking them in response, tasting the lip gloss I reapplied before leaving the office.

"I've been wanting to do that for days," he says, following the movement of my tongue.

"What?" It comes out breathy, and I should be embarrassed at how turned on I am. But we're alone here, shut away from the world, and gosh, I'm supposed to be giving up control, aren't I? Isn't that the whole point of this move, of this new job, this new life? I'm supposed to be trying new things. Being more adventurous.

What's more adventurous than kissing my boss? What's more adventurous than seeing if the real thing can live up to my naughty fantasies?

I teeter on the step, clinging onto his shirt, feeling the press of his fingers into my flesh.

"Been wanting to taste whatever it is you put on your lips," he responds. "The gloss you wear drives me crazy, but not as crazy as when you paint your lips bright red."

My breath staggers. Lee's free hand moves to my cheek, his thumb brushing over my chin to tilt it up.

It's happening. We're doing this. I'm going to kiss Lee Blair, the star of my naughtiest fantasies, my new boss, the man who owns my debt. I'm going to kiss him, and for once in my life, I won't worry about what'll happen next.

His head dips, his hand pressing against my jaw to keep me steady. I part my lips—

And the door flies open.

I jump right out of my skin, my foot slipping off the stair tread. Arms flailing, I scream as I teeter over the edge. Lee grabs me by the waistband of my jeans and pulls me closer, but the force of his yank sends us both falling toward the stairs.

I land on top of him as he lets out a low *oof*, his long body slamming into the stairs in half a dozen places. Scrambling to get off him, I accidentally knee him in the groin, then apologize, then elbow him in the gut.

By the time I'm up, I'm flushed and flustered. Lee's still lying on the stairs, wincing, curled around his abused crotch. We both look at whoever is standing in the open doorway.

Simone arches an eyebrow. "Was I interrupting something?"

"No," I answer, and can clearly see that Simone doesn't believe me at all. "We were just talking."

"Talking," she repeats, cocking a hip. Her red hair is silhouetted in the doorway, and it looks like her head is ablaze.

"Yeah. About the money I owe him."

Lee rubs his sternum, right where my elbow connected. He sits up, grimacing, shamelessly readjusting his groin in the process. "We've come up with a new payoff plan." His voice is strained, and I can't help wincing in sympathy. I didn't mean to knee him in the balls. It just happened.

"A new payoff plan," Simone repeats again, the smile clear in her words. "Sounds...interesting."

"It's not like that," I blurt, flushing. "I'm attending an event with him. Get your mind out of the gutter."

"I didn't say a thing." Simone lifts both hands in surrender, then drops them again. "This is an interesting place to undertake business negotiations, though. All alone in the dark."

"Oh, be quiet," I snap, aware that my entire head is

bright red and about one degree away from bursting into flame. "We were just leaving. Sebastian is waiting for us."

"The sexy cowboy? What's his story, anyway? I think he and Georgia know each other."

"He's not that sexy," Lee grumbles.

"He's sexy," I say emphatically. Maybe a bit *too* emphatically because Lee cuts a glare my way.

"Sebastian is creating an installation for the Fringe Fest," Lee tells Simone. "He's here to come up with a plan. No one knew he was coming. I thought we'd be meeting through video conference."

Simone clasps her hands at her breast. "An artist. Wow."

"Does Wes know you lust after other men like this?" Lee says, finally standing up. He brushes himself off, patting his jeans with violent movements to brush off imaginary dust. I don't know if it's the unfulfilled lust or the talk of Sebastian's hotness, but Lee seems very angry.

Simone, being Simone, just smiles wider. "He sure does. It's one of his favorite qualities in me—but probably because most of the time it's Wes I'm lusting after." Simone gestures at us. "You two lovebirds mind if I squeeze by? I need to go upstairs."

"We're not lovebirds," I say.

"Sure you aren't," Simone says, slipping past me. "Next time, try to find somewhere you won't be interrupted, though. Take it from someone who knows."

She swishes her hips all the way up the stairs, opens the door at the top, and throws me a wink over her shoulder. Then Lee and I are alone again, with the sunlight streaming through the open doorway at the bottom of the stairs.

Sebastian appears in the opening. "Everything all right, folks?"

"Wonderful," I grumble, stepping out into the sunshine at last.

THE DAY ISN'T OVER. After speaking to Sebastian about the particulars of his newest project, Lee and I head back to the office. My body burns with unnatural heat, and every time I hear the sound of his footsteps—because apparently, I can tell which footsteps are his now—my heart starts to beat a little bit harder.

Earlier, I asked him to let me ride on the back of his motorcycle. After what happened in the stairwell? No way is that going to happen. As soon as the clock strikes five, I jump out of my chair, call out a hasty goodbye to our small team, and make my escape.

It's not until I'm home that I let out a breath. A small part of me wilts with disappointment, because I can only imagine how exhilarating it would've been to feel the wind whip over my body while I wrapped myself around Lee's torso.

But I learned my lesson this afternoon. It's too risky. If I get too close to him, I'll lose control.

With so much change in my life right now, I can't afford to slip up. Not like that. Not with him.

13

LEE

I FLOP onto my couch just as the doorbell sounds. Groaning, I lean my head back and close my eyes. I'm worn out. My balls still hurt—both from the torture of having Nora in my arms and not being able to do anything, and from the pain of the unfortunate knee she placed a little too accurately—and my chest feels like it was hit with a sledgehammer. My back is sore from hitting the stairs, but worst of all, I'm simply strung out.

Getting off my couch and walking all the way to the front door seems about as easy as climbing Everest. But before I have to heave myself up to my feet, the door opens and my brother Mac enters.

"Hello?"

"In here," I call out, flicking on the TV.

Mac enters wearing a motorcycle jacket and dark jeans. He frowns at me. "Your door was unlocked."

"We live in Heart's Cove, Mac."

"You should be more careful."

"I think stepfatherhood has rotted your brain. You probably want to wrap me in bubble wrap, too." I turn back to the TV. "Next thing, you'll be giving up your bike because it's too dangerous."

"Unlikely," my brother responds, lips twitching.

I grin and jerk my head toward the kitchen. "Grab me a beer from the fridge?"

"You want to go for a ride instead? Your bike still runs okay, right?"

I grunt. "Couple of scratches. Getting the paint work fixed this weekend."

"Dad wasn't so lucky."

"Nora feels terrible," I hear myself say, and it sounds a lot like I'm defending her.

"I heard you came to an agreement with her. She's doing a payment plan?"

I nod.

"And you're the one carrying all the expenses?" My brother sits down on the sofa next to me, slouching down as he glances at the screen.

"Yeah."

"You don't think that's a little risky? What if something costs more? What if she skips town? You'll be left holding the bag."

"She won't," I answer.

Mac is quiet for a moment. "No?"

"I trust her."

Mac's shock radiates from him. In my periphery, I see him turn his head to look at me. "You do?"

I meet his gaze with an arched eyebrow. "Is that so surprising?"

"After Drea? Hell yeah, it is. You haven't trusted a woman in years."

"Nora's different." The words fall out of my lips and even though I can't explain them, I know they're true. She *is* different. She wouldn't turn her back on me. She wouldn't betray me. She wouldn't walk away.

Mac makes a noncommittal sound and turns back to the television. We sit in silence for a while until I let out a breath and heave myself up. "Fine. Let's go."

Mac grins. "Don't act like I'm forcing you."

"I can feel you vibrating with tension beside me, and I don't feel like answering any more questions. At least if we're on our bikes, I won't have to listen to your sermons about women and love."

"Love?" He arches an eyebrow.

"Oh, fuck off. You know what I mean."

"I was talking about a thirty-grand debt, Lee. I didn't say anything about love." His teasing grin makes me want to sock him in the face.

Instead, I stalk to the front door and grab my bike jacket and boots again. "Let's go."

As MUCH AS I hate to admit it, my brother was right. The short drive from the office to my house wasn't enough to calm me down, but as I follow him along a favorite route of ours through the nearby national park, the tension ekes out of my muscles. We drive through winding roads, surrounded by tall cedars and lush ferns, only to shoot out along a rocky cliff. Precariously slim bridges take us over crashing waves, then the road dips back in through impossibly tall trees.

I love this place. There's nothing like a motorcycle ride to make me feel connected to my home. The touch of danger, the rumble of the asphalt beneath my tires, the wind whipping around the leather of my jacket—it makes me feel part of my town in a way nothing else can. It makes me feel alive.

I want to share this with Nora.

The thought pops up, unbidden, and I'm not sure how to react to it. A few hours ago, she asked to ride on the back of my bike. I knew—I just *knew*—that having her on the back of my bike is exactly where she should be.

Then Drea happened. The stairwell happened.

When she practically ran away at the end of the day, I didn't want to chase her in front of the other members of our team. But I watched her mash the elevator button, decide it was taking too long, then rush down the stairs as if all she wanted to do was get away.

From me.

That thought stings more than I like to admit.

My brother slows down as we circle back to Heart's Cove and cross the town limits. Mac waves to me as he drives off toward his place, where he lives with Trina and her two kids. I take the turn onto Cove Boulevard, slowing down as I hit the main artery through town.

When I see a familiar shape peering at the display window in front of my friend Rudy's real estate office, I slow the bike down. Nora turns at the sound of my approach, straightening. She gives me a tight-lipped smile and a small wave, walking toward me as I cut the engine.

At some point between the end of the workday and now, Nora put on fire-engine-red lipstick. My jeans are suddenly tight. Her painted lips never fail to drive me fucking crazy.

I jerk my chin toward the window of the real estate

brokerage, where a dozen or so posters with available properties are displayed. "Window shopping?"

"Something like that." Nora tucks a strand of midnight hair behind her ear. "I figured I should start being an adult at some point this century, and buying a house seems like the next step."

"You know the internet exists, right? Most people house hunt online."

Her lips tilt into a smile that seems more real than the last one. "I'm aware, thank you. I wanted some takeout and got distracted."

I swing my leg off my bike and pull off my helmet, joining her near the window. "Any of these catch your eye?"

Nora hums, leaning toward the window. She's dressed in a loose navy top and tight, dark-wash jeans, and she looks like a present that needs to be unwrapped. By me.

Boss-employee. Debt hanging between us. She'll probably leave, anyway.

I try to reach for all the reasons I shouldn't be looking at her like this, but they buzz in the back of my mind like mosquitos at a cookout. Annoying, but not bad enough for me to stop leaning close to her, trying to soak in a bit of her warmth.

"I like this one," she announces, pointing to one of the posters. "Three-bed townhouse on the nice side of town. It's near Lily's place, which would be great. I miss her being across the hall from me."

"Lonely in that apartment all by yourself?" I hear the words come out of my mouth, and I know my voice was rough as gravel, but I can't take them back.

Nora's golden-brown skin flushes a pretty shade of peach. She blinks at me, then turns back to the picture of the property. "It's only got one bathroom, but I could save up to have another one put in."

I grin. Normally I wouldn't like someone to ignore me so thoroughly, but when Nora does it, it turns me on. Big surprise there—everything she does turns me on.

"You should set up a viewing," I say. "You have Rudy's number?"

She shakes her head, and I pull out my phone. Rudy and I became friends later in life. He's a few years younger than me, but we met at a social flag football game about ten years ago. Been friends ever since.

Even though I know Rudy is happy with Lily and their new baby, it still makes the space between my shoulder blades itch when I watch Nora enter his phone number into her contact list. It's the same way I felt when she said Sebastian Finch was sexy. Or when she smiled at something Rick said.

I'm so jealous I taste it on my tongue. Acrid, bitter, and inappropriate.

It's dangerous.

When Drea and I were dating, I had this same possessive feeling, like I was perpetually on the edge of a cliff and I needed to cling onto her to keep from falling off. I feel pathetic for it. Like I'm too insecure to be a normal fucking guy who's rational and level-headed, who can have a decent relationship without turning into some possessive asshole.

But even as the thought crosses my mind, I know this isn't the same as how I felt with my ex. In the years that have passed, I realized that she delighted in making me feel uncomfortable. She'd flirt with other guys in front of me and look over her shoulder to make sure I was watching.

She'd needle at me and laugh, then we'd fight like crazy. She always said it was worth it for the make-up sex.

It was an unhealthy pattern that we both indulged in. That roller coaster became addictive. When it ended, I didn't know how to act. Didn't know what was normal. Hell, I still don't know what's normal. Is it normal to want to rip a man's head off because he smiles at his coworker?

The difference is with Nora, I don't get the feeling she would enjoy making me suffer. When she said Sebastian was sexy, it wasn't to make me jealous. The way she said it was almost like she was just...stating a fact. There was no emotion attached to it.

"Thanks," Nora says, interrupting my thoughts. "I'll call him tomorrow." She slips her phone back into her purse, and my jealousy dissipates. She's going to call Rudy because she wants to buy a house. Nora's a grown woman; she wouldn't play games.

I know by the way she's glancing down the street that she's going to leave. A deep yearning to spend more time with her opens up inside me, and I can't bear the thought of her walking away.

This could be a huge mistake. I should probably just let Nora stay away from me, cancel the plus-one to Drea's wedding, and keep things professional between us.

But I just...can't bring myself to do that. This is the first time since Drea left me that I've been interested in a woman beyond something physical. The first time that a woman has made me laugh, made me crave more of her. Would it be so bad to lean into that feeling? To see where things go?

I've already been through the worst thing I could experience with Drea. She left me at the altar like she's Sarah

Jessica Parker and I'm the fool who thought we had a good relationship. She's marrying my former best man. How much deeper can a betrayal cut? How much more painful can things get?

Seeing where this attraction with Nora goes would be nothing compared to the hurt I felt before. Plus, judging by what happened in the stairwell, Nora isn't exactly immune to me. When will I ever meet someone else that intrigues me so much? Am I really willing to go back to my boring, flat routine? Turn my back on the first woman that's interested me in years?

No. I'm not.

In that moment, when I know Nora's about to leave, I realize I want to see this through. I don't care that we work together, or that she owes me money, or that I've been hurt before. I just want to be near this woman for a little bit longer. Feel the small of her back against my palm. Lean in to taste her skin against my tongue.

So, before Nora can take her leave, I motion to the bike. "How about that ride?"

Nora's eyes snap back to mine. She opens those red-painted lips then closes them again.

I grin. "Scared?" Before she can make any excuses, I walk to the bike and pull my spare helmet out of one of the saddlebags. I lift it up and arch my brows as the tension between us tightens.

When Nora's teeth bite into her bottom lip, I watch with avid interest. She tucks a tendril of glossy black hair behind her ear and shifts her weight from one foot to the other, finally lifting her gaze from the helmet to meet my eyes. "Fine," she says.

A hard, heavy thumping starts in my chest. Stalking

toward her, I fit the helmet on her head and make sure the straps are snug. Then I strip my motorcycle jacket off and place it on her shoulders, zipping it all the way up to her chin. The jacket swallows her whole, only slightly snug around her hips and thighs, and I love it. I want her to wear nothing but my clothing from now on.

Once I'm satisfied that she's covered up, I put my own helmet on, hop on the bike, back it up, and jerk my head. "Get on."

"Yes, sir," she answers with a mock salute. Unsurprisingly, my cock responds to her sass with a mighty throb. Then her hand is on my shoulder and her gorgeous, shapely leg is swinging over my bike. She wiggles a bit on the seat behind me, and I bite back a groan.

Nora's touch is shy as she grips my waist.

"Tighter," I tell her. "Don't want you falling off."

She pauses for a moment, then shifts closer and clasps her hands around my stomach. I let out a quiet sigh at the feel of her glued to my back.

This is what I've been wanting. Waiting for. Craving.

No one else will ride on the back of my bike. That seat belongs to Nora now.

14

NORA

WELL. I didn't think this would happen after I ran away from work earlier. Yet here I am, wrapped up around Lee's back like a spider monkey. Wearing his jacket and helmet. Trying to ignore my heart taking off at a gallop.

He guns the bike and we fly. I only just manage to bite back the scream threatening to spill from my lips, tightening my hold on his waist.

Even through the exhilaration of riding a motorcycle, I can feel the hard pack of muscle beneath my palms. No doughy middle here. Actually, nothing about Lee feels soft. Not his broad back, clad in a thin white tee. Not his arms, where the muscles are standing out in stark relief as he guides the bike toward the edge of town. Not his flexing stomach muscles beneath my hands. Not his legs, which are pressed against the insides of my thighs.

He's made of marble. That's the only explanation for this inhuman hardness.

My mental baseball bat disintegrates. I'll never beat my libido down after this.

Lee takes a turn onto the freeway and speeds up, sending us careening along the asphalt and into the forests beyond. I gasp, poking my head over his shoulder to watch the scenery whip by, my stomach doing somersaults the whole while.

The vibrations of the bike travel through my behind, my thighs, all the way up to my torso. It's almost as good as my new vibrator—and that's saying a lot.

Blushing like crazy at the thought, I'm immensely glad Lee can't see my face right now. He takes us on a winding road through tall trees, his body shifting in sync with the bike. I try to copy his movements, leaning into the turns, leaning into him.

It's surprisingly easy.

For once in my life I'm ceding control, and it's not a battle. I close my eyes and let myself melt into his back, focusing on the feel of the wind whipping around my body, the vibrations of the bike, and the strength of the man in front of me.

The white-knuckled grip I have on my own psyche slowly loosens, and I just...let myself go. I lean when Lee leans, from side to side, forward and back. I melt into the bike, into his body, and for the first time in a long, long time, my mind is quiet.

It's heaven. Bliss. Euphoria.

Is this what I've been missing? This feeling of freedom? Have I been denying myself a high that feels illicit, like I've injected some drug into my veins without knowing it?

I've spent the past decades trying to control every little detail, and in the process, I've lost the chance to just *be*. When I met Eric, I twisted myself into knots to make him happy. I supported him and listened to all his excuses about why he couldn't get a job, why he couldn't help around the house. I just cranked myself tighter to take care of him. At work, I outperformed everyone and burned myself out.

And after the divorce, locking down my finances and digging myself out of that hole was just another exercise in control. How much joy could I cut out of my life to pay off my debts, and how fast could I do it? How much was I able to deprive myself in order to get out from under that crushing weight?

If I could just *make sure* that everything worked out, it would. All I had to do was try harder. Tighten the reins. Control everything—even my own wants and needs. I made a slow, restrained spiral into becoming a person I didn't want to be.

As we cut through the forest, I feel like I'm flying, weightless. I have no idea which way we'll go, what turns we'll take, how fast we'll go—but it doesn't cause me to panic. I know that the man I'm clinging to can handle whatever comes.

I *trust* him.

As soon as the thought enters my mind, I stiffen. I trust Lee Blair, and I shouldn't. Why would I? The last time I trusted a man, he broke me down until I was a shadow of my former self. He took advantage of my support, my finances, my generosity. He ruined my mind and my heart until I thought the putrid rot of our marriage was normal—then he fought the courts for me to continue paying for my stupidity for five long years after the divorce.

My ex-husband didn't have my back. He pretended he was there for me, but he just sucked me dry.

Am I really ready to do that again with a man I barely

know? With my *boss*? Who I happen to owe a huge amount of money to?

I'm giving Lee so much power over me. I'm handing him the power to do exactly what Eric did, except this time I won't even have a job of my own to fall back on.

The bike slows, and Lee's voice fills my helmet. I jump, then realize there must be microphones and headphones to allow us to talk. "You okay? You just went solid on me."

"I got scared," I answer. It's the truth—kind of.

"I'll slow down."

True to his word, Lee takes us on a leisurely ride through a forested area that opens onto the coast. To my left, cliffs fall down to the crashing sea, spreading out on the coastline like a serrated, rocky ribbon. We snake along the coast and I will myself to relax.

It's just a motorcycle ride. It doesn't mean anything. And earlier, in the stairwell, that was just... I don't know what that was. A mistake. I'm not the type of woman who dates a motorcycle-riding, festival-planning hunk. I'm the type of woman who plans, who controls, who makes a pros-and-cons list about every decision. I'm restrained and proud of it. That's how I survived my father's death, how I rebuilt myself after my divorce.

Except I wasn't restrained when I quit my job and moved to Heart's Cove, was I? When I accepted Lee's proposition? When I bought my first ever vibrator?

On the right, a small building appears nestled in the trees. A neon sign in front of it just says, "Restaurant."

We turn in, and Lee backs the bike into the far corner of the lot, away from all the cars. I hop off as soon as we're steady, legs feeling like water. When I pull my helmet off, I let out a long breath. I'm equal parts exhilarated and panicked. For the first time in years, I actually allowed myself to let go. Then my brain screeched at me to scrabble back to more familiar territory, and now I just feel confused.

Lee gives me a searching look, then jerks his head to the restaurant. "You hungry?"

I nod, even though my stomach is in knots.

Without saying a word, Lee reaches for my helmet, locks it into one of the saddlebags, tucks his own helmet into the one on the other side, then walks over to me and slips his hand into mine.

It's so casual that I hardly even realize he's done it until we're halfway across the parking lot. His hand is broad and warm, wrapped around my much smaller one. His touch feels right, comfortable, like we've held hands a million times before. It somehow makes me stronger, like he's lending me something through the contact.

It's intimate.

I haven't held hands with a man in ages. My ex-husband and I stopped touching each other pretty soon after the wedding. Even when we slept together, it wasn't a true connection. We didn't hug, didn't cuddle, didn't kiss.

Until right this moment, I hadn't realized how starved for physical contact I've been. How much I missed having a man take my hand just because he wants to walk into a restaurant holding it.

Tightness eases in my chest, and when my brain tries to howl at me that this is a bad idea, I build a large, sound-proof wall to keep it out.

I've trained myself to be a tightly-wound control freak. It was the only way I survived the barren desert of my marriage, the slow suffocation I endured from the lack of intimacy. Unable to influence the love my ex withheld, I turned to the rest of my life and decided to control what I could.

But what if things could be different? Maybe there's a handholding, motorcycle-riding woman inside me waiting to be let out.

"After you," Lee says, shifting his hand to the small of my back. Even through the thick leather of the jacket I'm still wearing, I can feel the pressure of his fingertips against my skin. It sends shivers coursing through my body—a simple touch that means a lot more than it probably should.

SIPPING a diet soda through a straw as we wait for our orders to be prepared, I lift my gaze to Lee's.

"What's that look about?" His eyes are smiling even though his lips stay serious.

"Do you still want me to go to the mayor's wedding with you?"

He blinks. "Yeah. Why wouldn't I?"

"Don't you think that things between us are...weird?"

He leans back, the booth's vinyl seat creaking. "Weird how?"

I put my cup down and fiddle with the straw. "We work together," I start. My voice is so thin, I barely recognize it. Where's the woman who stood on a chair at The Cedar Grove and copped to thirty thousand dollars' worth of property damage? Where's the confidence I've always relied on? "And there's the debt I owe you."

"Mm-hmm," he says, stretching an arm across the back

of the booth. His foot nudges mine under the table, and neither one of us shifts to break the contact.

My straw is suddenly very, very interesting. I study it in detail. "Then there was the moment in the stairwell."

"What moment in the stairwell?"

I frown, gaze flicking up. "Lee."

His eyes are laughing again. "Nora."

"Don't be obtuse."

"I'm just trying to understand what you think is weird."

"Are you being serious right now?"

"Very."

I pause, tilting my head. Then— Oh, screw it. I lift my fingers and start ticking things off. "We work together. I owe you twenty-seven and a half thousand dollars—"

"Closer to twenty-six and a half now. You've worked for two weeks and we knocked off two hundred, remember?"

I ignore him, ticking off another finger. "We obviously have some strange attraction to each other and we almost kissed. The bride whose wedding we have to go to is *your ex-fiancée*, and the groom is blackmailing you to attend. Nothing about this situation is *not* weird. Need I continue?"

"You think it's strange to be attracted to me?" He looks down at the huge slab of muscle and male sensuality that is his body, then back at me. "Or do you mean you think it's strange that I'm attracted to you?"

I huff. This conversation isn't going according to plan. He was supposed to tell me he changed his mind and he'd bring someone else to the wedding. He was supposed to let me off the hook.

"Look. I—"

Lee lets out a chuckle and leans forward, capturing one of my hands in both of his. "Nora," he says. "Relax."

Relax? *Relax*? Does he know what he's asking of me? How am I supposed to relax under these conditions? My life is slowly but surely slipping out of my hands. I used to know what would happen tomorrow and the next day and the one after that. Now I don't even know what's going to come out of my mouth when I open it.

He squeezes my hand and despite my best efforts, the stress choking me starts to loosen.

"How about this: we have dinner, I drive you home, then I drop you at home and say goodnight. Tomorrow, after work, you can tell me whether or not you want to come to this wedding with me. If you do, we'll knock two grand off the debt. I know it'll be awkward, and I know going to a wedding with a bunch of strangers isn't most people's idea of fun. So we treat it like work." He squeezes my hand again. "Don't worry about what happened in the stairwell."

Don't worry about it. Right. It was the first sexual experience I've had in years that I actually wanted, but sure. I just won't worry about it. I'll pretend I'm not craving more of it.

Inhaling deeply, I try to sort out my own rioting thoughts. I know what Lee's doing. He's throwing me a lifeline. He can see I'm freaking out, and he's letting us both take a step back. He's wrapping my fingers around the handbrake and telling me I get to decide when to pull it.

I wonder how he'd react if I told him that I'm not worried that we almost kissed—I'm worried that I'm desperate for it to happen again. My hand might be wrapped around the handbrake, but my foot is on the accelerator.

Our food arrives, and Lee pulls his hands away from

mine. Cold rushes over my skin at the lack of contact, but I just focus on my meal until my heartbeat settles.

When we're done, Lee pays the bill while I'm in the bathroom, then he does exactly what he said. He takes me home and drops me off at my door, flipping his visor up to say goodnight. I shuck off his leather jacket and hand it over, after only very briefly considering stealing it for myself.

He slips it on but leaves it unzipped. "'Night, Nora."

"'Night, Lee."

We stand there for a minute, staring at each other. I feel like a teenage girl with a crush. My heart is thumping so hard he can probably see the pulse jumping in my neck.

He nods to the apartment building behind me. "I'm not leaving until you're safely inside."

"Such a gentleman."

Dark eyes stare back at me. "Too much of one, I think."

True to his word, he doesn't leave until I'm safely inside. But even when he's gone, my heartbeat never quite settles back down to normal.

15

LEE

Sleep doesn't come easy. I toss and turn, too wired to relax. I wake up before the sun comes up and go for a run to help my blood simmer down to a manageable level.

I went on a date last night. At least, I think it was a date. It's the first date I've actually enjoyed since Drea left me standing at the altar. The first time I've sat across from a woman and actually enjoyed it. Didn't want it to end.

I should be afraid of what it means, but all I want is more.

After a shower, I head to the office early and get ahead on some work. Maybe the wedding won't be so bad. If Nora's beside me, how torturous could it be? If it means we get all our proposals approved by the mayor, then isn't it an easy price to pay?

Sitting down at my desk, I rub the heels of my hands into my eyes. I need to slow down. Nora hasn't agreed yet, and I could tell she was freaking out last night. The woman needs time. Care.

And God, she deserves it.

In less than a week, Nora's come up with a genius idea for the walking sculptural exhibit, and she's designed half a dozen spreads for the next issue of the magazine, and she's already planned photo shoots with local artists. That's exactly the kind of thing we need to do to keep the Fringe Fest growing. She's a valuable member of the team, which makes my feelings that much more complicated. I want her to know how special she is. I want to be the man who treasures her.

But she's trying to start over. She needs time.

As my coworkers start filtering through the door, I give them a wave from my office but stay at my desk. There are stacks of paperwork to get through, with red tape and the city's bureaucracy to navigate before we can get the approvals needed for the festival. I don't want to give Roger any reasons to reject our proposals. Who knows what will happen at the wedding? If he doesn't sign off on everything after I attend, we'll only have two weeks to scramble for a solution.

It's not until Nora steps through my office door carrying two coffees that I lean back in my chair. "Nora," I say, and her name tastes sweet on my tongue.

"Fiona said you like cappuccinos," she says, placing a takeaway cup emblazoned with the Four Cups Café logo on my desk.

"Thanks." My chest is warm as I grab the cup, pulling off the lid to take a sniff. Four Cups makes the best coffee in town.

"So, I thought about what you said yesterday," Nora says, lingering on the other side of my desk.

"Yeah?" Suddenly I'm nervous. Intellectually, I can tell myself that she needs time, that I want to give it to her.

But emotionally? Physically?

If she refuses to be my wedding date, I'm not sure I'll be able to go through with the event. Seeing Roger and Drea up there, saying their vows, remembering what I went through—

It all seemed so trivial when I was imagining attending with Nora by my side. But if I'm alone...

She should refuse. It would be the logical thing to do. I know she enjoys the work we do here, and she won't want to mess that up. She works for me and she owes me money. Those things alone should be reason enough for her to keep her distance.

"I'll go to the wedding with you." Nora's thumb plays with the edge of her reusable travel mug. "I don't need the whole day to think about it."

My heart leaps, and it takes all my self-control to keep my face steady. Relief crashes through me, cool and sweet on my skin. "Good. Great. That's... That's good news."

"But," Nora adds, and I freeze in my seat. She takes a deep breath. "I think it'll be better if we just treat it like a work engagement. It's just a task we need to do to get the city's approval for our festival plans. Right?"

"Right, yeah," I answer. "Of course." The words taste bitter on my tongue. I don't want it to be a work task. I want to be able to put my arm around Nora and introduce her to people as my date.

But Nora needs time. She's backed up all the way to the door, with one foot already out of my office. I know I'm a selfish piece of shit, but I'll take what I can get.

"It's two weeks before the Fringe Fest?"

"Yep," I answer with a nod. "Two Saturdays before the opening ceremony."

"Great." She turns to leave just as the elevator doors open. We both glance across the space, over the tops of the cubicles littered across the hard-wearing navy carpet.

Roger Percy, Mayor of Heart's Cove, strides into the space like he owns it.

He's wearing a three-piece suit like he's walking the streets of Paris instead of the offices of a hippie festival in a small town in NorCal. Dark hair with just enough grey to look distinguished, sharp blue eyes, and a jawline to make any politician jealous. His teeth are toilet-bowl white and perfectly straight, and I can see them gleaming even from this distance as he smiles at our receptionist.

I freeze in my seat as he scans the space, nodding when Olivia gestures toward my office. Through the floor-to-ceiling windows, I watch the look he gives Nora, scanning her from head to toe and back up again before his gaze cuts to me.

My blood boils. The man stole my fiancée, and now he doesn't even have the decency to keep his eyes to himself?

The mayor of Heart's Cove lifts a hand in a wave and makes his way across the office. When he stands in the doorway, Nora shuffles inside again. Roger deploys his best politician's smile.

I can't help the tightness in my chest. Roger used to be my best friend. We got close in college, taking all the same classes, even living together for two years. Then I met Drea, and I matured while he didn't. I settled down, and he kept partying.

Or at least, that's what I thought was happening. It all turned out to be a lie.

"Hello there," Roger says to Nora, and I tamp down the urge to vault over my desk and stand between the two of them. I want to shield her from Roger's eyes, from his touch, from any snake-like smile he might deploy to make her melt.

She sticks out her hand. "You're Roger Percy," she says. "I see your face all over the bus stop benches."

He grins, wrapping his fingers around her palm. "Nothing I like more than a gorgeous citizen of this town sitting on my face while she waits for a ride."

Nora blinks. "Oh. I. Um."

"Lee!" His voice booms in the small space of my office, and he finally, *finally* drops Nora's hand. She turns to give me a bewildered stare. I almost snort. Roger loves to say things that are inappropriate. He loves toeing the line of what's acceptable and what isn't. I think it's a power thing for him.

I stopped thinking it was funny by the time I was about twenty-five years old, but he hasn't seemed to grow out of it at all. As Nora gives him a sidelong glance, I make a note to check in on her and make sure his comments didn't bother her. Her gaze meets mine and she rolls her eyes behind Roger's back. My anger evaporates, and all I want to do is haul Nora into the crook of my arm and kiss her until we need to come up for air.

I haven't even tasted her lips yet, but I'm already addicted.

First, though, it's my turn to shake my former best friend's hand. "Roger."

"Drea tells me you RSVP'd verbally." The mayor drops down into one of the chairs on the other side of my desk, propping his ankle on his knee. "Fucking finally. Although it would help if you did it officially." He nods to the computer.

I give him a tight smile, pull up the email, and click the button that says "Yes, I will attend with a guest," before turning to Roger. "Happy?"

"Very." He glances at Nora, who has been drifting toward the door during our little exchange. Before she can escape, Roger motions to the chair next to him.

"Nora, an interesting proposal slid across my desk, and I hear you're the one who came up with it. Just a couple of weeks on the job and you're having great ideas. What I want to know is, where did Lee find you, and have you ever wanted to work in municipal politics?"

"We met outside his father's bar," she answers. "I was in the process of causing thousands in property damage." A pause while she considers Roger. "And no, I'm not interested in politics."

Her words are blunt, a little rude, and the sexiest damn thing I've ever heard. This woman definitely doesn't play games. She wouldn't dangle another man in front of me, flirt to make me angry, or leave me for my best friend. If she was through with me, she'd have the courage to say it to me straight.

Roger grins at Nora, and the echo of an old hurt yawns open inside me. I know he's marrying Drea, that he's committed to her. But I remember him grinning at her when she was supposed to be dating *me*. I remember the way they laughed, and how he turned up the charm to a level I couldn't compete with. I didn't even know I was supposed to be competing.

He's doing it to Nora now.

Full of poise, Nora folds her hands on her lap. "You've already taken a look at our sculptural exhibit proposal?"

"The walking map is a genius idea," Roger answers. "It

really takes the Fringe Fest up to the next level. It'll get festivalgoers to explore the town a bit more instead of remaining on Cove Boulevard."

"That's exactly what I was thinking." Nora beams, eyes darting to me.

"You're a great addition to the team, I can already tell." Roger shifts his gaze to me. "Shouldn't take long to get the approval. I'll push it through after the wedding."

I can hear the subtext of his words loud and clear. He's telling me that even though I RSVP'd, if I don't attend his wedding and show the world that all is forgiven between us, he won't approve whatever we need for the Fringe Fest. The approvals are conditional on me going to his wedding and proving that our past has already washed away under the bridge.

I hate it. I hate that Roger has power over me, over the festival. I hate that I'll have to watch him commit his life to the woman who walked away from me.

But I'll do it. I want this year's Fringe Fest to be a success, and I also want Nora's ideas to come to fruition. Every time she talks about a new idea for the next issue of the magazine, or the design of a brochure or a map, she gets this light in her eyes that makes me want to give her everything. I can see her coming alive right in front of me.

She told me she was stifled by her ex, that Heart's Cove is her fresh start. I could be the man to give that to her.

"It was nice to meet you," Nora says, standing. "I'd better get back to work."

She stands, and Roger's eyes coast down her curves. She's wearing one of those hot-as-blazes pencil skirts with a tight top under her matching black blazer. Her dark hair is tied in a high ponytail, and those lips are a deep, sinful red.

No other man should be looking at her like that. Imagining what her lips could do.

My hands tighten into fists when Roger catches her wrist, looking up at her beautiful face. Anger rises in me so fast I have to grip the arms of my chair to stay seated.

"You're Lee's plus-one, aren't you?" the mayor asks in a low croon.

Nora nods. "Yep. Thank you for opening your wedding to the two of us. I'm sure it'll be a beautiful event." Her platitudes are delivered smoothly—just as smoothly as she extracts her wrist from Roger's hold.

I relax back into my chair. This woman doesn't need me to save her. Far from it.

"See you then," Roger says, turning to watch her ass as she walks away. I want to carve Roger's eyes from his head for letting his gaze linger on her.

As soon as my office door is closed, Roger lets out a low whistle. "I don't blame you for dipping your pen into company ink, Blair. She is one hot piece of ass."

I grit my teeth until I'm sure I can speak normally. "Aren't you getting married in a week? I'd think you would be keeping your eyes to yourself." *And your hands.*

Roger laughs, that loud, boisterous sound that grates over my skin. I used to laugh with him. I used to be his friend. How did I ever think he was a good guy?

"A man can look, can't he?" Roger grins. "Unless you're feeling a little protective of this one."

This one. Because he got Drea in the end.

I meet my former friend's gaze, and something inside me rises to the surface. An old pain that I've nursed for years. A friendship I thought was real, until I realized I was only being used.

Whatever Roger sees in my gaze, it makes him shrug. "Old history, Lee. Let it go. You're coming to the wedding, right? So it's all good."

"Yeah," I grit out. "It's all good."

Roger stands and nods, straightening his tie and pushing back a strand of dark hair. "Good. See you then. I'll have the approvals signed in time for the festival."

With that last reminder of what's at stake, the mayor saunters out, detouring to cut beside Nora's desk before finally leaving. I blow out a breath when the elevator doors close on his handsome face. Scrubbing my face with my hands, I lean back in my chair until I hear a knock on my office door.

Nora pokes her head in, ponytail sliding over her shoulder in an inky wave. "Your ex is an idiot, and the mayor is a douchebag."

A laugh bursts out of me. I nod. "Yeah. Thanks."

"Thought you might have needed to hear that." Nora's impish grin makes the last of my tension melt away—and a new tension grip my lower half. She backs out of the door again and heads to her desk, throwing me a smile over her shoulder before sitting down at her computer.

And for the first time in years, thinking of Roger and Drea together doesn't make me want to break something. If Nora is by my side, I might actually enjoy their wedding.

16

GEORGIA

As I DRIVE toward Four Cups for my daily morning coffee, I end up behind a familiar-looking pickup truck. The blue tarp is gone and the bed is empty, but I still inhale sharply, knowing who's at the wheel.

Damn him. Damn his stupid sculptures, and damn his stupid smirk. He should have stayed on his ranch outside of Dallas where he damn well belongs. Isn't that what he so forcefully told me all those years ago? That he'd never leave?

Last time I saw Sebastian Finch at Four Cups, I ended up running away like a coward. Now, as we take the same turns through town heading toward the most popular coffee shop in the county, my heart starts to thump. Blood pulses everywhere in my body. In my neck. My hands. My eyelids.

Between my legs.

It's not that I want to sleep with him. I mean, heck, I literally *just* got through with my divorce, and I'm not joking when I say I'm scarred for life. I had no idea people could be so cruel to each other until I saw what my ex-husband turned into. When he realized I wasn't going to be the meek little woman he wanted me to be, he turned into a different person.

He cheated on me, and when I served him with divorce papers, he had the audacity to look shocked. He thought I'd stick around! The last thing I want is to get entangled with another man. I'm not interested in men. I've just met a group of women that might turn into great friends, I sold my business so I have a bunch of money to play with, bought a gorgeous home, and I'm now the proud owner of a cherry-red scooter.

Life is good. Great. Fantastic.

A surefire way to ruin it would be to start lusting after a guy.

Especially *that* guy. He was my first male mistake, and I'm not going there again. Not in a million years.

But the pickup truck pulls up outside the Four Cups Café, and I have no choice but to park my scooter alongside it. Pulling off my helmet and shaking out my hair, I avoid looking at the man who disembarks beside me.

"Well," a deep voice calls out. "Thought I saw someone on a silly little bike riding behind me."

Damn him. I have no choice but to respond. I cock a hip. "Silly little bike? Is that really the angle you're taking here?"

Sebastian grins, and there's a sharpness in his gaze. Against my better judgment, that cruel grin turns me on. It's all the crinkles and laugh lines in his face, the way his eyes shimmer in the morning sun. He's stupidly good-looking, but not in that slicked-back, oily way my ex-husband was. Sebastian Finch is rugged and worn around the edges in the best possible way.

It's infuriating. After everything that happened between us, everything he said, everything he *did*.

"What would you call it other than silly and little?" He circles my scooter, cowboy boots hitting the asphalt with a distinctive rap.

"Fun. Maneuverable." I pause. "Red."

He chuckles, and the sound reverberates deep inside me. "Fine. How's this: I thought I saw someone on a fun, maneuverable, red bike behind me. Morning, Sweet Peach."

"I told you not to call me that."

"Not even for old times' sake?"

"Especially not for old times' sake," I grit out.

He holds my gaze for a beat. "Mornin', Georgia."

A tight knot forms in my belly. I should run from this man. But my mouth opens. "Morning, Sebastian."

He whistles. "Been a long time since I heard my name on your lips. Do it again."

"Do what?"

"Say my name."

He's toying with me. I narrow my eyes. "Sebastian Finch, you are a colossal asshole, and I'm not surprised to know that hasn't changed."

He grunts, a distinctly satisfied noise that travels all the way down to the space between my thighs. I stand stunned for a moment because I didn't know grunts could do that.

Sebastian watches me from beneath the brim of his hat, his smirk telling me he thinks he's won this round. "A man could get used to that."

I roll my eyes. "You're laying it on a little thick here,

cowboy. Tone it down a couple of notches." I start walking toward the front door, keenly aware of him keeping step beside me.

"I don't think you want me to tone it down at all." His voice rasps along all the soft parts of me. I suppress a shiver.

A part of me agrees with him, but I just arch a brow at him and deadpan, "Wow. A man who thinks he knows what's best and ignores everything I have to say. How novel."

Sebastian just laughs, then jogs ahead of me and opens the café door.

Because my snark-meter is stuck on high, I just give him another glare. "And here I thought chivalry was dead."

"Age before beauty, darlin'."

I pause just inside the door and whirl around in time to see Sebastian throw back his head and laugh. He winks at me, then struts to the counter. "Black coffee and whatever my Sweet Peach is having."

Prepare a jail cell for me. In about ten seconds, I'm getting locked up for murder.

I cross my arms. "You're not buying me a coffee. And you are not calling me Sweet Peach ever again. Certainly not *your* Sweet Peach, you arrogant, overbearing asshole."

He leans against the counter and crosses his legs at the ankle. "She's got more bite than she did in high school. Maybe we should come up with a new nickname. Ain't so sweet anymore, but I guess I learned that lesson a long time ago, didn't I?" His eyes are hard chips of ice, his body vibrating with controlled tension.

I tear my eyes away from him to glance at the cashier, a tattooed younger man. "I'm not having anything."

The young man shrugs, and charges Sebastian for his black coffee.

"Georgia!"

Turning at the sound of my name, I see Rudy entering the Four Cups Café pushing a stroller containing a sleeping infant.

I can't help the smile that spreads over my face. "Rudy. Is this Liam?"

"Yep." Rudy's face is the picture of fatherly pride. He adjusts the edge of the swaddle wrapped up around the baby, tucks in another side of it, and finally straightens.

"He's gorgeous," I say, and it's the truth. Sleeping like a tiny, scrunched-up burrito, the baby makes something unfamiliar spread through my veins.

I never had kids. It never seemed like the right time, and I was happy with my life as it was. When my picture-perfect life imploded and I had to deal with the divorce, I kept telling myself I was glad there weren't kids involved to make it even messier.

But now...a strange sort of longing fills me.

"I don't foresee many margarita dates in our future," I note with a wry smile.

"Unfortunately not," Rudy says. His gaze shifts just over my shoulder and I turn to see Sebastian Finch beside me. The heat of his arm blazes next to mine, but I can't quite bring myself to step away.

"I remember that age," Sebastian says. "Not much sleep to be had, but every little smile makes it worth it." Then he sticks out his hand. "I'm Sebastian."

"Rudy."

I blink. Sebastian has kids?

Sebastian studies Rudy for a moment, then flicks a

questioning glance to me. I just barely resist the urge to roll my eyes. I can see a man's searching look from a mile away. Mr. Cowboy is trying to divine what kind of relationship Rudy and I had with the subtlety of a longhorn bull crashing through a china shop.

He hasn't changed a bit, fatherhood or not.

The door to the café opens, and I see one of Simone's friends. She's a beautiful, curvy woman with a sheet of long black hair. Nora, I think.

She smiles at us, then motions to the counter behind us. "Are you in line?"

"Go ahead," Rudy says with a kind smile.

Sebastian is still looking at Rudy with narrowed eyes. And I mean, really? We broke up when we had both just turned eighteen years old. Maybe it's the curse of the macho alpha male, to feel like they have ownership over every woman they stuck their dick into.

But I should clear the air for Rudy, at least. "Rudy sold me my house," I tell Sebastian.

An emotion flits across the cowboy's face. Relief? I can't tell. And more importantly, I don't care.

He turns to Rudy. "Maybe you could help me. You do any commercial properties?"

"What are you looking for?" Rudy rocks the stroller back and forth.

"Studio space. Somewhere I can weld and use power tools without bothering the neighbors."

My eyes bug. Sebastian is...staying?

No. *Hell* no.

Rudy nods. "I've got a few places I could show you."

Nora steps away from the counter as the barista moves

to make her order. She tucks her wallet into her purse and approaches us. "Excuse me," she says. "I couldn't help but overhear. You're Rudy Dorset?"

Rudy nods. "Yeah. Nora. Fallon's little sister, right?" He jerks his head toward the Four Cups kitchen, where a very large, dark-haired man is cooking up a storm.

She smiles. "Yeah. I've been meaning to call you, actually. I got your number from Lee. He said you could help me find a house." She glances at Sebastian. "Sorry to interrupt."

"No problem at all, darlin'."

I frown at the pet name, then realize I must have accidentally turned insane. I'm not actually *jealous*, am I? I don't even like pet names! I don't want anyone calling me darling or sweet peach or whatever the hell else goes through Sebastian Finch's head. He can call everyone and their dog darlin' for all I care.

Sebastian reaches into his pocket and pulls out a business card, handing it to Rudy. "Call me to set up a time where we can view those studio spaces."

"Will do," Rudy answers, and the three of us watch Sebastian walk to the door. He really does have a very bitable butt.

"Can I buy you a coffee?" Nora asks, gesturing to the register. "I'm on a coffee run for the office so I could even be cheeky and put it on the company credit card."

Rudy laughs and nods. "Sounds good to me."

The two of them move to order, and I realize I'm standing in the middle of the coffee shop, alone, with no coffee, all because Sebastian Finch is an expert at twisting me up in knots with nothing more than a look and a few choice words. I glance out the front windows and see him jump into his truck. He meets my gaze through the windshield, gives me a little two-finger wave over his steering wheel, then puts the truck in reverse and drives away.

Then, finally, I turn to the counter and order my drink.

17

NORA

RUDY DORSET IS a handsome man in his mid-thirties. When we ran into each other at Four Cups last week, he told me he could help me find a place. We talked about budget, needs, wants, and preferences, and I felt like I was doing something naughty.

Buying a house is a normal part of being an adult, but it feels oddly illicit. Like I shouldn't be allowed to do it, because I should have a hundred other financial responsibilities that come first. It's too risky to be something I could possibly do.

Still, the afternoon after I met him at the coffee shop, I went straight back to the office and applied for pre-approval for a mortgage. It came through two days later, which gave Rudy a budget to work with. Now I'm here, viewing a property for the first time in my adult life.

I take a deep breath and wave at Rudy where he waits by the front door of a duplex. He pushes a strand of blond hair off his forehead and gives me a warm smile. I've been in town just over three weeks, and I'm starting to get used to the friendliness and warmth of all the residents.

"Nora! Right on time. What do you think?" He sweeps an arm at the duplex.

I pause on the pathway leading to the front door, taking it in. The siding is white, and there are dark-blue decorative shutters lining the four windows on the front face of the house. The door is a complementary fire-engine red, the exact shade of my favorite lipstick. The front garden needs work. Weeds poke through every crack in the path to the front door, and the bushes lining the house are scraggly and unkempt.

I love it.

"Needs a fresh coat of paint," I say, and Rudy laughs.

"Come inside." He fumbles with the keys, then opens the front door for me to step through.

My heart explodes. The door leads to a narrow hallway that immediately opens up on a cozy living room. There's an old feature fireplace in the corner, and floorboards that are knotty and worn in places. Crown molding lines the top corners of the room, and a dramatic chandelier hangs in the center of the ceiling.

I inhale sharply, clasping my hands at my breast. "Oh," I say, falling more and more in love with this house with every minute that passes.

"Kitchen's through here," Rudy tells me. We pass a staircase, a powder room tucked under the stairs, and open up on a large kitchen/dining area. The countertops are old vinyl and a few of the cabinets hang crooked, but the light streams through the big windows, flooding the space with buttery yellow warmth.

"I love it," I tell Rudy. "I don't know if it's because it's the first place I've looked at, but I love it with my whole heart." I drift to the sliding glass doors and push one open, stepping out on a porch that looks newer than the kitchen. The current owners have installed a gravel area just off the porch. In the middle is a fire bowl with a charred log, a few comfortable looking chairs surrounding it.

"The lot is big, compared to similar properties," Rudy says from behind me.

I look at the vast expanse of lawn. "I could get a dog." I've always wanted a dog, but I knew Eric wouldn't take care of it and I never had the time to commit to a furry family member. But now...

"You want to see the upstairs?"

I nod, heart in my throat. The rest of the house is as lovely as the bottom floor. A children's room is tidy, and I immediately want to transform it into a reading room. The master bedroom is small, but why would I need a huge room? It's only me and my future dog. There's a third bedroom and a very roomy shared bathroom.

Rudy meets me downstairs in the kitchen. When he sees my face, he smiles. "Like it?"

"I want it," I tell him. "This is my house."

"You have got to be the easiest client I've ever worked with."

When he tells me the price of the place, I inhale. "That's the top end of my budget."

"I think if we offer, say, ten percent below asking, it'll be a competitive price. We can talk about conditions of sale like inspections and financing, and I'll put together the paperwork. Is that something you want to do?"

The old Nora would say no. She'd go home, pull up a spreadsheet, and make a long pros-and-cons list. She'd compare the rates and websites of half a dozen mortgage lenders and rework her budget a thousand times to be absolutely, completely, irrevocably sure that she could afford it.

Then she'd probably decide not to buy.

That's not the type of person I want to be. I want to let go of this stifling control, release myself from this crushing fear. Yes, I've been financially beat down by life and divorce and debt. But things are looking up. Maybe, in this new town, with my new job and new friends, I can be the type of woman who falls in love with a house and buys it.

I take a deep breath and dip my chin. "Yes. That's what I want to do. I want this house, Rudy."

He grins. "Well, let's go ahead and get it for you."

TRINA CALLS me and invites me over for a girls' night barbecue at her house the next evening. This is my life now. Less than a month as a permanent resident, and I'm already on the weeknight barbecue invitation list. While our food is grilling, I end up telling them all—Trina, Candice, Lily, Simone, Fiona, and Jen—that I just put an offer in on a house.

Squeals and cheers erupt, and a bottle of champagne appears from out of thin air.

I laugh. "It hasn't been accepted yet," I protest. "The owners haven't even responded."

"But you're doing it!" Simone claps me on the back and fills my glass. "Where's the house? What's it like? Show us pictures!"

My insides are effervescent. I'm full of light and

laughter as I pull up photos to show the girls, and we all jump when my phone starts ringing.

"It's Rudy," I breathe.

Lily grins at me. "First of all, tell him I'm mad at him for not telling me this as soon as he got home. Secondly, answer the phone!"

I swipe to answer and put the phone to my ear. "Hello?"

"Nora," Rudy says. "I heard back from the owners."

My heart thumps. "Oh?"

"They have a counteroffer. Do you have time to go through it tonight?"

"Sure," I answer, then glance at Trina. She gives me a thumbs-up. "I'm at Trina Viceroy's place."

"I'll be over in a few."

We hang up, and I let out a breath. "He's coming over."

"Just this once," Fiona proclaims, "we will allow a man to intrude on our sacred girls' barbecue night."

Simone laughs and from just over her shoulder, a baby starts crying. Lily is there in an instant, picking her son up from his carrier to cradle him in her arms. She kisses Liam's forehead. "You're hungry, aren't you?"

"I'll warm the formula," Candice says. "You go get settled in the rocking chair."

Lily does exactly that, and we force ourselves to quiet down a bit—until the doorbell rings.

"That must be Rudy." I head to the front door and open it to see Rudy on the stoop.

He smiles at me. "Am I allowed to come in?"

"Special exemption," Simone says from behind me.

Grinning, I pull the door open wider. We head to the dining room, which has pocket doors that can be pulled closed. Rudy spreads out some paperwork on the table and goes over it with me.

"They want the full asking price," he says, "but they're fine with having conditions on the financing and inspections. They were happy to settle quickly." He meets my gaze. "We can go back to them and try to knock off a couple of grand, but I get a feeling they'll hold firm on the price."

I blow out a breath. The asking price is high. I've been pre-approved for that amount by the bank, but it still means that until I'm done paying off the motorcycle debt, things will be tighter than I'm comfortable with. I won't have much of a buffer. And even with the pre-approval, it doesn't mean the bank will come through with the financing. Everything about this is a risk.

It's the opposite of safety and security and control. I should probably refuse and wait a few months.

But the thought of losing that house, of having to wait even longer to feel like I'm making progress in my life...

I nod. "I'll accept their counteroffer."

Rudy smiles and gives me a pen, showing me where to sign. Once it's done, he extends his hand to shake. "Congratulations, Miss Richter. You're going to be a homeowner."

The dining room doors burst open and a stampede of women tumble through. The champagne bottle has somehow duplicated, and now everyone is topping up their glasses and toasting my impulsivity.

I take a sip, watching as Rudy heads to the living room to greet Lily and the baby. He drops a kiss on Lily's head and runs gentle fingers over Liam's chubby little arm, his eyes softening in true love.

Watching them makes my heart twist. Just once, I'd like

a man to look at me like that. With devotion and affection, with his heart right there in his eyes.

But I take a deep breath and look at the neat stack of papers on the table and let myself be swept up in the congratulations of my friends.

I don't have a man who's head-over-heels in love with me, but I *will* have a house. And a dog. And a little bit less fear about making impulsive decisions.

18

NORA

Walking into work on Friday morning, I'm on Cloud Nine Hundred and Ninety-Nine. I woke up dreaming of the first day I'll walk into in my new house. Today, I'll start the process of getting the bank to give me the final approval for the financing.

It's six weeks until the Fringe Festival. I could close on my new house by then and move in before Jen and Fallon's wedding. Finally, *finally*, I can move forward.

For once in my life, I'm actually living my life instead of watching it pass me by—and all it took was me to stop letting my own need for control choke me. Yes, this house will push my budget and yes, it was impulsive.

So what?

It's a *good* thing. It's like riding on the back of Lee's bike. A little bit wild, but worth the risk for the sheer thrill of it.

I glide to my desk and smile at Rick.

"You're in a good mood," he says.

"Yep," I answer, turning on my computer. "Life is good. How are your kids? Did your son recover from his illness?"

"He was fine within a couple of days. Both boys are with their mother this week, so I have a lot of time to myself." He shifts in his seat, then finally stands and comes to lean on the edge of my cubicle. Adjusting his collar, he clears his throat. "Listen, Nora, I was wondering if you might want to grab a—"

"Morning," Lee says, dropping a coffee on my desk and handing one to Rick. "Any plans for the weekend?" He puts a hand on the back of my chair, and I suddenly feel very tiny, sitting in between these two men. Lee's knuckles brush the back of my neck, sending warm honey gliding down my spine. The touch feels far, far too intimate for my little cubicle.

Rick clears his throat, eyes darting to the small contact between Lee's knuckles and my skin. "Taking it easy. Might go mountain biking if the trails are clear and the weather holds. I'd better get started." He jabs a thumb at his computer and slips away. I watch as he fiddles with the lid of his coffee cup and ducks his head on his way back to his desk.

It all happens so fast, I have to sit still for a moment.

Rick was going to ask me out before Lee interrupted.

My life is out of control. Since when do multiple men want to go out with me? Since when do *I* want to go out with one of them? Since when am I seriously planning on mortgages and houses and dogs?

Head spinning, I can barely manage to tilt my head to face Lee. His leg brushes my thigh as he stands next to my chair, hand gripping the back of my seat. Sunlight streams through the office windows, glinting on his hair and the scruff on his jaw.

He looks delicious. I want to kiss him so badly I could cry.

In other words, my life is very quickly spiraling out of control.

"You feel like riding on the back of my motorcycle tomorrow?" Lee asks, spinning my chair around completely so I'm facing him. The raw hunger in his eyes makes heat explode in my abdomen. "Been a while since we went out together. We could grab some lunch, come up with a strategy for the wedding."

"A strategy?" I arch a brow.

"What we tell people about us."

"We tell them we're coworkers."

"Why would a coworker be a plus-one?"

"We tell them we're friends," I amend.

"Are we friends?" Lee's voice deepens.

I shrug. "Sure."

He grimaces. "Friends."

"You say it like it's some form of torture."

"Maybe it is." He holds my gaze for a moment. "So? You want to ride with me?"

My throat is rough as sandpaper, so all I can manage is a nod and a croak. "Yeah."

"Good." Lee raps his knuckles on the edge of my desk and walks away.

I watch every step before turning back to my computer, wondering what the hell I just agreed to. The past couple of weeks have been a kind of truce between us. Ever since I agreed to go to the wedding with him, it's like we've put our attraction on the back burner. It's still there, simmering just under the surface.

But I just agreed to go on a motorcycle ride, and I have a feeling things between us are about to change.

SATURDAY MORNING USED to be a busy time for me. When I was married, it was the only time I had to do a big clean of the house. Eric never helped, of course, because he said it was women's work to cook and clean and obviously he couldn't be expected to lift a finger. He was a man, after all. So after working all week, I'd spend my weekends doing chores.

After we divorced, not much changed. In a lot of ways it was easier because I wasn't cleaning up after someone else. There were the same chores to do, but less mess. Less laundry. Fewer eggshells strewn over the floor for me to tiptoe over.

This Saturday, I pace my spotless apartment and wait for a phone call to tell me Lee's outside, straddling that hot bike of his, waiting for me to hop on behind him. We're meeting to discuss our strategy for the wedding, which is a flimsy excuse, at best. I would have agreed to anything if it meant riding on the back of his motorcycle.

Seriously, how did this happen?

Before I can analyze the hundred decisions that led me to this moment—before I can wrestle control back from the lusty demon inhabiting my body and brain—my phone buzzes. I grab my cross-body bag as I head for the door, putting my phone to my ear. "Coming."

"See you in a minute." Lee's deep, rumbly voice travels all the way down to my toes. And a minute later, I'm letting the lobby door close behind me as I take in the big Harley Davidson being straddled by the sexiest man I've ever seen.

How is he that hot? How can he kick the corner of his lips up and send heat tumbling into my thighs? In what universe is it fair for one man to have that much power over someone else?

"Hey," I squawk.

"Hey yourself." He extends my helmet to me, and I realize with a jolt that I already think of it as mine. Once I've got the helmet securely strapped onto my head, he grabs a leather jacket laying across his lap and hands it over. "Put this on."

I shake out the jacket. It looks a lot like the one Lee's wearing, but older. The black leather is faded around the pockets and the zipper, and the lining is splattered with half a dozen patches that look sewn on with a clumsy hand. I slip it on and it comes down to mid-thigh, but it feels like being wrapped up in a blanket on a rainy winter's night.

"My old jacket," he says, tugging me closer to zip it up to my chin. Manhandling me. "You can keep it until we get you one of your own."

That makes my heart kick, because the only reason I'd need a biker jacket of my own was if I'd be riding on the back of Lee's bike regularly. And doesn't that just make my pulse speed up to dangerous levels?

"Get on, gorgeous," he says, and I know I'm stepping into dangerous territory. By my getting on the back of his motorcycle, we're making a decision to leave our tangled situation behind—there's no work between us, no debt. I can sense it in my bones, that this ride will be different.

Because I know what's coming.

I know the rush of having my arms around him, of ceding control to him, of letting myself go. As I swing a leg over the navy leather seat and fit myself against Lee's much bigger, broader body, I realize I've been craving that feeling since the last time he took me out on his motorcycle. It's the same feeling I got when I signed the papers to buy the house. A weightless, toppling feeling somewhere in the vicinity of my navel.

And when the throttle opens with a roar, my heart does a few quick cartwheels along with it.

This time, I know what to expect. I know that Lee will drive the bike with absolute mastery, and all I have to do is let myself lean into the turns and not fall off. I know that my arms fit perfectly around his waist, and I'm prepared for the feel of his hard pack of muscles shifting under my touch.

But I'd forgotten the magic. I'd forgotten the buoyant feeling in my throat, in my gut, between my legs. I'd forgotten how good it felt to lean on someone else.

No. Not someone else.

To lean on Lee.

I tighten my grip on him as he merges onto the highway, the motorcycle's vibrations a steady purr between my legs. I watch the buildings fall away and the forest take over, inhaling the scent of clean, fresh air deep into my lungs.

When Lee's voice speaks into my ear, I don't jump. "You doing okay?"

"I'm great," I answer.

Lee accelerates in response, overtaking a slow-moving camper van as we make our way to the coast. The cedar and pine trees open up to reveal the Pacific Ocean, a shimmering carpet of blue extending all the way to the horizon. The roar of the motorcycle drowns out the crash of the waves, but I can feel them against my skin, deep in my soul.

This place has etched itself on my bones so quickly, I wonder if its name was always written there. No matter what happens, I'm glad I came here. I'm glad I took the leap.

We ride for an eternity, for the blink of an eye. Time ceases to exist. I'm tethered to the earth only by the feel of Lee's ribs on the inside of my arms, his thighs along mine, his shoulder against my cheek, and the leather seat beneath my bottom. Nothing else exists—not really.

When my brain tries to stutter and make me panic, I don't let it. I don't let fear grip me when I think of how much trust I'm putting in the man in front of me, how little control I have over this situation. At one point I close my eyes, and I let him lead me somewhere new.

The slowing of the bike finally brings me back down to earth. We take a snaking road down a steep cliff face, around hairpin turns that Lee maneuvers with an expert hand. When we reach the bottom, a small, crescent-shaped beach opens up in front of us. Lee parks the bike on a patch of gravel at the side of the road and sets the bike on its kickstand.

Wobbling slightly, I dismount and pull my helmet off, eyes on the view in front of me. Waves lap at white sand while trees sway gently in the sea breeze. It smells of salt and seaweed, fresh and earthy and familiar. A tangle in my chest loosens.

Lee takes the helmet dangling in my hand and hooks it on one of the handlebars. He moves to a saddlebag and pulls out a bag and a blanket, jerking his head toward the path leading to the beach. We toe off our shoes and let our feet sink into the sand.

It's not yet summer, and there's a definite chill in the air. The top layer of sand is warm from the sun, but just below is cool and comfortable. We make our way to one side of the crescent beach, and Lee flips open the blanket, setting one boot on each corner and motioning for me to do the same. I unzip my jacket—I call it mine, because there's no way I'm ever giving this one back—and sit down facing the water.

"Wow," I breathe.

"Like it?"

"What is this place?"

"A hidden gem," he answers, setting a bag between us and pulling out a couple of plastic-wrapped sandwiches, a carton of pre-made fruit salad, and two bottles of water. Seeing my curious gaze, Lee's cheeks turn very faintly pink. "It's not much of a spread, but I figured the view would make up for it."

There's a foreign object in my throat. I try to swallow it down and shake my head. "It's perfect."

"You're not allergic to anything, are you?" Lee asks, frowning at the sandwiches. "I didn't know what you liked. I just went with roast chicken and homemade aioli."

The man made homemade aioli and he's worried it's not good enough. I'm not going to survive this.

When in doubt, go for a casual quip. "Even if your aioli sucks, the view will *definitely* make up for it."

The redness in his cheeks fades, and he gives me a wry grin. "Good." He settles back on the blanket, long legs stretched out in front of him. His feet are bare, with a few grains of sand clinging to the toes. I'm not sure why the sight makes my stomach clench, like I'm seeing something I shouldn't.

Lee unwraps one of the sandwiches and takes a big bite out of one triangle. He took the time to cut the sandwiches into triangles. Why does that make my heart thump? Who cares how he cuts his sandwiches?

I care.

Every minute I spend with this man, I find myself wanting to know more. I want to know just how dark he likes his toast, and if he spreads the butter all the way to the edges. I want to know how he loads his dishwasher and what temperature he likes the shower to be.

I want all the other things too—the hot, sweaty bodies. The whispered words. The twisted sheets.

But that's not all I want.

It terrifies me, that wanting. It's wrong. I'm not supposed to want anything except my own house, a dog, and a steady job.

With trembling hands, I follow his lead, unwrap my sandwich, and groan as I taste the first bite. Faintly garlicky, rich, and perfectly balanced, with thick, fresh bread and the crunch of fresh lettuce. This is a near-perfect sandwich.

It's only when I feel Lee's gaze on me that I look over to see his darkened eyes, his food suspended in midair.

I swallow. "It's good."

His gaze circles my face, then he gives me a jerky nod and turns back to the view.

"I put an offer in on a house," I say, then clamp my lips shut, surprised. Why did I feel the need to share that?

Lee straightens. "Yeah? In town?"

I nod, brushing a few crumbs off my fingers and crumpling the sandwich wrapper into a tight ball. "One half of a duplex. It has a huge yard. I'm thinking of getting a dog."

"Sounds serious." He leans back on his elbow, his long

body stretched out beside me. Once again, I feel an intimacy with this man that I have no right to feel. I pop the lid off the fruit salad and eat a strawberry, then another.

"It's crazy," I admit.

"What's crazy?"

"Buying the house."

Lee frowns. "Why?"

"I just... It's impulsive, is all. Usually I'll hem and haw and agonize over a decision like that. But I just walked into the house and knew I had to have it." I clear my throat, working up the courage to speak the truth that's building up inside me. Maybe it's the crash of the waves or the cool spring breeze. Maybe it's the fact that we're both barefoot, or that Lee took the time to make us a picnic this morning. Whatever it is, I feel the need to be honest with him, to make him understand how much I appreciate it. Him. "If you hadn't offered the payment plan on my debt, I wouldn't have been able to put an offer in," I tell him, shifting my gaze to meet his. "I'd be in Tahoe living with my mother, begging my boss in Reno for my old job back. I'd be stagnant."

He's silent for a beat. The waves crash a steady beat in front of us as a bird trills in the trees behind. A bird of prey circles overhead, making large, gliding circles across the sky. "Is that how you felt before you moved here?" Lee finally asks. "Stagnant?"

I snort. "And then some."

He hums, and I know he understands.

Still, I feel the need to speak. I want to say things out loud that have been building up inside me, things that I haven't wanted to admit, even to myself. "My dad died when I was young," I tell him, eyes on the horizon. Lee goes very still beside me. "I was a daddy's girl, and it devastated me. Fallon dealt with it by rebelling, but I was the opposite. All of a sudden, I needed to control everything. My clothing. My hair. The food on my plate, how it was arranged and what order I ate it in. My mother was fraying, so I started helping around the house. I got a part-time job to chip in at home, taking care of my mom while she was grief-stricken and barely treading water. I started managing our household finances, started taking on all these responsibilities that I shouldn't have needed to take on. But it felt good—the control. To know that as long as I was doing my job, everything would be okay. We'd manage because I would make sure of it."

When my words stop coming, Lee shifts until he's lying on his side, facing me. "What happened?"

I shrug. "I just...kept doing that. Taking care of my mom, trying to control every aspect of my life. There were moments, in college, when I dreamed of something more. I was studying design and I thought I could find some way to make my life mean something. But I had student loans and my mom needed help and my brother was in prison, and I just... I made rational, reasonable decisions. I always considered every aspect and tried to predict outcomes that were completely out of my control. Like my marriage," I add with a bitter laugh.

"He didn't treat you right?" Lee's voice has an edge, and I look over to see his eyes dark and steady as he studies me.

I shrug. "He used me, and I let myself be used. I got a good job and supported him while he wasted weeks and years 'looking for his passion,' which was code for playing video games all day. I followed this path of how my life was supposed to go. Go to college, get a good job, get married, maybe have a couple of kids, live happily ever after. I thought if I just ticked all the boxes, everything would go according to plan. I was willfully blind, and I let myself get caught up in a toxic, codependent relationship that sucked me dry."

It's scarily easy to talk to Lee. He's steady beside me, quiet but attentive. I can feel him listening to every word, soaking them up, understanding them. These are deep truths that I've rarely brought out into the light. Aspects of my personality that I pretend are qualities, but are slicked in shame and embarrassment. I should have quit my job years ago. I should have enjoyed my thirties. I should have seen Eric for who he was, but I was too focused on making sure I ended up married and employed and on track. In control.

"Is that why you moved to Heart's Cove? To start fresh?"

I lie back on the blanket, staring up at the clouds. "Partly. I think I just wanted to take a risk—any risk—just to see what happened. I was finally financially secure enough to quit my job, and every day felt like I was on the verge of exploding with this need building right here." I put my hand on my stomach. "And then I went and toppled over fourteen motorcycles and caused nearly thirty thousand dollars' worth of damage."

Lee chuckles, and my lips kick up in response. I love the sound of his laugh. It's like wrapping cold hands around a warm mug.

I take a deep breath. "I guess what I'm saying is, you offering me the job and the payment plan allowed me to move forward, instead of back. And I'm really, really grateful. After so many years of inaction, going backward might have broken me completely."

When I turn my head, I find Lee watching me. His head is propped on his elbow, his long body stretched out on the blanket beneath us. Slowly, he reaches a hand toward me and traces the line of my cheekbone. He tucks a strand of hair behind my ear, then slides the tips of his fingers along my jaw.

"It was selfish, mostly," he says in a low rasp. "You joked about moving back in with your mother, and I just... I couldn't deal with the thought of you slipping through my fingers."

My heart kicks against my ribs so hard I expel a breath.

Maybe pouring my heart out was a bad idea. The motorcycle ride was a bad idea, as was the romantic beach and the picnic. Because suddenly, with the salt-laden breeze coasting over my skin and the solitude of the coastline wrapping us in a little cocoon, I feel stripped bare.

I can't hide behind the pretext of our boss/employee relationship. I can't pretend that the debt hanging between us will stop me.

I'm attracted to this man in a way I've never felt before. He's awoken something inside me I didn't even know existed, and no matter how many times I've tried to vibrate it away with my new toy, it's only grown stronger. That feeling I get on the back of his bike—the weightless trust, the wings he gives me—I want that all the time.

But—

How can I even think of letting go when it could all go so wrong? I'm already risking my finances with this house. I'm risking my career with my new job, because even though it excites me to work for the Fringe Festival, I know that it'll look like a step down on my resumé. Can I risk my heart? Can I risk letting this man in when the last man I trusted ruined me so thoroughly?

"Drea left me at the altar," Lee says, jolting me from my thoughts.

My eyes widen and I find myself turning onto my side, propping my head on my elbow to mirror his position. There's only a foot of space between us. I push away the picnic bag and clear the space between us so I can see him more clearly. His lips twist as he catches a piece of my long hair between his fingers, feeling the strands between his thumb and forefinger.

"We'd dated for over a decade. Her friends were my friends. I thought she was The One. I finally proposed and she cried and said yes, but then we kept pushing the wedding date back." He lets out a sigh and falls onto his back, threading his fingers behind his head. "I should have known. She'd agonize over the font of wedding invitations and flowers and whether we should go with blush pink or millennial pink for the accent color, whatever that meant. The date would get pushed back six months, a year. Two years. Three." He pauses, blinking slowly as he stares at the sky above. "We were engaged for four and a half years. We'd been together nearly a decade and a half, and it still felt like she wasn't sure. I should have seen it—that she didn't want to marry me, that she was panicking—but I was blindsided. Drea left me standing there in front of all our friends and family, sending her mother up the aisle to tell me her daughter wasn't going to show up."

"Oh, Lee." I reach over to rest my hand on his chest.

"Roger went to go comfort her." He lets out a snort. "He said he was going to get an explanation for me, find out if we could patch things up. They slept together that night. On my wedding night."

Heat prickles at the back of my eyelids and lower, in my chest. Anger. Outrage. "I'm sorry."

"I'm not." Lee turns his head to meet my gaze. "Marrying her would have been a disaster."

"You're still allowed to grieve the relationship. Marrying my ex-husband was a disaster but divorcing him still broke my heart."

His eyes are steady, serious. "The wedding will be awkward," he warns. "People will be talking about me, watching for any sign of weakness. Roger will hold the city approvals over our heads until I prove to everyone that I'm happy for them."

"He's a douchebag."

The line between Lee's brows smooths as a quick smile flashes on his lips. "You mentioned that." He moves his hand on top of mine, his broad palm covering mine completely. I can feel his heart thumping beneath my palm.

I don't know what's happening. I don't know what any of this means. But I do know that when Lee finally meets my gaze again, something has shifted. The earth turns wobbly beneath me at the depth of his gaze. When his thumb brushes the pulse point at my wrist, I lose my footing entirely.

And that's when Lee moves, pushing me onto my back with a rough movement as he props himself on top of me. His eyes are fully dark now, his breath sawing out of his lungs as the weight of his body presses me into the blanket, sand molding around my body. A broad hand skates up my side as his thigh fits in between both of mine. The pressure of him against my core makes my body heat something fierce.

"I don't want to go to that wedding and introduce you as my coworker or my friend, Nora," he tells me. "I want you there as my date."

His words make a balloon expand in my chest, crowding out my lungs. Then, belatedly, my brain kicks in. It makes sense, doesn't it? He wants to show up with a woman on his arm to prove that he's over the pain of the breakup. He's just trying to make Drea jealous. An uncomfortable feeling squeezes my heart into a tight ball, but the world stops wobbling and things make sense again. Harsh, bitter sense.

I reach for something familiar, something to dull the surprising pain inside me, and find the debt I owe him. I make my voice casual, flirty. "Wouldn't that make me more of an escort?" I ask. "Seeing as you're paying me for my time and everything."

His weight on top of me is making my head spin. Lips curling into a dangerous smile, his brow kicks up. "How much would it cost me to kiss you?"

"A lot," I answer breathlessly, heart sending my heated blood to every corner of my body. "I'm very expensive."

"I bet it would be worth it." His gaze drops to my lips and he slides his tongue out to wet his own.

I'm not sure where today went wrong, or what is even happening between us. I thought we were attracted to each other but happy to keep our distance. Now...I'm not so sure. I've officially lost control of the situation, and I know that unless I wrestle it back to more comfortable territory, I could end up getting very, very hurt.

But his leather and pine scent is all around me, drugging me. His weight is draped over me, his breath coasting over my lips like a prelude to a kiss. This is a motorcycle ride on steroids. I'm flying through space, tumbling, unsure what's up or down.

And what if I just...leaned into the turns?

19

LEE

I'LL DIE if I don't kiss Nora. I felt the need build up inside me as she spoke, lifting up the curtain to show me her innermost thoughts. She did it casually, openly. She laid out her past hurts like cards on a table, face up, one by one.

There's no artifice, no subterfuge. She isn't like Drea, who would hide true meaning in layers of passive-aggression and vague metaphors, who would make me guess what I'd done wrong. Nora is open in a way that makes my chest ache with the need to touch her, to pull her over and hold her.

"You make me feel off-balance," she says, dark eyes wide as she looks up at me. "Nothing makes sense when I'm around you. I keep meaning to stay away from you but it doesn't seem to be working."

Her body is soft beneath mine, and I take care to keep most of my weight off her. I slide my palm over the silk of her hair. "The last thing I want is for you to stay away from me."

All it takes is a gentle touch of her fingertips against my

neck, and I'm dipping my head toward hers. Her lips are as soft as I'd imagined, lush and pillowy and perfect. She lets out a sweet moan and parts them, and that's the only invitation I need to taste her fully, to claim her mouth the way I've been imagining for weeks.

She tastes like strawberry. Sweet and fresh and mine.

I could pull away and tell her the truth—that I'd wipe her debt clean right now, because I don't care about the money she owes me. I never did. All I wanted was an excuse to see her, talk to her.

Kiss her.

Her fingers tunnel into my hair as our kiss deepens, my hand searching for the hem of her shirt so I can finally feel her skin against mine. As soon as my thumb touches the softness above the waistband of her jeans, an electric jolt hits me. I nudge her head to the side and kiss her neck, inhaling her scent deep in my lungs.

She sighs, body softening. Her knees spread and I find myself cradled against her hips, my cock a steel bar between us. I want her so much it makes my head spin. I want her all the time. In the office. In my house. Late at night and first thing when I wake up. I've wanted her for months, since the first time I saw her, standing on the sidewalk while her mother was dragged out on a motorcycle ride with the rest of the geriatrics in town.

There's an honesty in Nora I can't resist. The way she squares her shoulders and faces life head-on. Stands up on a chair in a crowded bar and tells a group of bikers she knocked over their machines. Pokes her head into my office and tells me the mayor is a douchebag.

She blames herself for the failure of her marriage, but she shouldn't. She thinks it's a flaw to try to control her life, but it's just a need for honesty. Sense. For things to happen the way they're supposed to. The same honesty with which she approaches life is what she wants reflected back. It wouldn't have occurred to her that a man could deceive her the way her ex did.

"Kiss me," she says, breathless and open in that direct way of hers.

And who am I to resist that command? I capture her lips again and groan. She nips at my bottom lip—more honesty that tells me she wants more. So I give it to her. I let my hunger for her show in my kiss, let my hands grip her as tightly as I want to. She arches into my touch, lithe and beautiful and perfect.

Her hands claw at my shirt, so I help her remove it. I'm rewarded with a darkening of her coffee-colored eyes and the smooth touch of her palms against my chest. Then it's my turn to undress her. I pull her shirt off and kneel between her spread thighs, palms resting on her waist.

Beautiful.

"I like this," I say, running a finger along the bottom edge of her lacy black bra. My palm sweeps over the fabric to cup her breast, squeezing gently.

Her eyes are at half-mast, watching me touch her. "We shouldn't be doing this," she rasps.

I squeeze her breast again, letting my eyes coast down to her navel, to the button of her jeans. "Give me one good reason why not."

"We work together."

"I said a good reason."

Her laugh is breathy, but there's real hesitation in her eyes. "I owe you money. We're not coming at this on equal footing."

I pause, letting my hands slide down to rest on her thighs. "Do you feel like you need to be doing this because of the money you owe me?" My brows twitch together. If she feels at all coerced...

Nora huffs, then lifts her gaze to the sky. "No. I feel like it *should* bother me, the money and the job, but the truth is, it doesn't." There's a line between her brows that won't go away.

There she goes with that bald honesty again. My hands tighten on her thighs and I force myself to loosen my grip. Something feels off, and even though need for her screams through me, I have to figure this out. "Tell me what's bothering you, Nora."

She keeps looking at the sky. "Sex will complicate things."

God damn. Even hearing her say the word *sex* makes my cock throb. With gravel in my throat I say, "And that bothers you?"

She blinks and shifts her gaze to meet mine. She pauses, sucks her bottom lip between her teeth, then lets out a breath. When she speaks, it comes out as a whisper. "I'm scared."

My heart stutters. "Of me?"

"Of everything."

I ease out from the vee of her thighs and lie on the blanket beside her. Then it's just a matter of wrapping my arms around her to tug her back against my chest. She settles in like it's the most natural place for her to be. Her fingers inch up to tangle with mine against my heart, and I use my other hand to make soft, long sweeps down her side.

Her hair tickles my nose, and I close my eyes. The air is

cool against my bare skin, but it feels too good to have her in my arms to do anything about it. We stay like that for long moments, until Nora speaks.

"I've spent the past couple of decades with a steady routine. My life was predictable. Even through the divorce and after, my day-to-day life didn't change a whole lot. Now, in a matter of weeks, I find myself in a new place with a new job and a house, and..." She inhales. Exhales. "I used to be able to plan my weeks out almost to the minute. Now I feel like I'm losing my grip on...everything." She shakes her head, her cheek rubbing against my bicep. "I shouldn't be telling you this. You probably just wanted to hook up and here I am spilling my guts to you. It's embarrassing."

I tighten my hold on her, falling onto my back and taking her with me so she's sprawled over my chest. I keep my grip tight, holding her to me. "It's not embarrassing. It's honest."

"Those aren't mutually exclusive," she mumbles against my chest, her hand teasing through my chest hair.

A laugh rumbles through me. "That's true. But I like that you talk openly like this. I like that I don't have to guess what you're thinking." I squeeze her. "Let's take things slow. We have all the time in the world to figure things out. And you're right about sex causing complications we don't need. If I was capable of thinking with anything but my cock when you're wearing nothing but tight jeans and a lacy bra, I'd probably be able to come to that same conclusion on my own."

A breath gusts out of her, just a huff of laughter, and I feel her relax against me. "You're not mad at me for stopping?"

Using a finger, I tilt her chin up toward me. Her eyes are

uncertain, and I hate that this confident, beautiful woman is looking at me like that. "How about this, Nora. You're in control of this—whatever this is between us. We'll go as fast or as slow as you want."

"That's a lot of responsibility for little old me," she says, but her lips tip up at the corners.

"I think you can handle it."

"You'd wait for me to sort out the mess in my mind?"

"If you could see the brambles in my own head, you wouldn't ask that." I take a deep breath and decide it's time for a little honesty of my own. "I like you, Nora. I want to see where things go between us. And I'm a patient man." *I feel like I've been waiting for you for years. What's a few more weeks?*

Her hand rests on my chest, and I let my fingers trace its outline, every knuckle and nail. Finally, she nods. "Okay."

Desperately, I want to tilt her face up to mine and press my lips to hers. But I just let her extricate herself from my arms and tug her shirt back on before wrapping her arms around her knees and watching the waves lap against the shore.

I'm patient. I'll wait for her, give her all the time she needs.

But once she finally comes to me, when those shadows are gone from her eyes and she isn't trembling like a trapped animal beneath me, I won't hold anything back.

20

NORA

THE NEXT DAY, on Sunday, after a sleepless night and far too many thoughts of what happened on that beach, I visit my brother. He lives with Jen in a small apartment in town that's overrun with plants. Jen has a hell of a green thumb.

Fallon buzzes me up and has me sit in the kitchen while he cooks dinner, moving in the tiny space like a dancer on stage. He started cooking when he got out of prison and cleaned his life up, and watching him now, I wonder if I'll ever be able to do something so easily, so fluidly.

Everything feels like a clunky, clumsy effort for me. Fallon pokes a boiling potato to test it in an easy, practiced movement. Maybe I *could* be easy and free. I'd just need to loosen up with myself. Stop being so afraid of failure and disaster.

I could call Lee and tell him I'm ready. The deep end beckons, and I'm itching to find out if I can swim.

"How's the new job?" My brother tastes a bit of his gravy and adds a pinch of salt.

Putting down my wine, I nod. "Really good."

"Better than the law magazine?" He glances over his shoulder. "More room for creativity?"

I nod. "It's probably a step down, career-wise, but the work is really interesting. My ideas are actually appreciated. I can talk about content instead of just layouts and advertising space. I came up with this idea for a sculptural exhibit for this year's festival, and we're running with it." A smile tugs at my lips. "It's fun."

"Doesn't sound like a step down to me," he says, lifting the foil tented over the cutting board to start carving up the roast chicken.

The front door opens, and I peer around the corner to see Jen walk through. She moves with purpose, dropping her keys on a hook placed near the door for that purpose, kicking off her shoes and lining them up neatly along the wall, and finally walking into the kitchen carrying a box from the Four Cups Café in one hand, and a plant in the other. She drops the box on the kitchen counter like it's a sack of garbage and gently cups the potted plant in both hands.

"You finally found the pink princess philodendron?" Fallon says as she places the plant down on the windowsill on the far side of the kitchen, where it opens onto the living room.

Jen hums, repositioning the plant ever so slightly to the left. Its deep-green leaves are cut through with bright pink, unusual and beautiful. Jen touches a fully pink leaf in a gentle caress. "Yeah. It's looking a bit rough, but I think I can bring it back." Finally, she turns to Fallon, lifts herself up on her toes to kiss him, then nods at me. "Hey, Nora."

"Hey. Cool plant."

"Been looking for one for months," Jen says, reaching for a wine glass.

"Is that your most recent iteration?" Fallon asks, jerking his chin to the box.

Jen blows out a breath. "Simone's wedding cake wasn't this hard. Neither was Fiona's. I don't know what I'm missing."

She flips open the box, and the smell of something sweet wafts toward me. I groan, standing up to look in the box. "That looks amazing."

It's a small, six-inch cake iced in rich white frosting, with different piping techniques attempted on various sections. "Lemon?" I ask, sniffing.

"Lemon cake with blueberry filling and lemon buttercream. The blueberry overwhelms it. It's all wrong." Two lines appear between Jen's brows, and she plants her hands on slim hips, glaring at the cake.

"My mother mentioned you were doing your own cake," I say.

Fallon gives me a warning glance.

Jen clicks her tongue. "I'm a professional baker. It shouldn't be this hard."

"Why not hire someone else to do it?" I say despite the loaded glare Fallon sends my way. "Wouldn't it be less stressful than doing your own? You'll nitpick it. I'm sure it's delicious."

Jen closes the box and stuffs it in the fridge. "I'm not having someone else make my own damn wedding cake." She closes the fridge with grim finality, then stalks off.

I arch a brow at my brother, who shakes his head. "I tried, Nora. She's doing it herself and driving herself crazy trying to make it perfect." His gaze shifts to the open doorway, and his lips curl into a smile. "But in the end, she'll succeed."

He turns back to the food he's cooking, and I sit there, thunderstruck. It's not that I doubted my brother's affection for his soon-to-be wife. They've been together long enough now that I know they care for each other. He gave her our mom's old ring, after all. I'm shocked because seeing the love laid bare on his face like that makes me feel off-balance.

After Eric, I guess I assumed it didn't exist—that kind of steady, predictable, beautiful love that grows between two people who are meant to be together. I convinced myself love was either disruptive or destructive because that's the only kind of love I've ever experienced.

Whatever feelings I have for Lee, I've dismissed them as purely disruptive at best. At worst, they're feelings that will undoubtedly turn destructive if I give into them. They're getting in the way of my nice, steady, orderly life.

But my brother loves Jen with his whole heart, and he believes in her completely. He's not annoyed by her strong personality the way Eric was with mine. He isn't trying to change her or mold her into something he wants. He's just taking her as she is and loving every bit of it.

Kind of like the way Lee backed off and let me be in control yesterday. It didn't bother him. He just took me as I am.

Not wanting to delve into thoughts of Lee, I glance at my brother again.

I've spent my whole life seeing Fallon as someone a bit wild. After our father died, Fallon went a little crazy. He made mistakes and paid for them, and I saw his life spiraling out of control. I was the one who knew what she was supposed to do, who always did the right thing. I graduated, got married, and ticked all the boxes that were laid out in front of me.

But somehow I got it all wrong, and he's figured life out in the meantime. We've switched spots without me even noticing.

"Mash the potatoes for me?" my brother says, drawing me from my thoughts. He extends a potato masher to me and points to the pot of steaming boiled potato.

I nod and do as I'm told, trying to wrestle my thoughts back to neutral territory.

Lee pops into my mind again. His arms were steady as he held me under the afternoon sky yesterday. His skin was warm against my own, and after my minor freak-out, I felt safer and calmer than I've been in a long time. I reach inside myself and try to find that feeling, but it slithers away like a slippery eel.

I wish he were here—and isn't that a dangerous thought? What if I'm just clinging onto the first man who makes me feel safe when the rest of my life is in flux?

Shaking my head, I take out my frustration on the potatoes. Jen reappears, changed and showered, and we share a nice meal. When it's time for dessert, Jen begrudgingly lets us test her latest iteration of her wedding cake, and I hate to say she's right. The blueberry completely overwhelms the delicate lemon flavor.

"What about raspberry?" I ask. "I know it's kind of cliché, but you could do some sort of freeze-dried powder in the buttercream? Or a raspberry filling or something? When you did the *Boss Baker* show, didn't you do some sort of swirl in crème pat? You could do a raspberry swirl in a lemon-flavored custard to put between the layers. Sweet and rich and tart..."

Jen tilts her head, eyes steady on mine.

"I mean, you're the expert," I say, fumbling over my words. "I just watch cooking shows. I don't even bake. I didn't mean to assume—"

"Raspberry could work." She stands up abruptly. "I need to go."

"Want a ride to Four Cups?" Fallon asks, cutting himself another slice of cake.

"No, I'm fine. Don't wait up." She kisses his cheek, grabs her keys, and is out the door in seconds.

I sit there, stunned, and when Fallon looks at my face, he just laughs.

"Don't worry," he tells me. "She'll probably thank you later. When she gets an idea in her head, she has to work through it."

"Is she going to bake cakes right now? At this hour?"

Fallon's smile is easy. "Yep. I'll go check on her in an hour or two." He takes a big bite of cake and chews thoughtfully. "I don't mind the blueberry."

"Don't tell Jen that."

My brother laughs, and I can't help but grin in response. When I head home a while later, Fallon leaves to go check on his wife-to-be, looking as happy as I've ever seen him.

MONDAY MORNING COMES QUICKLY ENOUGH, and I'm surprised to see things aren't at all awkward between me and Lee. Even though the approvals haven't come through for the road closures and permits we need for the festival, Lee tells us to work as if they're in place.

Only he and I know they're conditional on him attending Roger and Drea's wedding.

The week zips by, and I only look at the listing of my potential new house about two hundred times. I'm the picture of restraint, really. The bank has received my application, but they didn't tell me how long it'll take to get approved for the mortgage. Rudy assures me it shouldn't take too long since I was pre-approved, but every day seems like an eternity.

Now that I've decided to embrace life with both hands, it's hard to live patiently and sedately. It's hard to go back to my old ways.

On Friday, Lee takes me out on his bike again, and we go to a nice fish and chips restaurant in the next town over. We walk hand-in-hand on the beach after, me wrapped up in my leather jacket, feeling warm all the way down to my toes.

When he kisses me goodnight, I almost cave and ask him to come upstairs, but there's something in me that holds back. With the debt, the wedding coming up, with my mortgage being processed...there's so much change in my life that I still feel off-balance.

I don't want to jump into something with Lee just because I'm getting addicted to the feeling of being free. I don't want to ruin everything I have in Heart's Cove by rushing things with him.

In other words, I'm a big ol' chicken.

"Your lips taste so good," Lee says, my face cupped in both his hands.

"It's the lip gloss," I answer, head spinning. The words still won't come out. *Would you like to come upstairs?*

The darkness in his eyes tells me he'd say yes without hesitation. Hell, my body is screaming at me to do it. But I just...

I can't. I'm scared. Everything is changing, and my feelings for Lee are growing so fast I can hardly keep track. I'm terrified of getting physical with him and falling so hard I lose all semblance of control. I only *just* recovered from my divorce, and Eric and I parted ways eight whole years ago. Things are changing rapidly. I just know that sleeping with this man will push me over the edge.

"Can I call you tomorrow?" His thumbs brush my cheekbones as he presses a kiss to my forehead.

I shiver at the tenderness of his touch. It feels so damn good to be in his arms. "Yeah," I say. "I'd like that."

When I get into bed that night, the sheets are ice-cold.

21

LEE

AFTER OUR DATE on the beach, things change between Nora and me. There's a current of intimacy that wasn't there before, an understanding that we're heading in a new direction. At work, Nora is professional, but still manages to throw me glances and grins that make me crave her something fierce.

Planning the Fringe Fest is busy, so I don't notice the weeks slipping by. I feel...light. Happy in a way I hadn't realized was missing. I look forward to the next day, and the next, and the next. The team drives the festival planning onward without Roger's final signature. It's a risk, but the alternative is not having a Fringe Festival at all. There's a hum in the office, a pleasant buzz of productivity. I find myself next to Nora's desk multiple times a day, but I notice other people do too. She's the sun that we're all drawn to.

Outside of work, Nora's still hesitant to make things physical between us. We spend a few evenings a week getting a meal or going for a short drive. Weekends are saved for longer rides. And although I'm prepared to wait for as long as it takes for her to feel comfortable, I can't deny that my need for her grows. Truthfully, the time since our picnic on the beach has been a sweet kind of torture. I've wanted Nora more and more every day. I've fantasized about pushing up her pencil skirts and fucking her on top of my desk. I've imagined her red lips wrapped around my dick so many times I should be arrested.

Still, I appreciate the time we have. I've never taken it slow with a woman, ever. Sex has always been what came first for me, and everything else came after.

With Nora, it's the opposite.

Nora fits on my bike like it was made for her. Weekends riding with her settle my spirit in a way I didn't know was possible. We drive all over the area, stopping off at lookouts, tourist attractions, and lush forested spots that I'd normally blow past on a drive.

Slowing down to enjoy every sight is something I haven't done in a long, long time. Maybe ever. Every smile that Nora gives me is a gift, every kiss a treasure.

This kind of intimacy is new to me. Even with Drea, we moved quickly from fucking to dating to living together, in that order. Spending time with Nora is entirely different. We're not rushing toward a goal, we're just...being. Taking sex out of the equation makes me realize how shallow my relationships have been since Drea left me. How shallow a foundation Drea and I had to begin with.

A part of me finds the depth of my feelings for Nora terrifying. She's burrowing deeper and deeper under my skin, leaving a mark that won't go away. But the fear is eclipsed by everything else she brings with her. Peace and contentment and a deep, settled feeling in my heart.

As spring starts showing the early signs of summer, I'm

a new man. Like a snake shedding its skin, I've shucked off some old, dead carcass that had been lingering over my soul for a long time. Weeks are busy, evenings are late, and weekends are spent exploring Northern California with Nora at my back.

Instinctively, I know to be careful with her. The light in her eyes brightens day by day, and I don't want to be the one to push her. I feel protective of her in a way I haven't felt before, and I want to nurture this new, adventurous side of her as much as possible.

Maybe I'm nurturing something within myself at the same time. A tenderness I thought had calcified when I spent those long minutes waiting at the altar for a woman that would never show up.

TWO WEEKS before my ex's wedding, on a Friday, Nora lets out a whoop and rolls away from her desk. I lean against my office doorway and meet her eye above the cubicles, eyebrows arched.

"My mortgage was approved. The building inspector is scheduled for Monday. I'll be closing on my house within a month."

Olivia cheers from the reception desk, jumping up. "This calls for cake. I'm taking the company credit card, Lee, and I'm getting cake and coffee for everyone."

"Fine by me," I say with a smile.

Olivia cuts across the office to give Nora a hug, then heads out the door. Rick is next to give her a one-armed side hug, and I consider it a miracle that the green monster inside me doesn't rear up.

Maybe because even while he's hugging her, Nora's eyes are on me, shining bright and happy.

THAT EVENING, I pick Nora up at her apartment building. She slides onto my bike in a practiced motion, then guides me across town to her future home. We stop in front of the duplex, get off the bike, and look at the big "SOLD" sign on the front lawn. I sling an arm around Nora's shoulders, leaning over to press my lips to her temple.

"I was worried they'd reject me and I'd lose the house," she admits.

"That's because you can't deal with things that are out of your control."

She jabs me with an elbow, then clicks her tongue in agreement. "I know you're right, but you don't have to say it out loud."

Laughing, I tug her closer and tilt her chin toward me. When I press my lips against hers, she shivers and curls her fingers around the nape of my neck.

I nudge her nose with my own. "How are you feeling?" It comes out as a growl, because having her so close to me —dressed in my old leather jacket, with the light of the fading sun glinting off her lips—makes me want to carry her over my shoulder and tie her to my bed.

God, I'm an asshole. I'm trying so damn hard to be a good guy, but she looks like a goddess and I just want to drop to my knees and worship her. My patience is fraying. I need...I *need*. Her. Us. Everything.

"I feel good," she says quietly, pressing on the back of my neck to silently demand another kiss.

I comply. I'd kiss this woman until I died of starvation if she'd let me. I'd do a hell of a lot more.

Nora lets out a sweet little moan, and I nearly break. "We need to get somewhere private," she says. Her breath comes out in hot little pants that make my jeans feel tight. "I...want you. I'm ready, Lee."

I pause, my lips coasting over her neck. My heart thunders so loudly I can hardly hear myself when I say, "You sure?"

When I pull away to look in her eyes, they're luminous. She nods. "Yeah. I'm sick of waiting." Her eyes drift to the duplex, and I know she's thinking about the purchase of her new home. For her, this is more than four walls and a roof. It's a symbol of risk and reward, of new beginnings.

And us, together—that's a new beginning too.

Her lips curl as she cuts her gaze back to meet mine. "My place?"

My whole body jerks. There's no hesitation. No doubt in my mind that I need this woman like I need air.

I grunt. "Fuck, yes."

My cock is so hard I can't sit comfortably on my bike, but I don't give a damn. I open the throttle as soon as Nora's sweet, luscious ass is behind me, and tear the street up on my way to her building. We make it there in three minutes. I park on the street, turn the bike off, and throw Nora over my shoulder.

She laughs, still wearing her helmet. "You need to let me down for me to unlock the door."

I do, keeping my hands on her hips as I spin her around to face the entrance to her building. Every pulse of my heart makes my cock throb thick and heavy between my legs. It's happening. She tears the helmet off her head, her black hair flying everywhere, and glances over her shoulder to curl her lips into a teasing smile. Her lipstick is coral pink, and all I want to do is smear it across her lips, undo her a little.

Look at her, with her back to me like this, ass pressed into my lap. I could push her up against a wall when we get inside, kick her legs apart, and take her rough and hard.

No. No. Not unless that's what she wants. She deserves the best. This isn't just fucking—it's more. It's always more with Nora. But God *damn*.

With trembling hands, Nora unlocks the door. Then she's thrown back over my shoulder with a squeal, and I take the stairs two at a time. She's breathless and laughing by the time she directs me to her door, and I pluck the keys from her hand to open it myself.

I should be patient. I should slow down.

But I *can't*.

Two steps, and I'm inside. A quick glance tells me Nora is extremely tidy, but my brain is far too busy to take note of anything else. I kick the door closed and push her up against it.

"Lee," she pants, thrusting her hands in my hair.

I kiss her harder than ever before. My body is on fire. Fitting my hips against hers, I pin her to the door and take her jaw in my hands to deepen the kiss. I'd fuck her right here if she let me, with her back banging against her front door.

I've lost my fucking mind. She tastes like heaven. When I pull away, Nora's eyes are dazed, and her lipstick is a delicious mess on her mouth. Unable to resist, I kiss her again, harder, loving the way she pulls me close and grinds her hips against me.

There's no reason to be afraid of this. No reason to wait. If this relationship crumbles and leaves me battered and broken, so be it. It's worth it for this moment right here.

Weeks—it's been weeks. Of wanting, craving, fantasizing. Waiting at my desk and watching the door just to see what color Nora's lips will be. Night after night spent gasping with my hand around my dick, wishing her legs were wrapped around my waist.

Hooking one of her legs over my hip, I grin when she gasps. "Feel what you do to me?" I rasp, pushing my cock into where she's softest. *Yes.* My body jolts at the contact, brain short-circuiting at the thought of finally, *finally* getting inside.

Nora lets out a breathless kind of moan, arching her hips into me. She's hot between her legs. So fucking hot, and I bet she's wet and soft and perfect.

"I—"

A knock on the door makes us both jump.

A voice calls through the door. "Nora. Are you ready?"

No no no no no! Not now! Please, no!

Nora closes her eyes and swears softly. She drops her leg and pushes me back, putting a hand to her forehead.

"Who is it?" I hiss.

"Simone," she whispers back. "Tonight is Girls' Night."

I blink. "So? Cancel."

"I can't cancel on Girls' Night," she says, outraged. "Especially not after what happened last time."

"Just...pretend you're not here." I hook my fingers into the waist of her jeans and tug her closer. Her eyes go blind when she collides with my chest and my hand slips between her legs.

"You guys know I can hear you, right?" Simone says

through the door. "And I can see shadows moving over the peephole."

We both freeze. Nora gives me a flat stare, straightens her clothes, pats her hair, then turns around to open the door.

Simone has her arms crossed, hip cocked, and eyebrow arched. "I just want to know—is it me? Do you guys plan these make-out sessions so I can interrupt you? Is this a kink?"

"Oh, be quiet," Nora says, cheeks turning bright red. "I forgot about Girls' Night, okay? How did you get in the building, anyway?"

"Wendy from the grocery store let me in the front door." Simone jabs a thumb over her shoulder, in the direction of the front door. She grins evilly. "But what could make you forget such a momentous event as your second-ever Girls' Night, I wonder?" Her eyes flick to me. "Could it be...a *man*? Because let me tell you, Nora, that is *not* a good enough excuse."

"You're talking like Girls' Night is some sacred ritual," I say, my erection now painfully uncomfortable and not getting the message that the moment has passed. I keep my lower body shielded behind Nora.

But then she glances back at me, and my cock turns to steel again. I think it's Nora's lips that are confusing me. The smeared lipstick is messing with my brain. I've imagined it so many times, and seeing it in person... *Fuck*, it's hot. Hotter than I ever imagined.

"Girls' Night *is* a sacred ritual," Simone says, clearly offended as she lifts a hand to her chest.

Nora huffs and gives me a sideways look. "She's right."

Thoughts clunk in my head, heavy and clumsy. "Can I

at least drive you to the bar? Make sure you make it there safe? Take you home when you're done?"

"Only if you don't bother us when we get there," Simone proclaims. "Nora was busy dealing with angry bikers last time, and tonight..." Her eyes flick from me to Nora and back again. "Tonight, the girls and I will have some questions for her."

Strangely, that makes Nora laugh. Her shoulders relax and she gives me the kind of smile that makes my chest ache. "Rain check?"

No! Fuck no. Never. "Sure."

Nora lets out a breath. "Fine. Let's go."

Simone arches a brow. "You might want to take a look in the mirror first, girlie. I'll wait downstairs."

With that, Simone struts away, Nora closes the door, and I try to will my body back under control. When Nora goes to the bathroom, I hear a scream. "My lipstick!"

I lean against the wall, letting my head fall back, and start laughing.

"Why didn't you tell me?"

"I had other things on my mind," I admit, readjusting the rod in my pants that's going down far, far too slowly for comfort.

A few minutes later, Nora re-emerges looking as put-together as ever, but the sight of her undone will stay burned in my head for a long time. I just hope I get to see it again.

And soon.

22

NORA

THIS TIME, GIRLS' Night goes off without a hitch. I don't cause tens of thousands of dollars in property damage, but I do end up hungover on Saturday morning.

Lee drove me to The Cedar Grove then left, saying he'd give me space to hang out with my girls. It was a shock to realize what he said was true—they're my girls. Somehow, I've fallen into a vibrant friend group that's accepted me without a second thought.

Of course, half the night was spent with said friends extracting information from me like professional interrogators, until I blushingly admitted that Lee and I had kissed. More than once. Quite passionately.

Now, as I huddle on the couch with a coffee in my hands, my stomach knots. I glance at my front door, where Lee had me pressed and panting less than twelve hours ago. If Simone hadn't interrupted, I would have had sex with him. Possibly right there against the door.

God, yes. I want that.

The thought blazes through me, right before my phone dings.

Lee: Not too hungover, I hope. You up for a ride today?

I stare at that little emoji, a yellow head with a sideways smirk, giving a whole new meaning to the word "ride"—a meaning that doesn't involve a motorcycle. My body comes alive in an instant, cutting through the haze of my hangover. Between one heartbeat and the next, my panties are wet.

My libido has officially entered the building and made herself Almighty Queen of the World. A baseball bat wouldn't do shit against her. I read the message over again, thumbs positioned over the screen, wondering how the hell I'm supposed to answer.

My text message flirting skills are sadly lacking. I grew up with a Nokia brick cell phone where text messages cost a fortune to send and receive. Then I got married, and texts were mostly just grocery lists and "I'll be home late tonight" texts. My brief foray into internet dating was, quite frankly, scarring.

I don't know how to respond, or where I want to take this exchange with Lee. So I decide to only acknowledge the first part of his message, because I'm a coward.

Me: Girls' Night is dangerous. You were right to leave before it got messy.

He answers right away.

Lee: I didn't want to.

My heart thumps. I'm sitting on my sofa in an old T-shirt and cotton panties, feeling like my skin is too tight. I'm torn. Half of me wants to jump head-first into whatever is happening with Lee, and the other half wants to pump the brakes.

We've fooled around, but we haven't crossed that final barrier. What if sex ruins our working relationship? What if after everything, I realize that I don't enjoy sleeping with him, either? Maybe I'm destined to be sexless and alone. How could I keep working for the Fringe Festival with him in the same building if I discovered that fact while he was inside me?

My phone buzzes again.

Lee: I'm taking the bike out for a long ride today. You want to join?

And just like that, he gave me an out. The same way he did at the beach and at the restaurant. He rewrote his first text to make it seem like he was talking about motorcycles and made it easier for me to ignore the sexual undertones.

Paradoxically, it makes me want him more. I've never met a man who is so in tune with how I'm feeling, so perceptive. He can tell when I'm shying away and when I need him to crowd me against a door.

And because I'm powerless to resist him, I tell him I'd love to join him. A short while later, we're roaring down the street and the wind is whipping away the remnants of my hangover.

. . .

LATER, after we spend the day traveling miles and miles along the coast up to Oregon and back, Lee drops me off at home and gives me another scorching kiss. He looks in my eyes for a moment, then kisses my forehead so tenderly my heart gives a violent thump.

"I'm going to let you get some sleep tonight, Nora."

Another thump in my chest. His words are a promise— that one day soon, there will be nights where he doesn't let me get any sleep at all.

And when I'm back in my apartment, slumped on the sofa almost exactly where I began the day, I'm starting to wonder if I'm the one being conned. Lee is giving me space, handing me the reins, and telling me he'll follow my lead, but he's also making himself irresistible.

This isn't merely physical anymore. It's a whole lot deeper.

And *that* is truly terrifying.

23

NORA

TWO MORE WEEKS PASS, and I manage to find my footing just in time for Roger and Drea's wedding. Sort of. The contracts for my house purchase are executed, and the closing date is set for the week of the Fringe Festival. My debt with Lee shrinks as I make a large payment, feeling slightly more in control of my financial situation. I start looking at rescue shelter websites to see about a dog. I throw myself into work.

And I spend time with Lee. We kiss and hold hands and talk, and I finally admit to myself that we're dating. But still, something is holding me back from taking things all the way physically. It's this one last element that I can hold back, cling onto, control.

As long as we don't have sex, we can always take a step back. As long as things don't go too far, I can retreat.

I've lived an orderly life. A normal, boring, stable life. Even with my father's death, Fallon's incarceration, my divorce, with all the small hurts that came along the way, my life has been neat. Those traumas rocked me, but the keel that keeps me upright was always dropped deep into the rolling ocean. Before everything, when I was a school-girl in Reno, I was too Indian for the white community and too white for the Indian community. I bore that wound and sorted it into a compartment inside myself. I couldn't control the way others tried to alienate me, but I could control my reaction to it.

From the moment I was born, there were challenges. I've always been able to weather them. Control them.

Early on, I promised myself I would always survive—and part of survival is always having a clear exit plan. I know that's why I'm keeping Lee at arm's length. I'm waiting to see if all these recent impulsive decisions will rise up and slap me down. Sleeping with Lee is stepping off a cliff into the blackness of open space. I'm not quite ready to let go of the last part of me, the flimsy piece of string keeping me together.

As I slip on one of Trina's many formal dresses—a wrap dress that fits over my more generous curves—I let out a gust of air.

This doesn't feel like surviving. It feels like much more than that. I'm attending a wedding with Lee Blair, and I'm giddy about it. We're two secret agents infiltrating an enemy's lair. Over the past couple of weeks, it's become a bit of a joke between us. I've actually been looking forward to it.

It's not about the Fringe Fest approvals or proving that Lee's past is forgiven. This event is something altogether different.

My hands shake as I set my hair into loose curls, spritzing them with product to make them glossy. I wipe sweaty palms on a terrycloth towel, checking my makeup one last time before slipping my favorite gold earrings into my ears.

Right on time, the buzzer sounds.

"Hey," I say into the intercom. "Be down in two minutes."

"See you soon." Lee's voice sends a thrill tripping through my stomach, the same way it has for the past month.

I slip my sensible, three-inch heels on, grab my purse, and head downstairs. Nothing about what I'm doing is neat and orderly, but it makes sense. Things always make sense when I'm meeting Lee. It doesn't matter how many times I tell myself he's my boss, that there's money between us, that I should stay away from complications. When I'm with him, the unfamiliar chaos of risk settles into a comfortable hum of energy, warm and inviting.

He's waiting for me beside a vintage baby blue Corvette.

I grin. "Why am I not surprised? Of course you have more than a hot bike. You also have a hot car."

"This old thing?" Lee slides a palm over the curves on the hood of the car, appreciative.

"At least it's not a convertible." I fluff my hair.

"I'm not completely clueless." He hauls me closer with an arm banded across the small of my back, dark eyes staring down into mine. "I'll mess up your lipstick if I kiss you. Convince me that's a bad idea."

There's a pause, when I decide whether or not I care about walking into the event looking like I've been kissed senseless. I touch his lips with the tips of my fingers, over the surprising softness of that male mouth. "It would look like you're trying to send a message to Roger and Drea."

He sighs, forehead touching mine. "Damn it. That's about the only thing you could have said to stop me."

"Is it bad that I'm feeling a sick kind of curiosity about today?" I ask, letting my fingers drift to his jaw. It's smooth; he shaved recently. "It's like I get to be the ultimate voyeur in some small-town drama."

"Dorothy and Lottie will be on tenterhooks waiting for your report."

I grin. "They cornered me this morning when I went to Four Cups for a coffee. Said they expected me to tell them everything tomorrow. Seems I've been accepted by the community."

"I think that happened a long time ago, Nora." Amusement dances in his eyes, one corner of his lips curled up. "Come on. Let's get this over with."

"Words every woman dreams of hearing."

His chuckle is deep and warm, sliding like velvet over my skin. I nod in thanks as he opens the car door for me, then sit inside and let him take me to the wedding.

We choose a pew halfway up the church. I sit primly, my purse on my knees, while Lee hooks his arm behind me and lets his knee touch mine. Sometime around the vows, I realize I've shifted close enough that my side is plastered to his.

Drea's dress is a lovely, elegant thing. The back has a row of hundreds of tiny buttons marching down from mid-back to the hem of the small train, while the front is a simple silk bodice dropping down into a fluttering trumpet skirt. The ugly, jealous part of me wishes she'd worn something gaudy and awful, but she looks every bit the beautiful bride.

Roger, to his credit, looks enamored with her. When

they finally kiss, he clamps his arms around her and dips her low, to the delight of the cheering audience. I steal a glance at Lee and see his face grim, but not in pain. He meets my gaze and curls his hand over my shoulder, letting his thumb brush the side of my neck.

When the guests are spewed onto the church steps a short while later, I let out a breath.

"You doing okay?" Lee says close to my ear so I can feel his breath on my cheek.

"Shouldn't I be asking you that?"

He just grins in response, and we follow the herd of well-dressed people down the street to the Heart's Cove Hotel. The event space in the hotel is small, but it's been decorated beautifully. Tables dot the space, all the way into the open courtyard. DJ equipment is in the corner, with a young, tattooed man bobbing his head along to the music.

Lee's hand is warm against the small of my back as I take in every detail of the room. The beautiful floral center-pieces, the lush tablecloths, the gauzy fabric draped along the walls.

"Well, I have to say I'm surprised to see you here," a male voice says behind us. I turn to see an older man, maybe in his mid-to-late fifties, looking at Lee with amuse-ment in the turn of his lips. "I probably wouldn't have showed up if I were in your shoes."

Lee shrugs, a movement smooth as water. "I wanted to congratulate the new couple. They deserve every happiness."

Shrewd eyes hold Lee's for a moment, then the man huffs. "I can't tell if you're lying." His gaze turns to me. "Who's this?"

"Michael, meet Nora Richter, the newest addition to our

Fringe Fest team. Nora, this is Michael Allen. Distinguished town council member and former fire chief."

The man snorts, sending his mustache quivering. "Distinguished, am I? Since when?" He extends a large paw that swallows mine whole. "Nice to meet you, Nora. Did he bribe you to come along to this thing?"

"Actually, yes," I answer.

Michael laughs. "Smart woman. What do you do at the Fringe Fest?"

We fall into easy conversation, and I find out he was a fireman for decades, until he took a bad fall and had to have his knee replaced two years ago. Small-town politics wasn't his first choice, but it's easy enough when you have the kind of respect around town he does. He doesn't say that directly, but I can see it in the set of his shoulders and the way he casts an eye across the room like he's observing his loyal subjects.

We find our seats, and I'm relieved to see we've been put at the back of the room with the other rejects. At least here, I won't feel like I'm on display.

The reception begins with the grand entrance of the bride and groom, flowing on to speeches, and finally the meal. The other guests at the table are a distant aunt and uncle of Roger's, a couple of family friends, and a sixteen-year-old cousin of Drea's who spends most of the time looking at her phone. As good a table as I could ask for, really. No one seems to care about Lee or me or our relationship.

Lee keeps his arm on the back of my chair and introduces me to everyone who comes to the table to chat. I keep stealing glances at him to see if he's looking at the bride and groom with any longing or pain. I wonder how he's coping. But every time he catches me staring, his eyes soften in a way that makes my heart tumble in my chest.

The only time I see tightness in his jaw is during the first dance. He sits perfectly still, watching Roger put his arms around his bride—the woman that was supposed to be with Lee—and grinds his teeth so hard I can almost hear it.

Then the dance is over, and he turns away from the dance floor to face the table. He's still for a long moment. Then his hand drops to my thigh. "Dance with me," he says.

I frown. "Really?"

"It's a wedding, isn't it? If we're going to make a show of being good guests, we might as well dance."

"I've got two left feet." My protests fall on deaf ears, because he's already hauling me up and dragging me to the dance floor. And when his arms encircle me, the heat of his chest is like a blaze against my front.

Just like that, I forget we're at his ex-fiancée's wedding. When the music swells, there's only him and me.

24

LEE

NORA IS soft and sweet against me, her lips cherry-red and tempting. I won't kiss her, though. Not here. Not when it feels like we've been walking a tightrope all afternoon. Instead, I slip my hands around her waist and sway with her. Her body fits into mine like we were made for each other, and every minute in her presence proves it. We're two halves of a whole.

"You okay?" she asks quietly, for my ears only. Another piece of proof. She sees my face and can read everything in my expression, even the things I try to keep hidden.

I chew on her words for a minute, then meet her deep brown eyes. "Yeah," I answer, and it's the truth. "I'm good."

"We can leave whenever you want."

"So keen to leave my arms?" I tighten my hold on her, rewarded with the flash of her eyes.

"When we have an audience, I am."

I lean into her, sinking into the feel of her in my embrace, taking the scent of her skin in my lungs. "What if we didn't have an audience?"

The shiver that courses through her delights me to my core. That simple words could elicit that kind of reaction from a woman, from *this* woman...it feels too good to be true. We dance among the other couples, and an old, hard knot hidden in my heart starts to unravel.

"Thank you for coming," I tell Nora, sliding my hands down the small of her back, feeling the sweep of the muscles on either side of her spine. Everything about her is smooth and curved. Every inch of her calls to me, makes me so hungry I could cry out.

Even the teasing, wry smile on her lips.

"Did you forget you paid me to come here with you?" She touched up her lipstick after eating, and I'm pretty sure she did it purely to tempt me to mess it up. Then, quietly, she adds, "You're welcome."

Today would have been different without Nora at my side.

Earlier, I watched Drea and Roger share their first dance. For those long, endless minutes, I saw the man I was three years ago. Ten years ago. Twenty. It was me who was supposed to have Drea in my arms, who should have been in Roger's place. I put myself up there in my mind's eye, knowing how it would have felt to have her as my wife. I would've been puffed up with pride, head over heels in love with a woman who didn't feel the same way about me.

The pain was old and familiar, buried deep under layers of scar tissue I've laid over the wound Drea left behind. I watched her dance up there, in front of everyone, with stars in her eyes for another man.

Then the song ended, I blinked, and I came back to myself. I turned to see Nora beside me, not looking at the couple on the dance floor, but at me. Searching my face, seeing everything that was written there.

And I realized I've changed.

The pain in my chest was an old friend. A keepsake. Something I've kept in a velvet box, locked away safely so I could bring it out whenever I wanted to be reminded of all the ways I've been wronged. It was a memory of a memory. A ghost of the real thing. A snow globe shaken up at every opportunity, suffering kept safe behind glass where I could admire it anytime I liked.

It wasn't real.

Sometime over the past three years, I've stopped hurting because Drea left me on our wedding day and started hurting because it was familiar. Comfortable. I couldn't tell you when the change happened, from righteous suffering to pure gluttony for punishment. How self-indulgent of me. I should have seen it earlier.

It was the work of a moment to let it go. To lay my hand on Nora's thigh and feel the warmth of her there, thrumming and alive beneath my palm. Between one breath and the next, I stopped hurting. I put the snow globe down and let the tiny flakes settle like an ivory carpet, until all that existed was the memory, stored in a glass ball, ready to be set on a shelf and forgotten.

Nora did that for me just by existing. We haven't even slept together, and I feel more connected to her than anyone, ever. How could I think that we *weren't* meant for each other? How could I stand in this room, at this event, and think that it wasn't destiny that brought us together? Fate shoved the truth in my face and said, *See? Aren't you glad you didn't end up with Drea as your wife?*

And all I can respond is *hell yes*. Because now I get to stand here with Nora in my arms.

"You're looking at me funny," Nora says, sliding her palms up to rest on my shoulders then all the way to the nape of my neck.

"Am I?"

"Like the cat who got the cream."

I couldn't stop my grin if I tried. "That's how I've felt for weeks. You should have seen me when I got home after our first picnic."

"Lord help us when we sleep together. You'll be insufferable."

"'When?' Not 'if?'" I repeat, grin widening. "You're saying it's inevitable." My cock throbs at the thought. I've been hard since she walked out of her apartment building wearing that gown, with her lips painted bright red, but my desire for her blazes hotter.

"Lee." I turn to see Drea beside us, in all her resplendent white. She ditched the veil at some point and changed into a shorter dress that dips low to show the valley between her breasts. She always did know how to use her body as a weapon. My ex-fiancée smiles at me warmly. "Thank you for coming."

I keep an arm around Nora as I nod. "Of course. Congratulations."

"The ceremony was beautiful," Nora adds, and Drea blinks, as if she just realized Nora was there. Annoyance sparks in my chest.

My ex's eyes take in the lack of space between us, and her smile turns a bit wooden. It brightens in the next instant. "Thank you." A graceful nod to Nora.

"There you are," Roger's voice booms. He tugs his wife

against his chest and kisses her, splaying his hand over her cheek as he grips her tight. "Wife."

I feel Nora's eyes on me. Glance down at her. I wink and she relaxes against me.

"Congrats, Roger," I say, extending my hand to my former friend.

Roger pumps my arm twice, then lets go. "Thank you. Glad you could make it. I'll be in touch next week. We leave on our honeymoon on Wednesday, but I'll get everything squared away in the office before then." He nods, rakes his eyes over Nora's breasts, then drags his bride away.

I let out a heavy breath.

"I'm guessing we passed the test," Nora says wryly. "He'll approve our plans for the festival?"

"Sounds like it. Let's get out of here."

"Finally." She lets out a laugh. "Let me grab my purse."

We take the side door out of the hotel to avoid the lobby, where Dorothy and Margaret are likely to be loitering. The last light of afternoon is settling over town, with the last rays of sun burning orange across the sky. It smells like rain, and the damp patches on the pavement tell me it sprinkled while we were inside. Nora inhales deeply, then lets it all out. I thread my fingers through hers and start walking to the church, where my car is parked.

Clean air fills my lungs, and I exhale out the last few hours. I'm tired in a way that has nothing to do with sleep. I realized some things today, and I feel stripped raw. I need a motorcycle ride, or a drink, or a week with Nora with no clothes on. Or all three. Something to cleanse my mind of everything that happened today: from the memories, to the realization that I'm completely over Drea, to the vague oily feeling Roger left in his wake.

It only takes three or four steps for Nora to squeeze my hand. "Lee," she says.

"Yeah?"

"Will you take me out on your bike tonight?" She blinks those wide, brown eyes at me and bites her lip, getting red smears all over her teeth. "I mean, if you're not too tired. You didn't drink anything tonight, right?"

This woman. She'll be the death of me. It's like she cracked my head open and read exactly what I wanted her to say.

I hold her face in my hands, cupping her cheeks and running my thumbs over the silk of her skin. Then I kiss her.

I stand by what I said on the beach all those weeks ago —the ball is in her court. I won't push things too far, too fast. I won't make her feel any bit of discomfort if I can help it. We'll go at her pace. She's in control.

But damn. I'll die if go another minute without tasting her lips.

She melts against me in an instant, gripping the lapels of my jacket tight as her mouth parts for me like she was starving for me too. I lick the red off her teeth and groan at the taste of her, so perfect. So sweet. So *mine*.

When we pull apart, panting, Nora's eyes are glazed. "I'm guessing that's a yes on the motorcycle ride?"

"It's a yes," I confirm. "I'm driving you home so you can change into something sensible, then I'm taking you out on my bike."

"We can let the breeze wash that wedding off our skin."

I kiss her again, just brushing my lips against hers. Once. Twice. Three times. She lets out a little whimper that goes straight between my legs, then blinks big brown eyes at me.

Her thumb swipes at my lips. "Messy. I should stop wearing such bright lipstick. It got all over your mouth."

"You should not stop wearing lipstick," I growl. "Ever."

Her smile is shy, with an edge of deep pleasure. "Take me home, Lee. I want to go for a motorcycle ride."

Sliding my arm across her shoulders, I lead her back to my car, and it feels like we've walked like this a thousand times. When I drop her off, it almost hurts to watch her disappear into her building, but I'm back in less than twenty minutes on my bike, and she's already waiting for me, leaning against the wall beside the front door of her apartment building, wearing dark jeans and my old biker jacket.

She looked good all dressed up and refined today, but she looks even better when she's strutting up to my bike and swinging her leg over the seat.

25

NORA

A YEAR AGO, I would've been comfortable at a wedding and uncomfortable on the back of a motorcycle. Even a stranger's wedding would have been preferable.

Today, I couldn't wait to get out of that stifling room. As soon as I fit my body against Lee's on the back of his Harley, the fist that had been wrapped around my chest starts to loosen. When the motor revs and we take off along the street, it feels like coming home.

A month ago, he told me we could take things as slow as I needed. He gave me the control I so craved, like he'd seen the contents of my heart and decided I was worth the effort.

Now, I want to give that control right back. I want to fly, to let go, to feel the strength of him in front of me. As we leave Heart's Cove behind, the wind starts tearing at the cocoon I've wrapped around myself, ripping away the layers of protection that I've used to shield my heart.

We drive fast, along winding roads that cut through old-growth forests, onto the coastal road that never fails to take my breath away. The sun sets over the Pacific Ocean, gilding the waters and painting the sky a thousand shades of orange and pink. There's soft beauty all around, and an edge of danger as we ride.

It's addictive, this feeling. I could get used to it.

We drive and drive and drive, until the sky fades to the bruised purple of late dusk. I don't want it to end. My mind is clearer than it's been in years, my body both relaxed and on edge. I feel every inch of the man in front of me, melting against his strong back.

I don't remember the last time I felt comfortable being so close to someone physically or emotionally. My arms fit against his ribs like that's where they belong. My legs mold along his, squeezing as we lean into a turn and relaxing when he opens the throttle on a straightaway. We are one on this motorcycle, in this moment.

I don't want it to end.

The person I was before needs to disappear. I don't want to be crippled by my worries, by the need to feel safe and in control. I don't want to stay stuck in a job I hate for years, just because I crave the steadiness of a paycheck. I don't want to settle for a marriage to a man who tears at the fabric of who I am.

I want *this*. Motorcycle rides in the light of the setting sun. Slow dances at a wedding that should be awkward, but somehow aren't. The feel of a strong, powerful man pressed against my front. Drugging kisses and hips pinning me to my apartment door.

By the time we turn toward Heart's Cove, I realize my body is tight as a bowstring. I've soaked through my panties without even realizing it was happening—and I know it's because I wasn't stuck in my own mind. I was free.

"You ready to go home?" Lee's voice resonates in my

helmet, sliding over my skin until I feel it everywhere. My breasts ache against his back, so I press myself a little closer.

I pause, arms wrapped tight around his torso. Finally, I answer. "No."

Lee doesn't respond. Instead of turning toward my apartment building, he takes a road leading to the far side of town. We slow down until we take a turn onto his street, pulling into the driveway in front of his home.

"You hungry?" Lee asks, turning the bike off. "I could make something. You didn't eat much of the food at the wedding."

It takes me a minute to synthesize everything he just said. First of all, apparently the man can cook. We've mostly stayed away from each other's homes over the past weeks—probably because that felt too intimate. But now I'm learning he knows his way around a kitchen. Second of all, he was paying attention to what I ate and wants to feed me. If that just doesn't warm the cockles of my heart —and every other part of my body—then my name is Betty Sue.

"Sure," I finally answer, sliding off the bike. My legs wobble a bit as I pull off my helmet, my body not quite under my command.

Lee takes the helmet from me and leads me to the front door. Last time I was here, I barely got a peek over his shoulder at the interior. This time, he opens the door for me before kicking off his motorcycle boots and tossing them into the hall closet. He unzips my jacket and hangs it up on a hook by the door before doing the same to his own.

Padding down the hallway behind him, my heart beats unsteadily. This house smells like him. We walk into an open-plan space with the kitchen on the left and a sunken living room on the right.

"Beer?" Lee asks, angling for the fridge.

"Sure." I accept the cold bottle, my fingers brushing his. When Lee reaches over to tuck a strand of my hair behind my ear, my heart thumps hard against my ribs. I take a sip just to do something with my hands, then wave a hand around the space. "Nice place."

"Thanks," he says, moving back to the refrigerator to pull out ingredients.

I take the three steps down to the sunken living room, noting the knickknacks on the built-in shelves and the big, comfy couch wrapping around in an L-shape. There are books lining the shelves—mostly biographies of sports stars and musicians, a few thrillers, and a couple of nonfiction titles about business and finance—along with a few dusty vases and a couple of photos.

I take a framed photo of Lee, Mac, and Hamish off the shelf. The three men are standing in front of their motorcycles, heads thrown back in laughter. Lee's eyes are crinkled, shut tight, his hand gripping his brother's shoulder. You can tell a lot about a person by the photos they display. This image tells me Lee loves his family and his motorcycle.

"We took that picture when Mac finally got his dream bike," Lee says from the kitchen, watching me. He's leaning against the counter, looming above me with a half-grin teasing over his lips. "Rode down to Las Vegas that weekend and met up with my dad's old college buddies. Good time."

"Did your mom ride motorcycles too?" I assume she took the picture. Or maybe Drea did.

Lee clears his throat, straightening. He grabs a knife

from the block on the edge of the counter and starts dicing an onion. "No. She left when Mac and I were kids. It was just us and Dad growing up."

He doesn't meet my gaze as I stare at him across the space. Every day I spend with this man, I uncover another layer. It wasn't just Drea who turned her back on him, it was his mother too. It seems like all the women in his life have let him down. I replace the black frame on the shelf and take a sip of beer while I keep snooping.

On the other side of the television are more pictures. Lee with Rudy dressed in athletic gear, looking sweaty and happy as they show off medals hanging from their necks. They have long, blue flags hanging off their hips. The photo looks fairly recent.

In the corner of the living room is an acoustic guitar propped on a stand. I pluck at one of the strings while taking another sip of my beer.

"You play?" Lee asks.

I laugh. "No. I'm far from artistic."

"You're literally an art director, Nora," he deadpans. A pan sizzles as he scoops the onion into hot oil.

I shrug, wandering back to the kitchen to watch those clever hands chop a red pepper into thin julienne slices. "That's different. There are rules to graphic design. The artistry makes sense. Music is different."

"There are lots of rules to music," he says, tossing the onion with practiced movements. He glances at me sideways, an unruly strand of hair falling onto his forehead. The man is a work of art. I could stand here and watch him cook for hours.

I slide onto a barstool at the peninsula counter and take another sip. "Maybe you can play for me after dinner."

His lips tilt. "Maybe."

"Can I help with anything?" I feel useless sitting here, drinking a beer. And maybe a little bit too turned on by watching Lee cook. I need to do something with my body.

"You can sit there and drink your beer." He glances over his shoulder while his hands toss the pan again. "You look good sitting in my kitchen."

A flush rises up my cheeks. "Beats being home alone." I tip my beer bottle against my lips, only to realize it's empty. How did that happen? Somewhere between snooping around Lee's living room and watching him cook, I drank the whole thing. Setting the empty bottle down, I push myself up to my feet. I'm too jittery to sit still. I round the counter and pick up Lee's knife, picking up where he left off with the red peppers. My slices are nowhere near as thin and perfect as his, probably because my hands are shaking and a strange, nervous excitement buzzes under my skin.

Large, sun-bronzed hands appear on either side of me. Lee's breath ruffles the hair at my neck as he leans closer, caging me against the counter. "I thought I said I didn't need any help."

"It felt wrong to just sit there." I pause my slicing, closing my eyes against the onslaught of sensation. The heat of him at my back, his lips near my ear, his rock-hard arms on either side of me. We stay utterly still for a moment, then I set the knife down.

I know that whatever happens, it'll be because I initiated it. The ball has been in my court for weeks. I can't keep ignoring this attraction. If I'm truly going to become someone new—someone better—I need to stop being such a coward and *act*.

Spinning around, I stand chest-to-chest with Lee,

knowing he's holding himself back with every fiber of his being. If I tell him to back away, to take me home, he will. If I lean in to kiss him, he'll kiss me back, exactly at the pace I set.

He's told me that a thousand times over the last month. He stopped when his body begged him to keep going, just because he could tell I needed the control.

Now, I'm not so sure. I'm unraveling at the edges, coming apart in his presence.

And I like that feeling. I *crave* it.

Tonight's motorcycle ride felt like a new beginning, being washed clean from what happened at the wedding. Maybe giving up my stranglehold on myself would be a good thing. I could let him touch me the way he wants to, let him take over. I could let go.

How would it feel to have those big, strong hands on my body, spreading me open for him to enjoy? How would it feel to let him set a punishing pace, to cede control to him?

The thought makes heat blossom low in my stomach.

Neither of us moves. Each breath brings my breasts closer to his chest, just brushing against the heat of him. I grip the counter with both hands, my pinkies brushing his thumbs. I feel trapped, but I don't want it to end.

There are two paths stretched out in front of me. One of them is familiar to me. It's the one where I pull away and go home alone. Where I stay in my safe little world, trying nothing new, treading water as I try to maintain a leash on every aspect of my life. The path where I cling onto my future with both hands and smother myself in the process.

The second path is full of tangled brush and overgrown weeds. It's dark under the shadow of tall, leafy trees, with each step taking me into the unknown. If I bring my lips up to Lee's and tell him I need him, I'll have to let go of a little bit of myself. I'll have to hand him my vulnerable parts in a neat little package, ready for him to tear to pieces. If I go down that path, I won't know where I'll end up. I might get hurt again. I might end up broken and alone.

But as the breath trembles out of me, I realize I'm already alone. Lonelier than I've admitted to myself. Even when I was married, I was alone. I'm a forty-one-year-old woman whose only real friend up until a couple of months ago was my own mother. A woman who hasn't ever enjoyed sex the way I'm supposed to.

How much worse could it get? If I can ride on the back of his motorcycle and feel the freedom of surrendering control to Lee in that instance, why can't I do it here too?

"Nora," he growls, inching closer. "You keep looking at me like that, I'm not going to be able to keep the promise I made to you."

Blinking up at him, I feel myself inching toward the overgrown path, my toes just brushing the edge of it. Then, uncurling my fingers from the counter to bring them to his chest, I take the first step.

"What if I want you to break it?"

26

NORA

THE AIR TURNS ELECTRIC. Lee's body, which had been tense a moment ago, turns to stone. His eyes are chips of obsidian.

"Nora," he grates.

My blood turns to honey at the sound of my name spoken like that. No one's said my name like that before. Like every letter is made of need, like my name is the definition of desire. On weak knees, I let my fingers curl around his neck. It only takes the slightest pressure to bring his lips down to mine.

He holds back. I can feel it in the tension of his arms, still caging me against the counter. In the muscles of his neck, hard and stark against my fingertips. In the soft brushes of his mouth against mine. He trembles as I comb my fingers into his hair, heavy silk against my skin.

"You sure?" Every word is torn from his throat, a hard rasp that makes my thighs tremble in anticipation. I know what he's asking. Am I sure I want this—him? Am I sure I want to take this step when I know there's no turning back?

Am I sure a little over a month was long enough for me to decide?

And I mean, damn. If a month wasn't long enough, how much time do I need? The Nora who moves to a new town and buys a house and knocks down a row of motorcycles also deserves orgasms from the hottest man alive. Right?

His lips brush mine softly, and an electric current darts through my core. I can almost feel the motorcycle seat beneath me, the wind whipping around me, the hard press of his back in front of me.

And I know.

"Yes," I answer. "I'm sure. I want you."

He goes solid in front of me.

I gulp, nipping at his lip. "I want you to..." I inhale, exhale. "I want you to do whatever you want to me. I want you to take control."

The next kiss isn't gentle or sweet or tender. It's a claiming. Hard, brutal, inescapable. Not that I'd want to escape the prison of Lee's arms. His hand moves from the counter to my neck, where he uses a thumb to tilt my head toward him. With deft little flicks of his tongue, he parts my lips and groans at the taste of me.

Desire blazes through me. Between one moment and the next, I've lost all sense of space and time. All that exists is the hard press of the counter at my lower back, the iron grip of Lee's hand on my jaw, and the heat of his chest against mine. My breasts tighten to hard points, abraded by the fabric of my bra. My clothes are suddenly rough. There are too many layers between us.

When I smell something burning, it takes me long seconds to realize it's the contents of the pan on the stove. An angry grunt, and Lee's tearing away from me to toss the pan aside and turn the gas burner off. Then his hands are on my hips and he's pressing me roughly to the cabinets.

Gosh, I love that. I like feeling small in his hands. I like knowing he can toss me around and pin me where he wants me.

He's hard as steel. I gasp at the feel of him on my belly, knowing that I want all that hardness deep inside me. It's an animal feeling. I'm wild with it. My hands move of their own accord, tugging at his plain white T-shirt until Lee helps me tear it off. His hair is mussed, his eyes dark as sin, and I love every damn inch of him. The patch of dark, coarse hair on his chest. The solid pack of bumpy muscle all the way down his stomach. The big shoulders that fill my vision.

I'm falling, spinning out, losing my mind. And I want more.

Exploring his chest with my fingers, my breath saws in and out of my lungs in quick, harsh pants. Heat winds through my core as my heart pounds a staccato beat, the feel of his skin beneath my palms sending pulses of fire into my thighs.

I don't know how my shirt ends up on the floor, or when exactly Lee got my bra unclasped, but it happens. Then his lips are on my breast and he's pulling my hard nipple between his teeth, and the last bit of my mind is shredded like tissue paper. All that exists is the physical sensations he gives me, the tidal wave of desire mounting inside me.

Broad, calloused palms sweep up my sides, his fingers digging into the soft flesh of my body. I used to hate when my ex touched my stomach and sides. It made me self-conscious, uncomfortable.

This is altogether different. Maybe it's because Lee

grunts against my skin, leaving one breast behind to lave attention on the other like he'll starve if he doesn't taste me. Right now, I feel beautiful and desirable and free.

When I reach down to palm the rod between his legs, Lee catches my wrist in his hand, his fingers reaching around easily. "No," he growls, breath hot on my skin. "Not yet."

"Please," I pant.

He catches my other wrist and brings it over so he can clasp both in his huge hand, pinning me against the counter. I can't move. My wrists are manacled at my front, my retreat blocked at my back.

Normally, I'd hate this. I'd want to be able to move, to be free, to be in control. But as tension rises and falls inside me, I sink into the feeling of his hand around my wrists and his hot, hard body surrounding mine.

His lips brush my neck. "This okay?"

I nod.

"I want to hear you say it."

"It's...good," I pant, closing my eyes as he runs his tongue along my pulse. "I...like it." God, could I sound more stupid? I've forgotten all my words.

The button of my jeans releases in a soft whisper of fabric. Lee pauses, glancing down at his hands, then over at the pan of onions. He turns his gaze to me. "Do not move."

I give him a jerky nod. "Okay."

He moves to the sink and carefully, deliberately washes his hands, like I'm not standing here topless and panting beside him. Using a clean tea towel to dry himself, Lee finally turns to face me. His lids drop immediately, taking me in.

"You look good standing in my house."

"You mentioned that," I manage to say between breaths.

"I like seeing you here." He prowls toward me, standing a bare inch from me. His palm moves to my breast, unhesitant and possessive. I melt, arching into his touch. He grunts in response, tweaking my nipple between his thumb and forefinger. A dart of pleasure ripples down my stomach.

"Are you wet for me, Nora?" Lee's voice is deep and dangerous as he runs the backs of his fingers from my breast down my stomach.

When his fingers dip below the waistband of my jeans, I give him a jerky nod. "Yes."

He lifts his fingers and slides his palm over the outside of my clothes, over the space where I'm already hot and damp. The heel of his palm presses against me, and I have to grip the counter to stay steady, back arched toward him. Lee takes a step forward, crowding my space, his hand palming me like he owns me.

I fucking love it. I close my eyes and sink into the sensation of his hands on my body, the surety of his touch, the absolute confidence of him. He knows what to do with my body. Knows what I need to give up control.

When he kisses me this time, with his hand between my legs, I whimper against his lips. His other hand moves to the back of my head to angle me where he wants me, and I lose myself in the taste and feel of him.

"I want you," I gasp against his mouth.

"You'll get me, baby, but you have to come for me first." His clever fingers lower the zipper of my jeans before sliding beneath my panties. At the first touch of his finger against my bare flesh, I give a violent jerk.

Lee's forehead drops to my shoulder as he slips his

hand deeper, feeling exactly how wet I am. Embarrassingly wet. My ex would have recoiled. He didn't like it when—

"Hey." Lee pulls away, searching my face. The hand in my panties moves slowly back and forth along my slit, teasing. "Stay here."

I grip his biceps. "I'm here."

He watches me for a moment as his hand parts my flesh and delves deeper, finding that hard nub at the apex of my thighs. "You have no idea how many times I've thought of this in the past few weeks," he tells me, voice low and rough. "No idea, Nora."

I let out another whimper, widening my stance as his fingers start circling that bundle of nerves. This is—wow. This is very different from my vibrator. It's both more and less intense. I can't think.

"Have you thought about me?" He places a kiss on the corner of my lips. "Have you touched yourself at night, wishing it was my hand?"

I gulp down a breath, shaking from head to toe. Another kiss on the other corner of my lips, and I nod. "Yes."

"What did you think about?" His fingers slide down to my opening and penetrate me in one strong, steady movement.

I gasp.

"What did you think about, Nora? Did you put your fingers inside like this?" One pump. Two. Three.

I'm losing my mind. It's gone. Never coming back.

"Talk to me." Another kiss, this time on my earlobe, followed by the brush of his lips against the shell of my ear. His lips are so gentle, but his hand is rough and demanding between my legs.

He's waiting for an answer, and I don't have the brain power to come up with anything other than the truth. "I bought a vibrator," I finally say on an exhale. "Bought it the first week I worked for you."

A shudder and a groan, and Lee's fingers work deeper inside me. The palm of his hand presses against my bud as his chest rasps against my pebbled nipples, each sensation overwhelming and delicious and exactly what I need. There are no thoughts in my mind other than sensation, need, lust. My nails dig into his biceps as my hips rock, and then Lee's encouraging me with words and with his other hand on the curve of my ass, guiding me to ride his fingers right here in the kitchen.

Release hits me out of nowhere. I cry out as soft, dirty praise is whispered in my ear. I'm his good girl, coming so beautifully on his fingers. Doesn't it feel good to give him this? He's been waiting to hear the sounds I make. So fucking good. He bets I taste even better. Muscles clench deep inside as my legs turn to water, and then I'm being swept up in Lee's arms and carried to the living room. He sits down on the sofa and arranges me on his lap so I'm straddling him, boneless against his chest.

Warm hands stroke my back as I come back to myself, head tucked into the crook of his neck. "Wow," I breathe.

A warm chuckle is the response I get, along with a throb from the area below his belt. I wiggle against him, wanting to burrow closer, under his skin, until all I feel is Lee.

"I didn't know it could be like that." I don't realize I've said the words out loud until I feel Lee freeze beneath me. His hands pause on their journeys up and down my back, and he shifts to pull his head away to look at me.

Heat creeps up my neck as I sit up, ignoring the contact

that causes between us down below. I put my hands on his shoulders and stare at his chin until Lee touches my face to bring my gaze up to his.

"You haven't been treated well, have you?" he asks quietly, searching my face. He's so calm while his cock is so insistently hard between us. It makes no sense, but it makes me feel warm and cherished, somehow. His thumb coasts along my cheekbone, a delicate caress.

Words stick to the roof of my mouth. I shrug one shoulder, letting my gaze slide away. Slight pressure on my cheek brings it back and we stare at each other until I'm able to speak. "I've never really enjoyed...sex. Physical intimacy. Any of it." I let out a huff. "This is probably going to give you an inflated ego."

"Can't get any worse than it already is." Lee's lips twitch, amusement dancing in his eyes. "Seeing you come the way you just did made me feel like the damn man."

I laugh. Words push at my lips, wanting to come out. What is it about this man that makes me want to spill my guts? Before I can stop them, I tell him the truth. "I haven't enjoyed sex since I was in my early twenties. After my marriage ended, I tried, but I just...it never felt right. I thought that part of me was broken or gone or something. I figured I was just getting old."

Lee's face is serious, brows drawing together. His thumb keeps at its gentle perusal of my facial bones while his other hand starts exploring the skin at my hip, my waist, my ribs, all the way up to my breast. "Nothing about you is broken," he tells me, no hint of humor anywhere on him. "You hear me? Nothing, Nora. You're a beautiful woman. Smart. Funny." He lets out a snort, shaking his head. "I wonder what goes on in that head of yours. What you'd think if you saw yourself the way I see you."

"You wouldn't want to be in there." I touch my temple. "It's a scary place."

His hand kneads my breast, the other palm still resting against my cheek. With every touch, heat winds through my core, wrapping tighter around me. A deep, aching emptiness opens inside me and I let my hips roll over Lee's body.

He groans, eyelids fluttering. "Nora."

I think I'm addicted to this man. I've probably been on my way to full-blown overdose since the day I saw him leaning against my apartment building wall all those months ago. He frees me from the shackles of my mind. When I'm with Lee, I'm not someone who's insecure and sexless, who needs to control every aspect of her life. I'm a creature made of want. Of need.

And right now, I need him like I've never needed anyone before.

His belt buckle gives me no resistance. As the backs of my knuckles brush the erection pressing hard against the placket of his zipper, my breath comes in short, sharp gasps. I slide off his legs and stand between his spread knees to pull the zipper down. I need to take all these clothes off.

Lee beats me to it. His hands hook into the waistband of my own jeans, which are still gaping open. He tugs them down and I kick them away, standing completely naked in front of him. A groan rips through his throat as his hands circle my body, kneading my ass as he brings his lips to my skin.

Kisses and bites all along my hips make me tremble. I

cling onto his shoulders, turning to putty in his hands. Lee grabs my leg and props it on his thigh, opening me up to him. As he sits on the sofa in front of me, I stand in the cage of his spread legs, his arms still wrapped around me, my body naked and open to him.

Then he brings his mouth to my center, and we both let out low groans. Pleasure jolts through me, lightning in my veins. His clever tongue teases my bud as I tremble before him.

"Please..." I grip his hair, and I don't know if I'm pulling him closer or pulling away.

"You taste like honey and roses," he growls, pulling me closer for another lick. "So fucking good."

"I want you." It's a breathless statement that slips through my lips without me noticing.

"You have me, Nora." His hands knead my ass, mouth devouring me. Then, without warning, I'm flipped on my back along the length of the sofa. Lee stands, pushing his jeans down and stepping out of them without taking his eyes off me.

His erection juts out, and it's enormous. My mouth waters. When a big fist wraps around that hard flesh, pumping once, twice, my body reacts by clenching hard.

"You look so fucking hot right now," he tells me, eyes dark, hand working faster on his cock.

I'm a beast of pure desire. Without my conscious permission, my body sits up and my lips part to taste the tip of him, that bead of salty liquid that's already seeping out. My hands splay along his hips, feeling the sparse, coarse hair that covers the top of his thighs. As soon as my lips touch his cock, he lets out a low groan.

"Wrap those lips around my cock, baby. I want that lipstick smeared all over your pretty face."

His deep, guttural words make the muscles between my legs clench so hard I nearly orgasm just like that. Without any physical contact whatsoever. I take him as deep as I can, hot and hard as he invades my mouth.

It's a shock to the senses. I shouldn't be enjoying this. Or maybe I should, and all those other times in my life were wrong. Maybe this is exactly how it's supposed to feel —like every groan and twitch from him is a gift I've given him. Like I'm powerful and sexual and I'm bringing this mountain of a man down with nothing other than my mouth. I suck and lick without thought, without worry, just because I want to.

I don't even know myself anymore.

An animal grunt is the only warning I get before Lee pulls away, pushing me back down to lie on the sofa. He hunts through the pockets in his jeans, finally pulling out his wallet. He opens it and money falls out, ignored. A foil packet appears between his fingers, and it's with practiced, efficient movements that he tears it open and rolls it onto his cock.

He kneels between my spread thighs, running a rough hand up to the juncture where I'm wet and hot for him. He pushes his thumb inside me then pulls it out and brings it to his lips with a groan.

This is unlike any sex I've had before. It's not a hurried coupling where the main goal is the man getting off. It's not painful or awkward or uncomfortable. Everything this man does tells me he cherishes me, all the way down to the way I taste.

"I'm going to fuck you now," he informs me, his voice rough as sandpaper. "That okay?"

Please. "Yes."

A rough tug with arms wrapped around my thighs, and I'm positioned where he wants me. My leg gets propped up on the back of the sofa while the other stays cradled in his elbow. Then, with sweat beading on his brow, Lee pushes inside me.

My body grows taut, arching into the feeling. It's... I'm... I gasp, then let out a surprised laugh, then gasp again when he hits bottom. Fills me up so perfectly I could cry.

"Okay?" His voice grates, like he can barely speak. His eyes are black as ink, every muscle in his body stark and hard.

"More than okay," I reply on a whoosh of breath. "Please. More."

Not one to waste any time, Lee starts moving inside me. Powerful. Indomitable. Relentless. Our bodies find a rhythm of slapping flesh and panted breath. He moves my legs where he needs them, grips my waist, and arches my back to get impossibly deeper. I let him. I want it. I want to give this up to him, to let go of the hold I have on myself and hand the reins over to someone who knows what to do with them.

I'm losing control, and I love every minute of it. I'm a doll in his arms, completely at his mercy.

The orgasm that tears through me nearly rips me apart. It happens the minute his fingers reach between us, finding that perfect spot to tease, always making sure I feel good. This man doesn't just take pleasure. He gives it. I fly apart, crying out as my body explodes in a flash of brilliant light.

"So beautiful," he grates out with a thrust that sends another spear of pleasure through me. "So fucking perfect."

When he finds release, I feel it. It turns me on like nothing before. I watch his eyes go sightless and his skin grow red, feral grunts escaping his clenched teeth. It shouldn't be hot. Honestly, it really shouldn't. But watching him orgasm while inside me is the sexiest thing I've seen in my whole damn life.

We collapse, panting, and I remain shattered in a million pieces for a long, long while. It's not until Lee gets up to deal with the condom that I take my first full breath, and realize that things will never, ever go back to the way they were.

And then my lips curl, because Lee comes back, gathers me in his arms, and hugs me to his chest right there on the sofa.

Things won't go back to the way they were—and I don't want them to.

27

SIMONE

It takes about four milliseconds to figure out what Nora and Lee got up to yesterday based on the looks on their faces when they walk into Four Cups on Sunday morning. They both look wrecked, like they've gotten no sleep, but deeply, deeply pleased.

Which I'm sure they are. I meet Candice's gaze across the café and a slow smile spreads across her lips.

Good for Nora. She deserves a decent man.

Lee has his hand on her lower back, scanning the space like he's ready to tear the head off anyone who challenges him. Men are truly ridiculous.

Dorothy, who's sitting beside me at one of the tables at the back of the café, arches her brows as she looks across the café at them. "Just *wait* until Lottie sees this. She's on her way down but she's going to hate that she missed *that* entrance."

I grin. "I'm sure you'll give her the play-by-play."

"Bold of them to saunter in here looking like that," Dorothy adds with a whistle. "Oh, to be young."

Candice sidles up beside me as the couple makes their way across. "You think it finally happened last night?"

"No doubt about it," Dorothy cuts in.

I laugh. "Have to say, I agree with Dor."

Candice giggles, dropping off our coffees as Jen emerges from the kitchen. She makes a beeline toward Nora, plate in hand, completely ignoring Lee.

"Nora," she says. "You were right." She lifts the plate to show a thin slice of cake. "Lemon with a raspberry swirl filling. Taste."

Nora blinks, then nods and does as she's told. Her eyes roll back in her head as she tastes Jen's newest creation. "That's incredible."

"I owe you one. Fallon said he'd cancel the wedding if I kept stressing about the cake."

"I'm sure he was joking."

Jen inspects a crumb of her cake with a critical eye. "I didn't want to take any chances. Hi Lee." She nods, finally acknowledging the man's existence, then turns around and heads back to the kitchen.

I laugh, leaning back in my chair. I love these people. Nora sees me and gives me a little wave, then orders her coffee before heading over. Lee lingers close, like he's afraid to let her get farther than touching-distance away. Cute. And ridiculous.

"Looks like you two had an eventful night," I say, unable to resist wiggling my eyebrows.

"I have no idea what you're talking about," Nora says primly.

Lee just stands beside her looking like the personification of male satisfaction. A lion who just finished a nice, big meal.

"Took you long enough," Dorothy says. "Oh! Lottie! Lee and Nora finally had sex." She lowers her glasses and looks at the two of them. "More than once, I'd say."

The other woman enters the coffee shop and lets out a whoop. "Finally! Took you long enough!"

Nora's skin turns red from the tips of her ears down to the neckline of her shirt. She puts her hands on her hips and stares me square in the eyes. "If any of you ladies start quizzing me on the size of Lee's penis, I will *not* be answering."

Lee finally snaps out of his post-coital daze to frown at Nora's words. "Wait. What?"

"Oh, never mind those details," Dorothy says with a wave of her hand. "Motion of the ocean and all that. Does Prisha know? Should we call her?"

"If you call my mother to tell her about my sex life, I will never speak to you again." Nora levels a glare at Dorothy, then swings it to Lottie and finally to me.

I blink at her, the picture of cherubic innocence. Or at least that's the look I'm going for. Judging by the arch in Nora's eyebrows, I'm not sure I quite nail it.

Oh well.

"So. Tell us. What happened at the wedding? Was it gaudy and awful? Did the newlyweds make a fool of themselves?" Lottie plucks a cookie from a plate in the center of the table and glances at Nora and Lee. "I've been dying to know. That Roger fellow gives me the willies."

Dorothy nods. "He's been good for Heart's Cove, but I wouldn't be surprised to hear he's skimming from the town coffers."

I kick a chair in Nora's direction, and she sits down. Lee takes the seat next to her and drapes his arm across the back of her chair. I try to keep the smile off my lips, but I'm just happy to see these two together. What can I say? I'm a sucker for a good love story. Now that Wes and I have our happily-ever-after, I have to get my kicks *somewhere*, don't I?

"So? The wedding?" Lottie leans forward. "Was it awful?"

Nora lets out a disappointed sigh. "Unfortunately, it was beautiful. I can't complain about it. Tasteful and elegant."

Lee grunts. "She's right. As far as weddings go, it wasn't bad."

Dorothy and Lottie exchange a glance, then sit back, surprised. I meet Nora's gaze, but her eyes slide away from mine.

Ha!

She thinks she can avoid the inquisition from the Girl Squad. But Candice is hovering, and Fiona just walked through the door. Even Jen will find us when it's time to get all the details from last night.

Nora will learn. She's our friend now. She can't escape us.

Especially not when she just bagged the last available Blair brother.

28

LEE

THE LAST THING I expected to do on Sunday morning after the best night of my life was sit around a table with a pack of cackling women. When Sebastian Finch walks through the door to the café, it's almost a relief to get up and cross the space to shake his hand.

"Any updates on the festival approvals?" he asks after we exchange the usual pleasantries.

"Still waiting," I reply, knowing not to trust Roger until the last T is crossed and the last I is dotted. "Feeling confident it'll come through, though. Will you still be able to deliver a couple of installations for the walking tour?"

"My new workshop is set up and operational. Shouldn't be a problem." His eyes scan the space, lingering on the table where Nora and Simone sit, then move away to the other patrons in the café. He's looking for someone.

"Rudy found you a space?" I ask after he orders coffee.

Sebastian grunts. "Warehouse across from a garage. I've seen you there working on your bike. Meant to walk over and say hello."

"Remy's place?"

The sound of a small engine cuts through our conversation, and Sebastian's eyes cut to the noise. We turn to the windows in time to see Georgia on her bright-red scooter, pulling up to the café. She dismounts, removes her helmet, and marches inside. When she sees Sebastian, she freezes. Then, visibly gathering herself, she approaches the front counter.

"You're later than usual this morning, woman," Sebastian drawls.

Georgia lifts a finger. "We're not doing that." Annoyance is written on every line of her face. "You're not calling me woman. Nope." She stops in front of him and arches a brow. "And are you keeping track of the time I get coffee every morning?"

Some silent conversation happens between them. Georgia's eyes narrow, then she huffs and sweeps past him.

Before I can ask him what happened there, Nora's hand appears at my elbow. "Want to get out of here?" she asks quietly. "I got my fix." She lifts her coffee cup. "Thinking I might like to enjoy the rest of my Sunday somewhere more...private."

My cock is hard in an instant. I'm like a damn teenager around this woman. I curl my hand around her shoulders and lead her to the door. "Sounds good to me, Nora. You know, my bedroom is nice and private."

A grin. "You read my mind."

AFTER A WEEKEND like the one I had, I almost expect Monday morning to feel different. In two short days, I managed to keep Roger happy, realize I'm over my ex-fiancée, and take the most beautiful woman in the world to bed for two whole nights.

But I walk into the office and there's paperwork waiting for me, emails to respond to, and an entire festival to plan in less than two weeks' time.

The rest of the team filters in, exchanging greetings, talking about their weekends, and sipping fresh coffees. Nora's the last to get here, which isn't surprising since she had to go home this morning to get showered and changed —and we woke up late and had a few, um, distractions before we could get going. She meets my gaze across the cubicles and through the glass of my office, a faint flush on her cheeks.

A notification pulls my gaze away, and I'm half-surprised to see Roger was true to his word. I forward the approvals on to the whole team, then walk out of the office with a triumphant smile. "Green light, people. We'd better get to work."

Cheers fill the space. Olivia claps. Nora beams. Rick laughs. Our junior intern, David, looks like he's about to cry. Then a buzz of excitement fills the space as plans are put in action. We filter into the conference room for a much-needed meeting.

We have only two weeks to finalize the plans for the festival. Roger didn't do us any favors by waiting so long, but then again, what more could I expect from him? The man walked off with my fiancée without even a word of apology.

"I'm going to get the magazines and the walking tour maps printed today. Everything's ready. Sebastian confirmed he can do two sculptures?" Nora looks up from her notebook to meet my gaze.

I nod. "Spoke to him yesterday. He'd like to take a look at the sites before doing the final setup."

Her lips twitch, and I know she's remembering what else we did yesterday. "Good."

Rick clears his throat. "The tables and tents are ready, and I've got deposits from every artist and business owner who wants to rent a booth. The main stage gear is still in transit, but I'll follow up with the company to make sure they can deliver it on time. We've hired the same company as last year to do the setup and takedown."

Ted pipes up and says, "The headliner band has confirmed. All the acts are lined up."

"Good." I nod.

"I just got an email this morning about T-shirts for the volunteers," Olivia adds. "We're expecting the delivery tomorrow, and we can start distributing them next week. I have almost all the paperwork for the volunteers, just waiting on a couple of release form signatures for some of the ushers we're going to put at the entrances."

Item by item, we go through the list of everything we need to put together in the last two weeks. It's like a dam breaking now that the approvals are in hand. We can finally get to work and bring this festival together.

The entire team stays late. When I finally turn off the office lights and head home, night has fallen. It's not until after nine o'clock at night that my doorbell rings. I open it, grab Nora, tug her inside, and crush my lips to hers.

"I've been starved for you," I say against her lips.

"Work definitely feels different after what happened this weekend."

I grin, then kiss her once more. She pulls away and

stares into my eyes, something written in her gaze that I can't read.

"What?" My hands slide down to shape her curves.

"I'm...happy."

My heart lurches. I lean my forehead against hers, inhaling the scent of her skin. "Me too," I say, pressing my lips to her eyelids. "Now kiss me."

A laugh, and she's doing exactly that. From there, our clothes vanish, and I'm inside her before we can move any closer to the bedroom. We take our pleasure right there on the hallway floor.

Later, when Nora is asleep on my chest in bed, I stare at the ceiling and wonder how I got to be so lucky. This woman just fell into my lap like a gift from the heavens. I was so stuck in the mire of my mind, so caught up in my own wounds, that it took her to yank me out of it.

And now she's here, soft and sweet and lightly snoring against my skin. Her fingertips curl against my chest, and I take them in my hand to kiss her knuckles one by one. My heart grows in my chest and I realize I love this woman. Love her like I've never loved anyone before. My feelings for her are a deep, deep river that looks placid on the surface but hides a rushing current beneath. Unstoppable.

I hold her tighter, kissing the dark strands of her hair until she sighs against me. "What's wrong?"

"Nothing," I tell her. "Go back to sleep."

She snuffles, an adorable noise, and is asleep in an instant. I run my hands over her body, rocked by my own emotions.

I survived my mother abandoning me as a child. I had my brother and my father, and we became inseparable. Drea leaving nearly killed me, but it would be a surface wound compared to what Nora could do to me if she walked away. This woman has inked herself on my skin like a tattoo that will never fade. She's carved herself into my bones. Maybe her name was always there, but it just took me four decades to learn to read it.

Never will I ever let her go. It's a silent oath I utter to myself before I fall asleep.

29

NORA

A MASS of wrought iron and old timber rises up from the middle of a patch of grass, all smooth curves and harsh materials. It's abstract, with the wood and metal curving around each other like splashes of water.

Sebastian Finch stands with his thumbs hooked into the belt loops of his faded jeans. "So?" He glances at me. "What do you think?"

I expel a puff of air. "How did you manage to manipulate the materials like this?" My eyes coast along the smooth curves and intricate joining. "It's breathtaking."

A grunt from the back of his throat. "Divorce was good for somethin', at least. Got all this scrap metal, a whole bunch of free time, and a serving of bitterness to use as inspiration."

I blink at the artist, shaking my head. "Honestly, Sebastian, I feel honored to have this in town. It belongs in a contemporary art museum."

"She's right," Lee says beside me. "Thank you for

contributing this to the Fringe Festival, Sebastian. Everyone who drives into town will slow down to look."

Faint pink blooms over his cheeks, and he clears his throat with a rough noise. "All right, then." He nods, pushing the brim of his hat up to scratch his forehead, then motions to the pickup. "Want to see the other one?"

"Can't wait."

I squeeze in between the two men on the front bench seat of Sebastian's old truck, and we drive over to Cove Boulevard. On the far end of the street is the new community garden that Dorothy and Margaret started last year. The plain wooden archway entrance has been removed and replaced with another of Sebastian's creations. Metal swoops and twists like two delicate waves meeting at the apex.

I sigh, shaking my head. "You're truly talented."

"That one's a donation," Sebastian grunts, leaning his forearms on the worn steering wheel. "Dorothy just about squeezed the life outta me when I told her it could stay."

Lee chuckles, his leg pressing into mine. "Sounds like Dorothy."

"Death by leopard print," Sebastian adds.

I giggle, then nudge Lee with my elbow. "I want to get a closer look."

We slide out of the vehicle and approach the arch. True to Sebastian's style, reclaimed wood is interwoven with the metal. Delicate leaves are carved, some half-wood and half-metal, creeping up the sculpture like vines. The whole thing is an ode to nature. Harsh, brutal, and somehow delicate and beautiful all at once.

"Okay," I say, remembering the camera hanging around my neck. "We'll get one of you next to the arch." I wave my hands to get Sebastian to move closer, then check the sun and position myself to take a photo.

Truthfully, we should hire a professional photographer. But the Fringe Fest budget is microscopic, and I'm not exactly mad about having more than one responsibility on the team. One of the things I hated about my old job was being pigeon-holed in my role. Content was handed over to me without consultation, and all I was allowed to think about was fonts and layouts.

Now, I get to be part of the entire process, from start to finish.

It's just one of the many things in my life that has suddenly blossomed into something beautiful. Like the weather around me, my entire being is being warmed by the sun, coaxed to life by the approaching summer. Finally, after four decades, I'm blooming.

It's not just my career, either. In seven days, I'll get the keys to my new house. I've been aggressively paying down my debt with Lee, and I should be able to wipe it clean by November. Most of the motorcycles are repaired already, a fact I learned at my last visit to Hamish's bar. None of the bikers held a grudge. Ted—the Hulk—even gave me a hug last time I was at The Grove.

And then there's Lee.

The physical part of our relationship is so new, but in a way, it's intensely familiar. All those weeks that we spent holding back allowed me to get comfortable with the idea of him—the idea of sharing this much of myself with another man. I've jumped on my mental motorcycle and given up control.

And it feels *good*.

More than good. It feels like living for the first time in my life.

Everything is falling into place. Three days after I take possession of my house, the Fringe Fest will begin, and I'll get to see the fruits of my team's hard work.

I check the camera's viewfinder and flick through the photos I've taken. Lee's bulk warms my side and back as he stares over my shoulder, grunting appreciatively. "One of those is a cover shot," he says, breath ruffling my hair.

Even though we're at work, everything inside me tightens. I can't help it. Serves me right for hooking up with my boss. Now every minute of the day is like being strummed like a guitar.

Still, I smile and go back to my favorite photo, where Sebastian has a booted foot leaning against a raised planter box, his gaze directed to the side. "This one."

Lee's hand slides along my lower back. "You're a woman of many talents, Nora Richter." The rumble in his words makes heat unfurl between my legs. My panties grow damp and I squeeze my thighs together in quick, violent clenches.

"We're at work," I say in a barely-there whisper.

His hand slides down a couple of inches, teasing the curve of my ass. "Shame."

This man will be the death of me. I'm not built for this kind of pleasure. My body can't withstand such violent sensations. Every time he touches me, I'm intensely aware of the path his fingers take, the distance between our bodies, the rough scrape of my clothes against my over-sensitized skin.

But what a sweet death it will be when I finally go over the edge.

I look up at Sebastian and nod. "We got everything we

need. Are you staying in town for the festival, or will you be heading back down to Texas?"

The sound of a small engine roars in the distance, and Georgia appears at the end of the road, riding her little red scooter. We all turn toward the sound, watching her dress flutter around her legs as she passes us and pulls into a spot in front of the Four Cups Café.

Sebastian clears his throat. "Think I'll stay," he says, then touches the brim of his hat and saunters toward his truck. His eyes linger on Georgia's scooter, then he hauls himself into the cab and drives off in the opposite direction.

Interesting.

I can't hide my grin. Now I understand why the girls were so giddy and pleased when they saw me with Lee. There's just something about watching two people circle around each other, obviously interested, that makes butterflies explode in my stomach.

Before I moved to this town, I thought I was too old for these feelings. I'd written myself off. I'd tried a serious relationship, it didn't work out, and I was ready to just lie down and wait for old age. The idea of being giddy about *anything* was so foreign, it might as well have been an alien language. I didn't get giddy, or excited, or enthusiastic. I just worked my boring, stable job, updated my financial spreadsheets, and took zero risks whatsoever.

I don't even recognize that woman anymore.

Now, life is laid out at my feet like a tantalizing adventure. One step forward, and I fall into bed with Lee. Another step, and I'm moving into a house of my own. Another, I'm getting a dog. My brain offers up all the financial disasters that could happen as a result of any of those choices, but I find I'm able to push past the discomfort. Whatever happens, I'll survive. And I might even thrive.

I *believe* in myself.

It's a heady, addictive feeling. I've been keeping myself in a tightly bound box of rigid control. I've been leashing myself, accepting less than I should.

Even my marriage to Eric was settling for less. I knew he wasn't as ambitious as I was. I knew he was lazy to his core. But I guess I thought... Maybe I thought that was all I deserved.

Not anymore.

I lift my gaze to the man beside me, tracing his blade-sharp jaw and his slightly crooked nose.

He meets my gaze, curling his lips in a rakish grin. "You're looking at me like I just hung the moon." His fingers touch my chin, tilting it up so he can press a kiss to my lips. "A man could get used to being stared at like that."

I duck my head, blushing furiously. "It's business hours," I hiss a bit too aggressively as my body comes to attention. "And we're in public."

"I don't give a fuck where we are, Nora," he says, catching my fingers in his. "You looked like you needed to be kissed."

"We should go back to the office. There's lots to do before next weekend."

Lee doesn't let go of my hand. He just wraps it in his much larger one and turns in the direction of the Fringe Festival offices. A comfortable silence stretches as we walk, hand-in-hand, proclaiming our relationship to all of Heart's Cove. I swear curtains twitch as we walk past. When we get to the Heart's Cove Hotel, Dorothy is outside with garden shears, trimming one of the hedges. She looks at our hands, then our faces, and a slow smile spreads over her lips.

When she reaches for her phone, I let out a low groan. All of Heart's Cove will know we were walking hand-in-hand, even Dorothy's archnemesis, Agnes. Their feud doesn't stop them gossiping like magpies.

Lee just laughs.

We walk on, until I can sense that Lee wants to speak. I feel it in the subtle tension in his hand, and the way his breath grows shallower with every step. When I glance at his face, his jaw is diamond hard.

"You okay?"

He glances down at me and lets out a rush of breath. "Yeah." He gulps. "I was just thinking... I was wondering..." He shakes his head in a violent, animal move, like a dog shaking water from its fur. "There's an opening ceremony on the first night of the Fringe Festival. I usually make a speech right before the headlining band comes on stage. We present a plaque to the featured artist. This year it's Sebastian. I was just thinking that I'd like for you to be there with me. We could open the festival together—you could hand him the award."

My heart stutters. "You want me on stage with you?"

I visualize myself up there, on the temporary stage that will block off one end of Cove Boulevard for a week. All of Heart's Cove—and an influx of tourists and festivalgoers—will be watching. They'll see me beside Lee in a place of honor.

I know it's work, and I know I'm part of the team, but something about the way Lee asked me makes me think it means more. Like he wants me up there beside him because I'm *me*. Because he wants to show me off to everyone who will listen, to tell the whole world that we're a unit.

And isn't that the most beautiful, terrifying, exhilarating thought I've had in a long time?

"It would mean a lot to me if you stood there with me, Nora," he finally says. "I'm just a barbarian male, because I find myself wanting to stake my claim on you in front of anyone who will listen."

Another stumble from the organ in my chest. A part of me thinks I should be insulted at his word choice—no one stakes a claim on me. I'm independent and strong and I belong to no one but myself. Hell, I'm only learning what that means after decades of hiding under the illusion of control.

But I can't deny that another part of me wants to belong to him. Wants to stand up beside Lee and stake my claim on him too.

A niggling worry pokes its head above the blossoming ground in my mind, whispering that I'm making a mistake. I'm opening myself up too fast. The consequences of my throwing myself headlong into this relationship with Lee will be disastrous.

I take a big rubber mallet and whack that mole right back into the ground.

"Of course I'll open the Fringe Fest with you," I finally say, throat tight. "I'd be honored."

30

LEE

THE WEEKS LEADING up to the Fringe Festival are always hectic and exhilarating. This year is no exception. With the late approvals from City Hall and the new walking art exhibits around town, there's extra pressure to put everything together.

But our small team is worth its weight in gold, and as the days slip from one to the next, a familiar hum of excitement builds inside me.

All the while, Nora is by my side.

In the office, we keep things professional, but I refuse to hide what she is to me. In any case, even if we wanted to keep our new relationship quiet, the Heart's Cove game of telephone has already reached everyone within a twenty-mile radius. Nora and I are officially an item.

About fucking time.

No man has ever been prouder than me to have a woman on his arm. I take her out on the bike every chance I get, wine her and dine her and take her to bed. I can't get enough of the taste of her, the feel of her skin against mine, the hot, wet clench of her core around me.

She's the hottest woman I've ever been with. No question. Everything about her attracts me, from the red, glossy lips to the lush curves to the frown lines between her brows when she stares at her computer screen. I love the way she tilts her head up to the sky and breathes in deep whenever we're outside. With every day that passes, she seems to unwind a little bit. Let go of that stranglehold she held herself in.

Control is still a big thing with her. She likes to drive herself places when we aren't riding the bike. She likes to send weekly summaries of her debt, including spreadsheets and graphs. Her work on the Fringe Fest magazine is precise, professional, exact.

But when I get her alone, I'm the lucky man who gets to watch her let go. I get to watch her eyes go sightless as she screams my name. I get to pin her arms above her head and feel her soften, like she's been dying to feel the weight of me on top of her. It's a gift, and I'm not going to waste it.

Being up on stage beside her as we officially open the Fringe Fest is significant to me. When she agreed to stand beside me, it felt like one last burl smoothing in the center of my chest. She won't leave me hanging, standing in front of all my family and friends. It's not a wedding, but it's a public declaration nonetheless. Nora and me, together.

A knock on my office door makes me look up from my computer. Nora's in the doorway, looking gorgeous and edible. With the weather warming, she's opted for a sleeveless white top with a high neck that hugs every curve, tucked into a navy skirt. A necklace glints against the white fabric, and her hair is in some sort of half-up,

half-down style that looks innocent and sensual all at
once.

"Hey," I say, my lips curving.

"Hey yourself," she replies. "Olivia just left, she said
she'd be in early tomorrow to start distributing the flyers to
local businesses. I told her it was fine to leave."

I glance at the empty office beyond my office glass,
surprised to see it dark. "I hadn't realized it was so late."

"Time flies," Nora says with a smile. She sucks in a
breath, wringing her hands. "Lee, I..."

I frown. "What is it?"

"Well, see, I'm supposed to meet Rudy tonight to pick
up the keys, and..." She bites her lip, looking at me through
her lashes. "Do you...want to come?"

Warmth spreads through my chest so fast I'm knocked
back in my chair. I swallow past a lump in my throat,
staring at the beautiful woman before me. "You want me
there when you walk into your new house?"

She nods, flushing slightly. "Yeah. If you're busy, it's
fine, I—"

Crossing the distance between us, I band an arm
around her back and crush her to my chest. "I want to be
there."

She smiles, red lips parting to reveal white teeth. "Good.
Thank you."

Resisting the urge to kiss Nora right now would be like
trying hold back a tsunami with my bare hands. I can't, and
I'm not even going to try. I cup her cheek in my hand and
brings my lips to hers.

With a soft sigh she parts for me, accepting my kiss like
it's water and she's been walking through the desert for
days. Melting into my body, she wraps her arms around my

neck. I feel the moment she lets go—that second when that last barrier falls as it always does between us. When she becomes mine, body and soul.

Walking her back toward my desk, I let out a low growl as I run my hands down her sides. "You look so damn hot right now, Nora." My hands slide around to her ass, taking two generous handfuls like they're my due.

I'll never get sick of this woman. Not as long as I live.

She smiles against my lips, nipping and kissing and licking at me in little sips. The woman drives me insane with need.

"We should stop," she mumbles, teeth dragging along my lower lip. "I have an appointment."

"We will," I reply, pushing her against my desk. "We'll stop in a minute."

"Okay," she sighs, arching into my touch. "In a minute."

But a minute later, I'm lifting her up onto the desk and standing between her knees. I'm reaching between her legs, along the smooth, bare skin of her inner thighs to the sweet, wet place where they meet.

"Anyone could walk in," she gasps when I push her panties aside. "Your office is made of glass."

"The cleaners won't come for hours, and everyone else has gone home."

My fingers delve into her folds, circling her clit. She lets out these addictive, breathy little moans. Her legs climb up my sides, ankles crossed behind me. When I reach lower and sink two fingers inside, we both release low moans.

"You feel so damn good, Nora," I breathe, curling my fingers slightly just the way she likes.

I'm rewarded with a trembling in her limbs and the sharp bite of her nails on my shoulders. "This is so bad."

"You want me to stop?"

"God, no." Her hips grind against my hand as she clings onto my shoulders, wrapped around me like she never wants to let go.

And I never want her to.

"Eyes, Nora. Give me your eyes." I work another finger inside, cock rock hard behind my fly. Half-lidded eyes meet mine, and I grin. "I love the way you look when I'm inside you."

"Yeah?" Her voice is a wisp of smoke.

"Yeah. Like you can't think straight."

"That would be correct," she breathes, arching her back. Her hands slide down to my pants and she palms me roughly, pulling a groan from my throat. "I need you. Please. Now."

With one glance through the windows to make sure we're still alone, I put an inch of space between us, find a condom in my wallet, free my cock, and sheathe it. Nora watches me through dark, dark eyes, and I think I could come just from her looking at me like that.

A growl rides my throat and I pull her roughly to the edge of the desk, stepping between her legs once more. She gasps, clinging onto the edge and falling onto her elbows. We're both fully clothed, but it doesn't matter. With my pants open and her panties shoved to the side, I push inside her with one hard thrust.

We both pause, panting. I meet her gaze and fall down on top of her, letting my forehead touch hers. "I'll never get over how good you feel," I say, driving into her again and again.

"I hope not," she says with a gasping laugh. "I think I'm addicted to you."

"It's mutual, babe." I grip her hips and we both let go. Right there on my desk, I fuck this woman hot and dirty and rough, and she gives me the gift of coming on my cock. When my orgasm hits, I see stars. I gasp into the crook of her neck, my mouth forming words that I haven't spoken to a woman in a long time.

I love you.

My lips shape the words against her skin, but there's no sound. I just hold her as we both tremble, taking long moments to recover. By the time I pull away from her, the words stick to my throat like glue. It's crazy to feel this way about a woman I met mere months ago, right?

Nora straightens her clothes and blots her face with a tissue. "Well," she says. "That was the most inappropriate thing I've ever done in the workplace."

I laugh, tucking her against my chest. "Let's go do a lot of inappropriate things in your new house."

I feel her smile against me. "Sounds like a plan."

31

NORA

MY NEW HOUSE IS AMAZING, and more importantly, it's *mine*. As soon as I walk through the door, I feel like my feet have left the ground. I'm floating through space, so happy I could cry.

Weekend projects pop up everywhere I look. A wall I'll paint a punchy color. A carpet I'll replace. A nook I'll install shelves in. Every step that takes me deeper into the house is an unfurling of all my deepest desires.

To have a home. To move forward. To take a risk—and have it pay off.

Rudy left after congratulating me and giving me the keys, and I'm glad to have this moment alone with Lee.

Body still buzzing from what happened in the office, I walk along the length of the central hallway to the back of the house. Lee follows close behind, his big body silent on my wooden floors. When I stop in front of the sliding glass doors and gaze out at the huge backyard, his hands slide over my hips and his chin comes to rest on top of my head.

I point at the lawn. "That's for the dog."

"The dog?" I can hear the smile in his voice.

"I told you. I'm getting a dog. I've been looking at rescues for weeks. But if you're a cat person, this might not work out between us."

"I've never had a pet," he admits.

I turn my head to look up at him, shocked. "Not even a fish?"

He shakes his head. "Nope."

"That's so sad. My dad loved animals. When our dog died, it was the only time I saw him cry."

Lee's hands tighten around me. "Did you get another dog after that?"

I shake my head. "My dad passed about two years later, and neither my mom or me or Fallon were in any shape to take care of a pet."

"But now you are," he says, wrapping himself around me so all I feel is his warmth.

"Now I am," I agree quietly, gazing out at the huge green space. They key in my hand bites against my palm as I squeeze it, heart so full it could burst. "I'm glad you're here with me," I say to break the heavy silence between us. "It would have felt different to walk through that door alone. Still amazing, but different."

A soft kiss on the crown of my head. "Wouldn't miss it for the world."

A little while later, we christen the kitchen counter. When we're sated and panting, my lips curl against Lee's skin. This house is more than a new beginning. It's a rebirth.

. . .

I SLEEP at Lee's house that night. With the Fringe Festival starting in two days and my lease on the apartment not up for a couple of weeks, I decide to postpone moving in until the festival is over. It's not ideal, but it's the practical thing to do.

The day before the festival is hectic. We have dozens of vendors and artists trying to get set up, road closures to put into effect, and a huge stage and a few marquis tents to install. Accommodation in town is already fully booked, and the influx of tourists gives Heart's Cove a vibrant buzz of energy.

"You still good with standing on stage next to me?" Lee asks as we watch the workers set up the big stage and sound equipment.

I glance over at him and nudge him with my shoulder. "Of course. As long as you're not going to spring some sort of speech on me at the last minute."

"You'll just have to hand Sebastian his plaque. No speaking necessary."

I grin, nodding. "Fine, then."

Someone calls him away to organize a pack of volunteers that don't know what to do, and I find myself angling for the Four Cups Café. There's a tent set up on the sidewalk outside the café, and the four owners—Fiona, Simone, Candice, and Jen—are in deep discussion about the decorative flower arrangements.

"Nora!" Simone spreads her arms toward me. "Help us decide. Do we line the flowers up neat and tidy, or do we go with a whimsical look?"

"Whimsical, for sure," I answer, casting an eye over their supplies. "Are you planning on wrapping the tent poles with that fabric?"

Fiona nods. "Yep. We're going for welcoming oasis full of coffee and pastries."

I smile. "It's going to look amazing."

Simone hands me a bolt of fabric and asks me to help her drape it. We work well together, and for the millionth time since I moved to Heart's Cove, I feel part of something bigger.

"Will you be watching the opening ceremony, Nora?" Fiona asks as she adjusts a planter box two inches to the left on one corner of the tent.

I nod, grabbing another piece of fabric with Simone to start wrapping the metal pole beside the planter box. "Yeah. Lee asked me to present the plaque to the featured artist, so I'll be up on stage for part of it."

The four women freeze.

I blink, looking at each of them in turn. "What? He said I don't have to speak. I just have to hand out the award."

Simone glances at Candice, who clears her throat. "Lee just hasn't had anyone do the presentation with him for a couple of years, is all."

I frown. "Oh?"

"He used to do it with his ex-fiancée."

I inhale. "*Oh.*" Sounds like this opening ceremony is an even bigger deal than I'd realized. Warmth fills my chest as I think about Lee's nervousness in asking me, and the way he smiled when I said yes. We're together, and I'm not afraid. I don't know what's going to happen next, but I know I want it.

"It's a whole thing," Jen says with a wave of her hand. "The couple who started the Fringe Fest were these old hippies who preached about love to anyone who would listen. When Lee took over from them, they insisted he continue the opening ceremony tradition and have his partner be beside him. Something about unity and love." She frowns at one of the planters Fiona moved, bending over to nudge it back two inches to the right.

Fiona just grins.

I clear my throat. "I didn't know it was such a big deal," I admit. "But he did seem nervous in asking me."

"He's basically proclaiming you as a couple in front of the whole town," Simone answers. "Fiona and I saw the opening ceremony the first year we were in town, and that was the last time Lee had a woman up there with him."

Candice tilts her head. "How do you feel about being up there now that you know what it means, Nora?"

I take a deep breath, trying to sort out my feelings. After asking him to walk into my new house with me last night, being up on stage beside him feels like the exact place I want to be.

"I feel good about it," I finally answer, lips curling in a broad grin.

My friends squeal. Candice, Simone, and Fiona huddle around me in a not-exactly-age-appropriate group hug. Jen pats my head and retreats to the flower arrangements again. I feel like a teenage girl with a crush, and I couldn't be happier.

THE NEXT DAY IS HECTIC. Like every year's Fringe Fest, Heart's Cove's population swells with tourists, who flock to Cove Boulevard to peruse stalls, eat food, and buy all kinds of artisanal products. As I run around with the rest of the team making sure everything is going smoothly, I'm glad to see people with maps in their hands admiring the sculptures dotted around town.

Along with Sebastian's two pieces, we have ten other installations. Big and small, abstract and otherwise, they've already drawn early festival attendees to the far corners of Heart's Cove. On my way to replenish the information booth with freshly printed pamphlets and maps, I pass by Four Cups and glance inside. The café is packed, as expected, with all four owners along with two baristas working like crazy. Fallon and Jen are in the kitchen with their heads down, creating incredible food.

Candice waves at me and shoves a coffee in my hands. "On the house, girl."

Grateful, I stand aside as she heaves a big tray full of coffees up and shuffles outside. There's a hum in here. A high vibration of energy and excitement, and I know it'll only get better. As I step outside, I glance at the stage on the far end of Cove Boulevard, where opening folk acts have already started plucking guitars and playing keyboards. The headliners aren't due to come on until about six p.m., with the opening ceremony scheduled for a few minutes before that.

Judging by how busy I've been so far, I know the hours between now and then will fly. I scan the crowd, but I don't see Lee anywhere. I want to share this feeling with him, the fullness. The joy.

We did this. Our little team, working tirelessly for the past many weeks, brought this festival together. I was a late addition to the group, but I can't help but feel like I've accomplished something worthwhile.

How long has it been since I felt this way? Have I *ever* felt like this in my working life? In *any* aspect of my life?

Unable to wipe the smile off my face, I decide to walk along the stalls and see what the residents and artisans of Heart's Cove have to offer. There's intricate handmade jewelry, specialty honey, fresh-baked bread. There are hand-whittled wooden spoons and bowls, a caricature painter, and an entire display showing off Mac's amazing pottery.

The Heart's Cove Hotel has a throng of people in front of it waiting for the next class to start.

This town is incredible. To be part of this...it makes me feel whole.

I can't resist anymore. I pull out my cell, intending to call Lee to find out where he's hiding—but my phone rings before I can unlock it.

My mother's name appears on the screen, and I let a smile stretch across my lips. She's planning on coming to town in the middle of the week to attend the festival and talk to Fallon and Jen about last-minute wedding preparations. For the first time in an eon, I don't feel that usual pull of guilt and worry at the thought of my mom. She doesn't need me to provide for her, to coddle her. Alongside Dan, she's living her best life. Maybe it's time for me to realize that—and do the same.

"Ma," I say, putting the phone to my ear.

"Nora," a man's voice answers. "It's Dan."

I stop, moving between two stalls to step out of the way of the milling crowd. Holding my cup in the same hand, I extend a finger to plug my opposite ear. I bend my head down. "Dan. What's up? Is everything okay?"

The pause that follows my words makes my blood turn to ice. It only lasts a second or two, but time slows to a crawl, and those seconds last an eternity.

"I'm sorry, Nora. Your mother had a fall."

My heart stops. "Is she okay?"

"She broke her hip on the step outside her front door. I was there, but I couldn't catch her. I stumbled like an idiot and—" He sucks in a hard breath. "They had to get her in surgery right away. They just took her away. I called as soon as I could, Nora. We rushed to the hospital and haven't had a second until now."

A weird croak comes out of my mouth. I look up to see the white canvas of the market stall in front of me. My mouth opens, closes, then opens again. "I'm on my way."

"I'll text you her room number just as soon as I can figure out how to use this phone. They think she'll have to stay here for a while, assuming surgery goes well. That's all I know, Nora. I'm so sorry. I know the festival started today. She was so excited to come visit, and—" Another choked sound, and I'm pretty sure my mother's beau is sobbing.

"I'll be there in a couple of hours, okay?"

We hang up, my hands shaking the whole time. I stare at the white canvas for a beat, feeling nothing.

Then the guilt rises up like a wave.

After being my mother's crutch, I left her in Tahoe with no support. I went from visiting her multiple times a week to almost completely ignoring her. Not because I meant to, but because I was wrapped up in my own selfish happiness. I've been dreaming about a house and a dog and a boyfriend when my mother has been on her own. I let her convince me to stop paying her bills—

Her health insurance.

She said she was eligible for Medicare, but—

I redial and put the phone to my ear. "Dan," I say as soon as he answers again. "Her insurance. It covers the surgery?"

He blows out a breath. "I don't know. She was so out of it they said she needed the surgery right away. They said it was an emergency."

"Okay. I'll be there soon." I hang up and sprint to Four Cups, shoving my way to the kitchen. Jen is on the right side of the kitchen, arranging pancakes on a plate. Fallon and another cook I haven't met are on the left, at the grill.

Fallon looks up, frowning. "Nora. What's wrong?"

"Ma had a fall. She's in surgery. I'm leaving for Tahoe right now."

He throws a dishtowel into a laundry bag in the corner. "I'll drive."

I glance at Jen, whose brows are pulled low. She must see the question in my face, because she just shakes her head. "Go. We'll manage."

The other cook nods. "It's all under control."

Fallon jerks his chin to the back door, and before I know it, I'm sitting beside him in the passenger seat of his car, trying to swallow down the panic threatening to choke me.

It's not until an hour later that I remember where I'm supposed to be tonight—on stage, beside Lee.

My hands are trembling violently when I pull my phone out of my purse.

Nora: Lee, I'm sorry. Family emergency. Can't do the ceremony with you tonight.

I'm cross-eyed, trembling, and hardly able to type on my phone. That's all I can manage for now, and I just hope Lee will forgive me.

32

NORA

DAN IS A MESS. He hugs me so tight when he sees me that I think my shoulders pop out of their sockets. Then he grabs Fallon and does the same.

All the while, he's mumbling apologies, explaining, saying he should have done more.

He's a good man, and the fall wasn't his fault. He fell right along with her but landed in the bushes instead of the hard concrete step. He has the scrapes on his arms to prove it.

I tell him not to blame himself, and he takes a deep breath to get himself back together.

Due to my not-quite-a-control-freak personality, I end up taking charge of the business end of the hospital stay. I fill out the paperwork, keeping my mind busy as I wade through hospital red tape.

And what I find out is not good news.

When my mother told me she didn't need to fund her health insurance, it's because she turned sixty-five and became eligible for Medicare. The hospital administrators tell me her surgery—due to the complication of a compound fracture and the potential need for a total hip replacement—is only partially covered by her plan. Anxiety knots in my stomach.

This could be a financial disaster.

I could have kept paying her policy. If I hadn't thrown all my plans and safety nets to the wind, I could have been prepared for this. If I hadn't stupidly gotten myself in nearly thirty thousand dollars' worth of debt, and if I hadn't signed for a mortgage I can't back out of, we would have avoided this.

She was on the best health insurance before this. I *planned* for this.

The seat beneath me is hard plastic, uncomfortable and cold. I drop my head in my hands as guilt rides me until my insides turn to an oily black mass.

If I hadn't been so hell-bent on letting go of control, I could have prevented this. It's my fault this is such a disaster. My fault. My responsibility. My stupidity. My selfish need to chase after a man.

I lean back in my chair, meeting Fallon's dark eyes across from me. My brother's chair looks even less comfortable, considering the size of him. It looks like a child's seat.

"I think I need to sell my house," I tell him, voice flat.

He leans forward, elbows on his knees. "Nora. You're spinning. Stop."

I shake my head. "I'm not spinning, Fallon. It's simple math. Mom doesn't have the money for this kind of medical debt. It's my fault."

A frown mars my brother's features. "How is that your fault? And we don't even know how much it's going to cost. It depends how long it takes her to recover."

"I've been paying her insurance since I left college," I say, staring at the beige linoleum floor. "She convinced me to cancel the policy when she heard about the motorcycles. Said she didn't want to keep holding me back. I should have refused."

Fallon lets out a gust of breath and scrubs his face with two big hands. "Fuck," he breathes. "I didn't know you were paying her insurance. Why didn't you tell me? We could have split it."

"We haven't exactly been close, up until you did the baking show. Plus, I didn't want to burden you. You have a wedding to pay for, and you've worked so hard to start your life over. This was my responsibility."

He stares at me for a beat, then drops his head. "I wish you wouldn't think that way."

I shrug. "It's true. I've been responsible for Ma's well-being for a long time, Fallon, and I dropped the ball. I thought I could escape life. Escape consequences. I thought I could move to a new town and turn into a whole new person, but I messed up. This is my fault."

"Stop saying that," he growls.

Dan approaches with three Styrofoam cups full of sludge-like coffee. I take one and sip the disgusting brew, mourning the fact that I probably won't get to have much more coffee from Four Cups. My life as the New Nora ends now.

My mom needs me. I'll need to find a higher-paying job, sell my new house, forget about the dog, and tell Lee that we were dreaming. I'm not cut out for a relationship. I'm not cut out for freedom and motorcycle rides.

I need to be the responsible one, because when I let go

of the reins, the horses buck and the whole damn carriage tips over.

My mom's fall isn't my fault, but I could have mitigated the consequences. Now all I can do is sit here and wait to hear how bad those consequences will be.

33

LEE

I SEE Nora's text in between delivering bottles of water to various stations around the festival and being called to an information booth to help a mother locate her lost child.

The words on my screen are painfully brief. She has a family emergency. She can't make it tonight.

As soon as I reunite the mother and child, I find a quiet place and try to call her.

No answer.

Frowning at my screen, I take a deep breath. Part of me wants to make sure Nora is okay. Part of me is clawing at my skin, knowing that I never should have opened myself up to a woman again.

Family emergency could be code for, "I don't want to do the opening ceremony with you." Just like Drea, she's going to leave me standing in front of everyone like an idiot.

I try calling again, with the same result, so I shoot off a text asking if she's okay. My mind spirals faster and faster, until Olivia finds me and tells me two of the vendors are having an argument, and I need to come calm them down.

For the next hour, I'm dealing with an irate pesto salesman and a jewelry maker who's threatening to make a voodoo doll pincushion to curse the pesto man for life.

Once that particular fire is dealt with, I check my phone again. No word from Nora. She hasn't returned my call or answered my text.

My initial reaction fades as worry settles in. What kind of asshole am I to worry about a stupid opening ceremony if something is truly wrong?

Across the road, I spy Fiona dropping coffees off at one of the tables outside the Four Cups Café. With a few long strides, I make my way there as she steps away from the customers.

"Lee," she says, gripping her tray. There are worry lines between her brows, and her usually full lips are pinched bloodless.

Something's wrong.

Guilt worms inside me for my earlier thoughts. Who cares about a stupid ceremony? Why should I worry about standing on stage next to Nora?

"Nora sent me a cryptic text about a family emergency," I say in a low voice. "You know anything about that? She's not answering my calls."

"Her mom's in the hospital," Fiona replies. "She left with Fallon a couple of hours ago. They're probably in Tahoe by now."

Shame slams into me like a punch to the gut. Thank fuck I didn't voice my thoughts out loud. I was worried about a stupid ceremony when Nora's dealing with something real? How could I be so shallow, so stupid?

"I wish I could go," I say, glancing at the stage. "I need to do the opening ceremony speech at five-thirty."

Fiona's brows arch. "I know. I've been waiting for a call from Fallon since he left to let us know what's going on."

I nod, thank Fiona, and move on. I only check my phone about ten thousand times before it's time for me to go up on stage. I make a wooden speech and paste a fake smile on my face, hand Sebastian his plaque, and scurry off to let the headlining band come on.

How fucking anticlimactic. All week, I've been building that speech up in my mind, imagining my arm around Nora. I made that ceremony into something big and meaningful in my mind, and it turns out it doesn't even matter at all.

Kind of like my failed wedding. In the end, it's just a blip in the story of my life.

As my foot hits the last stair as I exit stage left, my phone rings. I fumble with the device, letting out a long breath when I see Nora's name on the screen.

"Nora," I say as soon as the phone is at my ear. "I got your text. Are you okay?"

"Hi, Lee," she replies, and her voice is gossamer thin. "I'm fine. I'm sorry I missed the speech."

I find a quiet place between two nearby buildings and lean against a brick wall. "Don't worry about the speech, babe. Is your mom okay? Fiona told me she was in the hospital."

"She broke her hip. It was a compound fracture and they needed to bring her in for surgery immediately. She just got out a few minutes ago. They had to do a total hip replacement, and she might need the other one done if it's in the same shape this one was before the fall. They said she'll be asleep until tomorrow." That flat, lifeless voice doesn't sound like Nora at all. She sounds completely defeated. I want to reach through the telephone and pull her into my embrace. I want to fix everything that's wrong.

"What can I do?"

Nora inhales, like she's bracing herself. Then she says words I wouldn't expect in a million years. Not after the weeks we've just had. "Look, Lee, I'm going to need to take time for myself. There's a lot going on here, and my mom will need me. I'll make sure you get the money for the motorcycles back and I can work remotely to finish up the next issue of the magazine, but I'm not going to be able to continue. I'll send you my resignation letter as soon as I'm at my computer."

I'm speechless for a second. "But...your house." *And us. What about us? What about* me?

"I'm selling the house." She sounds determined. "I'll lose money on the real estate fees, but I just can't carry the mortgage payments right now. It was stupid of me to make such an impulsive decision. I should never have moved to Heart's Cove in the first place."

"Nora." I turn to face the wall, leaning my hand on the rough brick while I stare at my feet. "I think selling the house is an impulsive decision. Shouldn't you wait until your mom wakes up from surgery?"

"No," she answers, completely sure of herself. "I'm sorry, Lee. I had a wonderful time with you, but I won't be able to continue seeing you. I have to go."

"Nora, wait—"

There's a click, and I realize she hung up. I stare at my phone, dumbfounded. How could I wake up this morning feeling like a new man, only to end the day like this? Broken, alone, standing in a stinking alley while the woman of my dreams slips through my fingers?

I might not be standing at the altar, but these feelings are all too familiar. Once again, I'm not good enough. I'm not worth fighting for. I'm not the one that gets chosen.

The black, evil voice in my head cackles and tells me I should've known. I was a fool to get involved with a woman, and an even bigger fool to let myself fall. I'm destined to be alone. I've known that since Drea walked away from me. Nothing has changed.

Except...things *have* changed.

I've had a woman on the back of my bike and known it in my bones that she was supposed to be there. I took on her debt without a second thought because I knew it was the right thing to do, and I couldn't bear to have Nora leave Heart's Cove.

Am I really going to let her walk away so easily? Am I really not going to fight for this?

Nora belongs in Heart's Cove. Her friends love her. Our coworkers love her.

And I love her. Desperately.

This is nothing like my failed engagement. I let Drea walk away because part of me knew that we never should have gotten engaged in the first place. We kept pushing back the wedding because it never would've worked. I was just too much of a coward to break things off.

But Nora's different. Nora makes me laugh. She makes me feel whole. She's beautiful and smart and funny and she deserves to have a life that doesn't revolve around other people's disasters. She deserves to spread her wings and fly, knowing that I'm going to be there to catch her.

When I emerge from the alleyway, the setting sun casts a hazy glow over the street. There's music and laughter and a thousand people talking, admiring the festival that Nora helped put together.

She deserves to be here, and I'm not going to let her retreat back to her shell without a fight.

She wants to break up with me? She wants to sell her house and run away?

She'll have to tell it to my face.

34

NORA

AFTER MY CALL WITH LEE, I feel so defeated that Fallon takes pity on me and drives me to our mother's place. He orders takeout and sits with me until I eat a few bites, then puts fresh sheets on the guest room bed and tells me to go to sleep. I would've stayed at the hospital, but my mother's room was in the ICU with strict visiting hours. The nurses wouldn't let me stay even if I didn't feel like death warmed over.

I just sit on my mother's guest room mattress instead, staring at a spot on the wall, replaying my conversation with Lee.

Breaking up with him was the right thing to do. I need to fix this mess and make sure my mother is okay. She'll need help around the house, she'll need money, she'll need someone to lean on.

For that, I need to be here. I'll sell the house in Heart's Cove and live here, beg for my old job back, and make sure everything is okay. It's what I should've done when all those bikes tumbled to the asphalt.

It was stupid of me to think things would work out differently.

Like a movie in my mind, I replay the past couple of months. The exhilaration of riding on the back of Lee's motorcycle, the freedom and elation I felt with my arms wrapped around him. The ecstasy of being in his bed.

I grew addicted to him so quickly, it terrifies me.

But it's over now, and that's for the best.

If I keep telling myself that, I'll believe it, right?

I fall onto my side, curling into the fetal position, feeling sorry for myself. I'll allow myself one night, I decide. Tonight, I'll lie on this bed and let the awful feelings bubble up. Maybe, if I'm able, I'll cry myself to sleep.

Tears don't come. I just lie on my side and stare at a slightly different spot on the wall, not knowing what to do. All I can think about is Lee's choked voice when I told him it was over between us, and that painful ache that bloomed in the center of my chest. Now I'm just numb.

The life I thought I could have just slipped through my fingers, and I don't even have the energy to cry.

Then someone knocks on the front door.

I frown, but I don't move. Fallon can get it.

The knocks turn to pounding, and then the doorbell rings.

I sit up and stare at the bedroom door, until I realize Fallon told me he was going for a drive after he stuffed me in this room. He's not going to answer the door.

I lie back down. Whoever's at the door will go away.

But they don't. The doorbell rings again, and the knocking resumes. Then I hear a faint, "Nora!"

It doesn't sound like my brother.

My heart starts to pound just as my phone starts ringing. Lee's name lights up my screen and I inhale sharply, shaking my head. I told him things were over. Tomorrow, I was going to email Rudy and deal with the sale of the house remotely. I didn't even want to go back to Heart's Cove, except to grab my things from my apartment. It was always going to be temporary. Maybe that's why I only got a month-to-month lease. I knew it would end.

"Nora!"

I know that voice.

I stand up. My throat is bone-dry, but my palms are damp. On shaky legs, I pad across the thick carpet and exit the guest room, staring down the wallpapered hallway toward the foyer. When I get there, the tiles are cool on my bare feet. Through the half-moon window on the front door, I can see the top of a dark-haired head.

My heart takes off, banging against its cage so hard I put a hand to my chest to make sure the organ doesn't jump right out.

Then, with a deep breath, I open the door.

Lee's fist is raised for another knock and we both freeze. His hair is a mess and his face is blotchy and red. With wide eyes, he stares at me for a beat, then drops his arm.

"Nora."

I blink. "How did you find me?"

"Dorothy gave me your mom's address after I went to the hospital and couldn't find you. She told me your mom made it out of surgery okay, but couldn't tell me anything about you. Everyone's worried about you."

I shake my head, mostly just to clear it. Everyone is worried about me? I don't have anyone to get worried about me. I'm on my own, just like before. It's me against the world, with a mountain of medical debt incoming, personal debts to the man in front of me, and a stupid mortgage I never should have taken. I don't have friends or a boyfriend or anyone to rely on except myself. That's why I need to be better about planning for emergencies. Controlling uncontrollable outcomes.

But...

There's a whole town of people who care, apparently. And Lee is standing on my mother's doorstep, looking like he sprinted all the way from Heart's Cove just to make sure I was okay. He didn't actually run; I can see his motorcycle parked in my mother's driveway. But still.

He drove all the way here *after* I broke up with him over the phone, like the coward I am.

"I broke up with you," I say stupidly.

"I know, baby," he says, taking a step closer and wrapping me in his arms. I melt into his chest with a shudder. He lets out a low rumble, hand smoothing over my head. "Let's worry about that tomorrow, okay?"

I nod, inhaling the scent of his leather jacket with my hands clinging to his back like he's the only thing keeping me from falling apart.

Hell, he *is* the only thing keeping me from falling apart. As if he knows that my legs aren't working properly, he scoops me in his arms and carries me back inside, kicking the door closed behind him. The living room is only a few short steps from the front door, so Lee carries me to the couch and settles me on his lap. His hand makes long, slow sweeps over my arm while he lays soft kisses on my temple, my ear, my hair.

Exhaustion hits me like a blow to the back of the head. My limbs are made of lead, and all I can do is settle into the warmth and strength of the man who drove across the state to be by my side, even after I did my best to push him away.

"I'm sorry," I finally say to his shoulder. "I was horrible to you on the phone."

"You were fine," Lee answers, the smile evident in his voice. "It was the kindest breakup speech I've ever received."

Finding the strength to pull away from his drugging embrace, I meet his gaze. Before I can stop myself, my fingers are coasting along his stubble, feeling the warmth of him beneath my skin. He's *real*, and he's here. For me. "You're not going to let me break up with you, are you?"

His eyes crinkle. "Not in a million years, Nora. You mean far too much to me." With a hand on my hip, he lets his thumb coast over and back under the hem of my shirt. His touch makes me shiver, and I melt into his chest once more.

"My head is all messed up," I admit. "I feel like my mom's accident was my fault."

"That's because you're used to being the one who takes care of everyone," he tells me quietly, wrapping thick arms around me like a warm, comfortable cage.

We're quiet for a few minutes, until Lee takes a breath. "When I got your text, my first instinct was to be mad. I felt like you were letting me down, just like Drea did. I had this whole image in my head of the two of us up on stage together, and then all of a sudden it wasn't going to happen."

"I'm sor—"

He squeezes me to silence me. "But it took me all of thirty minutes to get over that and start to worry. When I didn't hear from you, I went to the café and found out about your mom. I wanted to jump on my bike and head straight here, but I had to do that stupid speech." He strokes my hair, laying a kiss on my temple. "And it was fine. I was up there alone, gave Sebastian his award, and the world didn't come crashing down. All that mattered to me was getting it over with so I could be with you. Because I love you, Nora."

I inhale sharply.

Lee keeps going. "I love you so much it's almost painful. It puts all my previous relationships to shame, because it feels like the first time I've really cared about someone else. I know you're hurting and you're worried, but I want you to understand what I feel for you. Whatever happens with your mom, I'm going to be here. Whatever financial worries you have, I'm going to help you. If you want to run away, I'm going to chase you. You're my future, Nora, and you can rely on me."

For the first time since I got the phone call from Dan this morning, a tear leaks out of my eye. My throat has a boulder jammed in it that I try to swallow around, but I end up just choking myself with a sob. Lee tightens his hold on me, settling me in his arms.

"I love you," he whispers. "I'm not going anywhere."

I nod, my cheek rubbing against the soft leather of his jacket. Tears fall from my face and I try to wipe them away with my palm, but they won't stop. Lee tilts my chin and kisses my wet cheeks, but that just makes me sob harder.

"I've never had someone to rely on," I say between sobs. "I've been alone for so long, Lee, I don't know how I'm supposed to function with someone else in my life."

Broad palms settle on my cheeks, and Lee places a soft

kiss on my lips. I'm trembling all over, terrified of what this means.

I can't run away from this man. I can't turn my back on Heart's Cove and retreat to my sad, controlled, comfortable life. That's been shattered like a cheap porcelain figurine. Now I need to sweep up the pieces and figure out what happens next.

I'll have to embrace change. Embrace the unknown. Embrace *Lee*.

That last one doesn't quite terrify me as much as the first two. Lee has been there from the start of my transformation, hasn't he? He's the one who offered me a hand out of the dark when he took on my debt. He's the one who gave me my dream job. He's the one who reawakened my body from its long, cold slumber.

He drove like a maniac to get here because he knew whatever I said on the phone, I needed him by my side. This is a man I can depend on. One who knows me, who sets me free and keeps me safe, all at the same time.

I blink at him, tears still escaping my eyes as he cups my face like I'm a precious jewel. "I'm in love with you," I whisper. "And it terrifies me. All of this terrifies me. I'm scared that I'll lose it all. You, the house, the job, the future..."

"So your solution was to throw it all away instead?" His brow is arched, but his voice betrays his amusement.

A snorting laugh falls out of me. "It sounds pretty stupid when you put it that way. I guess I thought if I made the decision to throw everything away myself, at least I was in charge of what happened."

If I threw away the house, the man, the job, and the new life, at least no one would take it away from me. At least I'd be in control—even if I ended up heartbroken, broke, and alone.

God, I'm glad he chased after me.

A soft kiss on my forehead, and Lee is pulling me back into his chest. "Tomorrow, I'll start a long campaign to convince you that your life won't fall apart if you stop trying to control everything." He runs his fingers through my hair. "But tonight I want you to let me take care of you, okay?"

My lids are heavy all of a sudden. A yawn cracks my jaw, and all I can do is settle against the man I've fallen in love with and let him take care of me. Just this once. "Okay," I mumble, and promptly fall asleep.

35

NORA

My mother is awake when I get to the hospital. When we walk into her room, Lee has his hand on my lower back, his eyes periodically scanning my face to make sure I'm okay. He's been like this all morning. Taking care of me.

I...like it.

"Hey," I tell my mom, hurrying to her side. "How are you feeling?"

"I feel fine, all things considered," Ma says. She smiles at me, but she looks tired. Her brown skin is sallow, and her normally glossy hair is limp on her head. "Dan tells me you rushed over here and missed the start of the Fringe Festival. You shouldn't have done that, Nora."

"Mom, you were in surgery. Why would I stay at a festival?"

Her eyes move to Lee. "And your man came too." She extends a hand, which Lee takes carefully in both of his. For such a big man, he's incredibly tender. My mother meets his gaze. "You're looking after my daughter?"

"Always," he says solemnly, and I feel that word in every corner of my heart. It sounds like a promise. An oath.

"I knew you were a good one," Ma says with a smile. She blinks slowly and leans back against her pillows, already exhausted by our interaction. I hate seeing her like this. I hate thinking that I've been neglecting her.

Dan walks through the door behind us carrying a tray of coffees. "Not as good as Four Cups, but it'll do," he says, handing the coffees out. Fallon, who had been parking the car, walks in and groans in appreciation when he gets a cup of coffee handed to him.

Then we sit around my mother's bed and make small talk. Lee takes the chair next to mine and slings his arm over the back of my shoulders in a pose that's casual and possessive and perfect. The guilt inside me recedes, and I look around the room realizing that my mother has a support system that extends beyond just me. None of this was my fault. None of it was within my control. Lee's face is illuminated by the light of the windows, the few coarse grey hairs in his stubble shining silver.

He's been here for me all along.

He catches me staring at him and leans over to press a gentle kiss on my forehead. I blush, then whisper, "I'm glad you're here with me."

"Nowhere else I'd rather be," he replies, tucking me into his shoulder.

My mother beams at me, and I can't help but blush. I might be a grown woman, but there's just something about a mother's gaze that makes me feel like a teenager again.

"Jen said she spoke to Dorothy, and we can push the wedding back a month or two to allow for your recovery—"

"Absolutely not," my mother snaps, whipping her head toward my brother. "The wedding will proceed as planned."

"Ma, you're lying in a hospital bed," Fallon protests.

"I'll be fine. The doctor said my stitches will likely come out as early as ten days from now. Your wedding isn't for three weeks!"

Fallon and I exchange a glance. Our mother is stubborn to a fault. She'll dig her heels in about this and probably drag herself to his wedding just to prove a point and sabotage her recovery in the process.

"Let's just see what the medical team has to say, okay?" I cut in.

She harrumphs, taking a sip of water with shaking hands. "I'm not an invalid, Nora."

"I know that. I just think we should listen to the professionals."

Right on cue, the doctor walks in wearing a pristine white lab coat over blue scrubs. "Morning, Prisha. Glad to see you awake."

"Doctor Kowalski," she says, handing her water to Dan before folding her hands. "I was just telling my son that I won't be missing his wedding in three weeks for anything. You agree, yes?"

The doctor hums, watching my mother over his wire-rim glasses. "Well, let's take a look at these X-rays, shall we?"

He flicks the lights on a board and sticks a couple of X-rays up on the wall. We all lean forward to look at the new ball and socket in my mother's hip. Guilt squeezes at me like a vise, but Lee puts his hand on my thigh and I let out a breath. The feeling passes.

The doctor tells us that the surgery went well yesterday,

and my mother's pain levels are better than average. He's tentatively optimistic about her recovery, which makes my mother nod at Fallon as if that settles the wedding issue once and for all.

"When am I getting out of here?" my mother asks once the doctor is finished explaining recovery times, physical therapy, and expectations for the next few weeks.

"Let's start by seeing how your physical therapy goes today, shall we?"

"Today?" I nearly screech. "Shouldn't she rest?"

"Outcomes of hip replacements are greatly improved when we start physical therapy immediately," the doctor says. "The sooner we get your mom moving, the better her recovery will be."

Shocked, I sit back. I wasn't expecting that. But my mother beams at me and gives me a curt nod. "See? I'll be dancing at Fallon's wedding on my own two feet. Just you wait."

"Let's not get ahead of ourselves, Prisha," the doctor says, grabbing the X-rays from the lighted board to tuck them back into her file. "We'll see how your physical therapy goes before we start tearing up the dance floor."

Ma nods, and the doctor leaves the room. Lee's hand is still on my thigh. Dan stands up and plants a big, wet kiss right on my mother's lips.

"That's good news, sweetheart," he says, beaming.

"You're all acting like you were worried I would croak," my mother answers, pretending to be grumpy. But she still presents her lips to Dan for another kiss.

We all stay with my mom until the physical therapist arrives, then promise to come back for a couple of hours in the afternoon. Fallon has to leave to go back to work at Four

Cups, but he resolves to come back and stay with her in the middle of next week, when the café is quieter. We come up with a roster between me, Fallon, and Dan, and before I know it, I find myself back at my mother's house with Lee.

We end up in the kitchen, where he backs me up against the cabinets and places his hands on the counter on either side of me.

"Now," he says, looking down at me with serious eyes. "We're going to talk about what happened yesterday."

I pretend not to know what he's talking about. "The ceremony?"

"I don't give a damn about the ceremony, Nora," he answers. "We're going to talk about the fact that instead of asking me for help, you pushed me away."

I bite my lip. "I did that, didn't I?"

His hand moves to my chin, tilting it up. "Do you believe me when I say I'm not going anywhere?"

The question settles heavily between us. He said the same words to me last night, but I was in such a daze that it seemed natural to sink into the warmth of his embrace and accept his love.

Now, I've had a good night's sleep and the panic of my mother's surgery has ebbed. I know things will be manageable. My mom is fine. I'm fine.

I reach for that familiar wall inside me, that spiky defensive mechanism that allowed me to call Lee to break up with him—but I find nothing where it used to be. At some point between last night and this afternoon, I've accepted that Lee is the man for me. I've let go of that part of me that uses guilt and shame and responsibility to control everything, to keep my life small.

Maybe it happened when my mother insisted that

Fallon not move his wedding. Maybe it was when she preened at the doctor complimenting her spirits and recovery so far. Maybe it was the X-ray of the new ball and socket, successfully installed, which would allow my mom to start physical therapy right away.

Maybe it was Lee's hand on my thigh, warm and comforting, through it all. He's not going anywhere. I know that to the core of my being.

And beside me is exactly where I want him to be.

"Yes," I say, lifting my hands to rest on either side of his face. "I believe you."

"And do you understand what I mean when I say I love you?"

My lips curl. "What does it mean?"

"It means you're it for me, Nora. You're the woman I want. You pulled me out of a dark hole and showed me just how bright and beautiful life can be. I'm not going to let you throw that away. I'm not going to let you hide under a rock because you can't control the chaos of life. I'm going to stick you on the back of my bike and ride until you smile again."

Chaos terrifies me. The unknown is my worst nightmare. But if I explore the great unknown on the back of Lee's bike, maybe it won't be so bad.

"You're not going to go easy on me, are you?" I ask, heart warming. There will be no more running away, now that Lee is in my life. No more hiding behind a steady job and a boring, safe existence. Together, we'll be embracing life, freedom, and love.

"I'll go easy on you," he says in a low rumble, lips dropping down to my neck. "I'll go easy until you're nice and ready. Then we'll see what happens."

His lips find mine, and when his hands start exploring my body, I know it won't take long for him to figure out I'm nice and ready for a lot of things already.

LATER, when we've said *I love you* in a million different ways with our bodies and words, Lee takes me out on the back of his bike. In this mountainous, beautiful area, with my arms wrapped around the man who dragged me out of my shell, I turn a page.

The next chapter of my life will be so much better than the last.

EPILOGUE

NORA

FALLON DELAYS his wedding to give time for our mom to get back on her feet. Jen takes the blame, telling my mother that she needed more time to finish her already-perfect wedding cake recipe. It had nothing to do with my mother's hip replacement, she says. The delay was purely to do with the cake. For that, Jen gets a permanent gold star in my books. I couldn't ask for a better sister-in-law.

Their wedding venue is the Heart's Cove Hotel, but not in the same ballroom as Roger and Drea's reception. Since the venue was booked out every weekend until October, Fallon and Jen decided to reschedule their wedding on a Friday evening. They use the huge green lawn at the back of the property and rent out massive marquee tents for an outdoor affair. How they managed to pull off the rush job of pushing back all the preparations, I have no idea. Then again, Jen was in charge. 'Nuff said.

I check the weather through my big sliding glass doors, happy to see it's a beautiful mid-August evening. I'll bring a shawl, but I should be fine in my sleeveless dress.

A yip brings my attention to the little furball at my feet. A crossbreed spaniel with big, floppy ears, Harley is the light of my life. "Okay, okay, calm down. You're getting your treat now," I tell my new rescue pup, to his doggy delight. I fill one of his KONG dog toys with peanut butter (his favorite) and place it in the big kennel in the corner of the kitchen.

Locking the gated enclosure around the kennel, I double-check that Harley has enough water for the couple of hours I'll be at the wedding. I know he'll be fine—he usually prefers being in the kennel anyway. It took him an entire week to come out and investigate the rest of the house after I brought him home. I had to pretend I didn't see him sniffing at everything, because any time I looked over, he'd hurry back to his enclosure.

Poor puppy. It broke my heart to see him so timid, but in a way, it made me feel closer to him. It took me a while to come out of my shell too.

Now, a few weeks later, he's warming up to his new home. Still not entirely comfortable, and he gets nervous around new people.

With me and Lee, though, Harley is incredibly affectionate. Every hour or so, he'll come over and stick his head on my lap, wherever I am, to request head scratches. Sometimes I think he does it because he can't believe that I'll actually pet him whenever he likes, so he comes over to prove to himself that I still exist. As he gets more comfortable in our new home, his little doggy personality is starting to blossom.

Kind of like mine did when I came to this town.

Lee's footsteps echo down the stairs and along the hallway. I turn to watch him enter, my mouth watering at the sight of my man in a well-tailored suit. He's not wearing a tie, and the top two buttons of his shirt are undone. A triangle of chest stares out at me, begging to be kissed.

So I do. I walk over and plant a big one right there in the hollow of his throat.

Then I notice the red mark from my lipstick on his skin and start wiping. Lee laughs. He's used to those red marks by now, yet still insists he loves the lipstick. So I wear it as often as I ever did.

And if I sometimes put an extra swipe on before certain —*ahem*—activities, well, that's between him and me and Miss Libido.

"You look beautiful," Lee says, letting his hands coast down my sides.

"Not bad yourself," I answer, wiping one last smudge of lipstick off his skin.

"When we get home tonight, I'm going to have fun taking this dress off you." His voice slides over my skin like velvet, and I can't help the shiver of anticipation that passes through me. A soft kiss on the shell of my ear, then he says, "And maybe we can use your magic wand again."

My cheeks flush. My trusty vibrator made a surprise appearance when I was moving from the apartment to this house back in June. It fell out of a box and rolled across the hardwood floors in the hallway to bump up against Lee's toes.

It was mortifying.

But then we used it together, and I got over the embarrassment. I got over the embarrassment a few times, actually.

"We need to go or we'll be late," I say, checking my lipstick in the big mirror on the living room wall.

Lee checks on Harley, who's happily exploring the contents of his KONG toy. Lee double-checks the water bowl, then extends his arm toward me. I take his elbow and let him lead me away.

FALLON AND JEN'S wedding is perfect. Literally perfect. Nothing goes wrong. Not even a single fairy light is off. Every single detail, from the centerpieces to the seating to the music to—of course—the cake, is well-thought-out and executed flawlessly.

With Jen at the helm, I didn't expect any less.

The ceremony is beautiful. My brother looks smitten. There isn't a dry eye in the place. Jen wears a tea-length, boatneck white gown, her blond hair gathered in a sleek French twist. She looks incredible. My brother is a lucky man.

Us old biddies kick off our heels as soon as the music starts, and I find myself surrounded by my friends, dancing up a storm under a big white tent like I'm twenty-two years old again.

My mother sits at a table with Lottie on one side and Dorothy on the other, presiding over everything like a queen. She's already up and walking, and has been busy navigating the complicated world of hospital bureaucracy and insurance without me. She refused my help in dealing with all the phone calls and paperwork, actually, and has been managing fine without me. Her hospital stay ended up being much shorter than I expected, and she assures me her payment plan is more than manageable.

I should have known she'd be okay. My mom has always been fiercely independent. A fighter.

An arm snakes around my waist as a song ends, and I'm spun around to face my lover, my champion, my man.

"My turn," he says, pulling me close. "Sick of watching you shake those hips without being able to touch you. You're driving me crazy."

I laugh, leaning my cheek against his chest. "That was a conga line, Lee. Hardly a sexy dance."

"Wrong," he says, letting his hands coast down to my ass. "Everything is sexy when you do it."

We sway for a few minutes, until Lee speaks again. "I got a notification from my bank this afternoon. The money hit my account."

I pull away, a smile stretching across my face. "We're square?"

"Twenty-seven and a half thousand dollars, paid off in full."

"Minus two thousand two hundred for the wedding and the drive home," I say. My chest feels warm and light. After everything that happened with my mother, I reworked my budget. I put off some home improvement projects and decided to delay purchasing new furniture for the house. It was important to me to pay the debt off. To move on.

To truly start fresh.

He leans his forehead against mine. "Worth every penny, because it meant I got to spend time with you."

Is it unhealthy to blush this hard? Instead of answering, I just pull Lee down and let my kiss do the talking instead. We don't come up for air until we hear wolf-whistles from the direction of my mother's table.

I laugh, pulling away, and drag Lee off to get us a couple of drinks to cool down.

Later, when we're alone, we pick up right where we left off.

GEORGIA

TWILIGHT IS my favorite time of day. When the sky is dark purple and the stars are just winking above, the world holds its breath as night creeps closer.

Right now, I'm holding mine.

Grass pokes at the peep toes of my shoes, cool and spiky at my feet. Gentle summer wind holds me in its embrace as I lift my head and take in the sculpture before me. The mass of metal and wood is as brutal as it is beautiful. It makes me feel...it just makes me *feel*.

I've never been an art person. Mostly, I don't get it. If a painting is beautiful, fine. I get *that*. It'll look good on my walls. But contemporary art? Abstract installations? The brainchild of a Texan cowboy transplanted into a small town in Northern California?

I want to cry, which is not like me at all. I didn't even cry when I found my ex-husband in bed with another woman. I didn't cry when he fought me in the divorce for everything I'd worked for in my own business. I didn't even shed a tear when I had to sell that business at the end of it all because I couldn't afford to buy him out. Even though I'd built it from the ground up.

No tears. I just moved on.

I'm pragmatic. The type of woman who gets her motorcycle license, takes lessons, and buys a scooter because she decides she wants to. I get things done.

But I find myself rooted to the spot, staring at a sculpture that makes me feel angry and heartbroken and hopeful and a thousand other emotions I can't name.

Maybe I'm getting my period. Last month, Nora's cute new puppy made me tear up.

Or— Oh, God. Maybe I'm well and truly starting menopause. Is it hot out here, or am I just paranoid?

"What do you think, Sweet Peach?"

Even with the pet name making me stiffen, Sebastian's low drawl sends a rush of desire to all the forgotten corners of my body. I turn slowly, watching him saunter toward me on loose limbs. His smile is easy, but his eyes are sharp.

A woman could get lost in eyes like that. Dark, sensuous, ringed with thick, black lashes.

I loathe that he has this effect on me.

"I think the pet names are getting old, cowboy."

A one-sided smile, and a long, lean dimple appears in Sebastian's cheek. My core quivers. Yes, *quivers*. And when his bare forearm brushes against mine as he comes to a stop beside me, my panties grow embarrassingly damp.

Okay, so I'm not suffering from vaginal dryness. Maybe I'm not starting menopause after all.

But more to the point—what the hell is wrong with me? Why do I have this reaction to the man? I hate this man! I hate what he did to me twenty-five years ago and I hate what he's doing now. Inserting himself into my town, my life, my head.

My body grows taut as a bowstring. I don't know if it's Sebastian's raw sexuality or the bitterness that rises within me every time he's close. Our history is complicated, fossilized, set in stone. I thought it was in the past.

But Sebastian is here, and his sculpture has remained a permanent installation in one of the main parks in town since the end of the Fringe Festival. I've had to ride by it every day on my way to the coffee shop, but I've never stopped to have a look.

Until tonight.

I turn back to the sculpture and reach out to touch a sensually curved edge of rough iron. "I heard this was an ode to your ex-wife."

A grunt is the only response I get.

"I wish I could make something like this for my ex-husband and dump it in his front yard in the middle of the night. He would hate that."

With a surprised snort, Sebastian meets my gaze. "Everyone else says they love it. You were always brutally opinionated, though. You always enjoyed cutting people to the bone."

I freeze. He thought I was cruel...on purpose? After everything he said to me? After everything he did? I choose to ignore his comment. "I never said I hated it. I said my ex-husband would."

Sebastian's face is carved in shadows. He's not wearing his hat, and his chestnut hair is tossing in the slight breeze. He meets my gaze, holding it for long moments.

Electricity fizzes inside me. My skin grows sensitive. I hate this man.

"I'm staying in town for a while," he says, voice full of gravel.

"Great," I answer sarcastically. "I moved away from one ex just to run into another."

"I don't think you mind me being here at all."

"I hope, one day, I'll meet a man who doesn't presume to tell me what I feel." I cross my arms, leveling him with a stare. I have to crane my neck because he's so tall. It takes away slightly from the intimidation factor I'm trying to achieve.

Damn him.

Then everything happens quickly.

Sebastian takes a step closer. I refuse to retreat. His eyes grow dark, his jaw clenching. Then, without warning, he bands and arm around my waist, pulls me tight to his chest, and crushes his lips to mine.

For a brief, fleeting moment, I'm pressed against the length of his broad, strong body. I'm engulfed in the scent of him, the feel of his hard muscles, the sheer power coiled under his skin. His lips are hard, but they soften against mine as he cups my cheek with his free hand.

He's kissing me.

Sebastian Finch is freaking *kissing me*.

What. The. Hell?!

My brain comes back online. I push him away with both hands until he stops kissing me, but he doesn't let go of my waist.

Of course he doesn't. He's a Texan rancher who's as overbearing as he is strong. He hasn't changed a bit.

I hate him. Hate him!

Anger roars in my ears. Before I can think—or admit to

myself that my body is begging for this to continue—I wind back my arm...

And slap him across his stupid, handsome face.

The story continues with Sebastian and Georgia in Book 8: Dirty Little Midlife Drama: http://mybook.to/DLMidlifeDrama

EXTENDED EPILOGUE

NORA

"I'm not sure I want to do this." My voice wobbles as I glance off the wooden platform to the ground far, far below.

"You'll love it." Lee is nearby, getting his harness fitted around his thick thighs. "Like riding a motorcycle, except you're two hundred and fifty feet above the ground."

The employee checks my harness once more, then checks the strap on my helmet. "You're all set," he says. He's a young man, mid-twenties, with tattoos on the backs of his hands and a neatly trimmed beard. He smiles a lot. In fact, he's smiling right now while nodding encouragingly, as if that will convince me.

I'm clipped onto the zipline above. I look at the thick steel cable and the mechanism that will allow me to glide along it. It looks chunky and solid, but it doesn't change the fact that I'm very far above the ground.

"Remind me again why we're doing this?" I ask, closing my eyes for a beat. The tree we're in sways in the breeze, its trunk creaking in an entirely unsettling way.

"Because it's fun," Lee answers.

Fun. *Fun.*

We have very different definitions of the word.

"You want to jump, or you want a push?" The guide asks the question as if it's entirely reasonable. For him, I suppose, it is. He's probably asked that question a thousand times.

I ponder. "Push," I finally answer.

"Okay. Remember to keep your feet up!"

I stand on a yellow line at the edge of the platform, in the area where the handrail opens onto empty air. Above my shoulder, I glance at Lee, whose brown eyes are glimmering, his hair and skin dappled in the midday sunlight. The forest smells like fresh rain from last night, and the bite of autumn makes me zip up my windbreaker to my chin.

It's been two months since Fallon got married to Jen. Two months of moving into my new home, driving back to Tahoe every weekend to visit my mother, and spending time with my new dog.

Two months of Lee.

Truthfully, they've been the two best months of my life. I've laughed more than ever. I've ridden on the back of his motorcycle. I've woken up with him next to me in bed almost every night, and I'm starting to wonder if I should ask him to move in with me.

After taking things slow, I find I want to rush now. Make up for lost time.

"Sit back in the harness," the guide tells me.

I do as he says, lifting my feet up.

Then he pushes me.

My stomach drops down, down, down as the platform disappears and I fly along the treetops. A squeak escapes my lips, not even enough breath to truly scream. Forcing myself to keep my eyes open, I watch the tree canopies zip by as I fly along a steel cable between them.

And...and...

Oh, it's magic. Air whipping over my body, just like on the back of Lee's motorcycle. Freedom. I laugh, casting an eye over the tops of the trees, wondering if birds feel this kind of elation every time they take flight.

Then, just as soon as it starts, it's over.

Another worker is there to catch me at the next platform. She grabs the cable and steadies me until I get my feet under me, unclipping one of the cords attaching me to the cable, but leaving a safety line clipped on. She shuffles me out of the way as I try to catch my breath, glancing back in time to see Lee gliding down toward us.

His long legs are held straight out in front of him. His arms are spread wide, and his face is one big smile.

My man. My handsome, beautiful man.

He lands with a thump and as soon as he's unclipped from the zipline, he crosses the distance to me and cups my cheeks. "So?"

"I loved it," I answer, heart jackrabbiting in my chest.

His eyes crinkle at the corners. "I told you so."

"Ready for the next one?" the woman asks. I nod, and she takes off to meet us at the next platform. The tattooed worker takes my harness and clips me to the next zipline behind her. So, just like that, we glide from platform to platform, flying through the beautiful old-growth forest, and I let myself go.

It's been like this for two months. Lee coaxes me out of the shell I've built around myself. He teases me with new experiences, gives me a taste of adrenaline and love and laughter.

And I eat it up.

On the third zipline, I find the courage to glance down. The ground is so far below that my stomach gives a lurch. I must jump, because I wobble up, bouncing on the zipline so far above the earth.

Then it's over, and my feet are on another platform.

Lee arrives behind me and gives me another kiss. We do it again. Again. Again. Until we've made a complete loop and are at the entrance of the adventure park, being swiftly divested of our harnesses and safety equipment.

Mac, Trina, her kids, and my dog Harley are waiting for us outside. There's an incredibly cool playground full of swings and platforms where the kids are playing, and Harley is living his best life getting endless belly rubs from Mac.

"So?" Trina asks. "How was it?"

"Magic," I answer.

A heavy arm lands across my shoulders and I'm unceremoniously pulled into Lee's chest. He lays a soft kiss on top of my head, then turns to his brother and Trina. "Ready for lunch?"

"Let's do it." Mac stands, grabbing his motorcycle helmet.

Trina calls the kids, then turns to me. "You riding with Lee, or you want to come in the car with me?"

I still feel unsteady on my feet after what we just did, but— Oh, what the hell. I want more of that feeling. More of the weightlessness. "I'll ride with Lee."

"Damn right you will." He crushes me to his chest and lays a big wet one on my lips. When we fall apart, I'm laughing. I'm always laughing with him.

Harley rides with the kids and Trina. Our little convoy heads out of the adventure park and down the freeway for a few minutes, then turns off to a picnic area. Nestled in the forest, we find a picnic table by a rushing river, and the kids run off to explore. Harley joins them.

When Lee produces chicken and aioli sandwiches, I feel a strange lurch in my chest. I pick up a triangle, my eyes suddenly blurry.

"You made sandwiches," I say.

Lee meets my gaze, his expression softening. "Home-made aioli and chicken okay?"

"The view's not bad either," I answer softly.

With memories of that day on the beach, I bite into the sandwich and let the flavors explode on my tongue. That spring day all those months ago, Lee handed me control over the pace of our relationship. Without me having to explain anything, he gave me exactly what I needed to come out of my shell.

He's still doing it. Dragging me out to that adventure park and ziplining with me—it's exactly what I needed today. A little thrill, a beautiful view, and the love of my life to share it with.

LATER, when we stop off at a hotel for the night before heading back to Heart's Cove in the morning, I find myself freshly showered and wrapped up in a fluffy bathrobe, lying on a king-sized bed. Lee emerges from the bathroom in a cloud of steam, a towel wrapped low on his hips.

Harley is on his dog bed, lying by the window. His ear perks up and he lifts an eyelid in our direction.

Lee sees me watching him exit the bathroom and cocks an eyebrow.

"Thank you for today," I say.

"The day's not over," he responds, and drops the towel.

And oh—wow. Before I can speak, he grabs my ankles and drags me to the bottom of the bed. Laughing, I let him tug me close.

Harley takes the opportunity to huff, then trot to the bathroom. I hear his claws click on the floor and then another huff as he settles himself down.

The bathrobe gives absolutely no resistance as he unties the sash and spreads the lapels. Then his lips are on my skin, my breasts, my neck. When he kisses my lips, I wrap my arms and legs around him and melt into the sensation.

"It's been a week since I started the birth control pill," I say as my lips brush his earlobe.

With his weight still pressing me into the bed, Lee lifts his torso and meets my gaze. "We can..."

I reach down between us and grip the hard length of him. "Yeah," I whisper.

His big body shudders against me, hands coasting down my ribs. It's the work of a moment for him to tease pleasure from me with those long, talented fingers, then with his tongue. When I'm gasping and writhing and begging, he gives me what I want.

The feel of him inside me is like riding on a zipline two hundred and fifty feet above the earth, times a thousand. The weight of him above me, the bulk of the bed beneath me, the scent of his skin, the look in his eyes—it all makes me feel protected and cherished and so incredibly alive.

We go slow, holding back, until I put my calves on his shoulders. Then, all bets are off.

With him standing at the foot of the bed, and me clinging onto the edge of it, our lovemaking turns feral and wild and perfect. I let go, the way I can only with him. I cry out as pleasure rushes to every corner of my body, and then I feel him empty himself inside me.

My heart thunders. I gasp, lying on the bed with my legs still on his shoulders as he strokes the top of my thighs, his body curved over mine.

"I love you," he rasps, hands tightening on my skin. "That was..." He blows out a breath.

"Yeah." It's all I can manage to say. It says it all.

After a quick cleanup, I discard the robe still hanging off my arms and climb into bed beside the man I love. He spreads an arm and pulls me tight to his chest. Harley has settled himself back in his bed now that the action is finished.

"Lee," I start, my voice small.

"Yeah?" He's sleepy. I can tell by his voice, by the absent-minded way his fingers are drifting up and down my arm.

"Do you want to move in with me?"

The fingers stop. He pulls away, nudging my chin up toward him. "Would you like that?"

My cheeks are burning. It's too soon. After everything, I should know that taking things slow is much, much better. Why rush it? Why did I bring this up now, shattering our post-coital bliss?

I swallow thickly, then shrug one shoulder. "I think so.

But if you're not interested, we can keep doing what we're doing. It's probably too soon, so just forget I said anyth—"

He silences me with a kiss. It's long and languid and warms me all the way to my toes. Then, forehead to forehead, Lee speaks.

"Yes, Nora. I want to move in with you. I can rent my place out. It's probably better for a family, anyway. Too much space for me on my own."

My heart does a cartwheel. "I don't want you to feel pressured—"

"I've wanted to move in with you since you got the keys, Nora. Since we christened the kitchen counter."

My heart stops cartwheeling and is now threatening to explode. "Really?"

He lets out a low chuckle. "Really."

"Why didn't you say anything?"

"I'm a patient man, babe. Figured I'd wait for you to realize we should live together." He lies back on the pillows, tugs me close, and closes his eyes.

Decision made.

Meanwhile, I feel like I've just done the hundred-meter dash. My heart is doing all kinds of strange things in my chest. My mind is spinning. My body feels hot.

I'm...elated. Excited. *Happy*.

The future is bright. Smiling against Lee's skin, I close my eyes and hope tomorrow is as good as today.

Somehow, I already know it will be.

The story continues with Sebastian and Georgia in

Book 8: Dirty Little Midlife Drama:
http://mybook.to/DLMidlifeDrama

ALSO BY LILIAN MONROE

For all books, visit:

www.lilianmonroe.com

Manhattan Billionaires

Big, Bossy Mistake

Big, Bossy Trouble

Big, Bossy Problem

Forty and fabulous

Dirty Little Midlife Crisis

Dirty Little Midlife Mess

Dirty Little Midlife Mistake

Dirty Little Midlife Disaster

Dirty Little Midlife Debacle

Dirty Little Midlife Secret

Dirty Little Midlife Dilemma

Dirty Little Midlife Drama

Brother's Best Friend Romance

Shouldn't Want You

Can't Have You

Don't Need You

Won't Miss You

Military Romance

His Vow

His Oath

His Word

The Complete Protector Series

Enemies to Lovers Romance

Hate at First Sight

Loathe at First Sight

Despise at First Sight

The Complete Love/Hate Series

Secret Baby/Accidental Pregnancy Romance:

Knocked Up by the CEO

Knocked Up by the Single Dad

Knocked Up...Again!

Knocked Up by the Billionaire's Son

The Complete Unexpected Series

Yours for Christmas

Bad Prince

Heartless Prince

Cruel Prince

Broken Prince

Wicked Prince

Wrong Prince

Lone Prince

Ice Queen

Rogue Prince

Fake Engagement/ Fake Marriage Romance:

Engaged to Mr. Right

Engaged to Mr. Wrong

Engaged to Mr. Perfect

Mr Right: The Complete Fake Engagement Series

Mountain Man Romance:

Lie to Me

Swear to Me

Run to Me

The Complete Clarke Brothers Series

Extra-Steamy Rock Star Romance:

Garrett

Maddox

Carter

The Complete Rock Hard Series

Sexy Doctors:

Doctor O

Doctor D

Doctor L

The Complete Doctor's Orders Series

Time Travel Romance:

The Cause

A little something different:

Second Chance: A Rockstar Romance in North Korea